# PILLAR OF FROZEN LIGHT

# PILLAR OF FROZEN LIGHT

BARRY ROSENBERG

GUARDBRIDGE BOOKS
ST ANDREWS, SCOTLAND

Published by Guardbridge Books,
St Andrews, Fife, United Kingdom.

http://guardbridgebooks.co.uk

Pillar of Frozen Light



Edited by David Stokes
and Terry Jackman

Cover art © Alex Storer

ISBN: 978-1-911486-37-4

*Barry dedicates this novel to his lovely wife, Judith.*

# PROLOGUE

*On the press of a button...*

*On the press of a button...*

The Tsadkah opened his mind and the phrase came to him. Turning it over and over, he considered his children. As young adults, they were fine. Fine, but not right. They were too fine to be right. He needed someone less fine, less right, more… An anticipatory glow in his eyes, he gazed toward the mountains.

Early the next morning, the Tsadkah kissed Hulva, his wife, and set off for a two day trek on a planet now more familiar than the one on which he'd been born. Although, he thought, this was the planet on which he'd truly been born.

That night, on the slopes of the mountain, he slipped inside a sleeping bag. With the press of a button, the bag separated from its base and anti-gravity lifted him out of harm's way. As the Tsadkah closed his eyes, the phrase *on the press of a button... on the press of a button…* kept circling in his mind.

The next day, he reached his destination, a column as smooth and dark as polished obsidian, a pillar of black light, yet one that felt more solid than the surrounding rocks. But when the Tsadkah touched the pillar with his mind, anyone watching would've been amazed. His solid body merged into the light, and holding his mind just so, the Tsadkah adjusted his awareness and allowed it to travel.

Guided by the thought, *on the press of a button…* his awareness sped towards Terra. Touching one mind after another, he finally found one who might be suitable.

# Chapter 1

Jonan felt the girl curl her naked body against him, but already bored with her, he pressed a button. The Screen came alive, presenting the night-time news. "People on Tumu Island claim that sea level rises are making it impossible for them to live there, and they demand refugee status in Australia. We now switch to the Australian Prime Minister in Parliament House."

"Never! Our shores are also disappearing." The Prime Minister banged his desk. "Plenty of other planets can be terraformed. Let them go there. Let them go off-world." His side of the House cheered. Even the opposition reluctantly nodded. Every country was closing up its borders.

"What d'you think about refugees going off-world?" the girl, Alyssha, asked.

"Good." Jonan, tall and contentedly plump, left the bed. "As long as it's not me going." With the Screen mumbling to itself, he picked up his minScreen and opened *Psychaeology Today*. "Hey, look at this! A new gadget for inducing deeper levels of hypnosis."

"Yes?" Alyssha peered over his shoulder. "Psychaeology, the science of digging into the strata of the mind."

With her firm breasts digging into him, Jonan felt sufficiently aroused to grab for her. "We also like to dig into the strata of the body."

Alyssha squealed but happily sank onto the floor as the Psychaeologist pressed his little paunch against her firm stomach. But he acted more out of indulgence than lust, and was almost glad when they finished.

"This'll have to be our last night for a while," Jonan said. "Uni starts next week so I'll be too busy." Seeing a wistful expression flash across her face, Jonan knew that she'd got his message: that this was probably the last time, period, and it was back to her fellow students after a taste of the highlife.

Returning to his bedroom, Jonan pressed a button to set his alarm, a second button for the morning shower, and a third for overnight room temperatures. The Psychaeologist loved pressing buttons. It made him feel in control.

As they lay between clean white sheets, the lighting gradually dimmed and the music became softer.

"Hypnotic," Alyssha murmured, her breathing becoming slower and slower.

Jonan, listening to her breathing, drifted into a light hypnagogic state. When his brain waves slowed even more, the light and music cut off. Jonan slept – if not the sleep of the just, then the sleep of the self-indulgent.

At seven the next morning, the alarm began its program by exuding a gentle haze and playing a mellow music. Jonan rolled over, only to fall asleep on his other side. The light and sound jumped a level. In reaction, Jonan rolled back again. But encountering a body, he froze. His eyes unshuttered. A body! A woman? Ah, yes, a woman. Who was it? Oh, yes, a student. A student and her name was… Alice? Alicia? No, Alyssha. Yes, Alyssha.

Jonan pressed the alarm before the melodic bird song turned into a kookaburra's shriek. At his movement, Alyssha turned and nestled into him. He reached down and began to stroke between her legs. The young woman made a sound, a purring deep in her throat. She opened her thighs and pulled Jonan into her. They moved together, still half asleep.

The alarm gave a final chime. Jonan groaned and rolled out of bed. He pulled Alyssha with him so that, without their weight, the blankets rearranged and his personal *son et luminaire* faded to nothing. In the living room, however, another program began. The Screen turned on, and a sleek man in a silver one-piece cheerfully started on the morning news.

"Another day over 40 centigrade," he announced. "Isn't it good we have air-conditioning? Carbon dioxide levels have reached 600ppm. Oops!" He banged the meter, and the level dropped. "Phew! For a moment there, I thought we were going back up again."

Jonan grimaced. "Thinks he's funny."

"Don't forget the usual water restrictions," the anchor continued. "Tune in to your local station for details." Maps appeared on the Screen. "If you're thinking of going overseas, fighting is still going on here… and here…, terrorist incidents, here. Meanwhile for the past quarter, the number of murders has remained stable and political rorts have diminished." The announcer grinned again. "But, as usual, that probably represents only the tip of the iceberg."

"Rorts!" Jonan snorted. "Politicians are always ripping off the system."

"You want people to move off-world?" Alyssha said. "Why not begin with politicians?"

"Wish I could. They make the most hot air."

They both grinned, and Jonan pulled Alyssha towards the bathroom. He pressed the button to start the shower program.

Alyssha laughed. "You don't speak to it first thing in the morning?"

"Speech recognition!" Jonan waved a dismissive hand. "Artificial Intelligence gets so far and then gets stuck." He scratched his head. "I'm not one of those people who think the mind can be uploaded and downloaded."

"Many do."

Jonan chuckled. "I'm an anachronism." After sharing a scented shower, the Psychaeologist added, "Of course, I could shout at the damn speech machine. But who wants to shout first thing in the morning? It's bad enough having to perform for students."

Alyssha pulled on her one-piece. "I thought you liked performing."

Jonan smiled. "First day back, I'm dramatizing."

With the towel wrapped around his slight bulge, the Psychaeologist studied himself in a holo-mirror. He carefully cultivated a small beard without any moustache, but detecting a slight shadow on his cheeks, he decided to rub on SlowShave™ cream. Good, no more growth for a month.

Jonan touched his beard. Didn't it make him look like an olde-worlde buccaneer? Didn't it, just? He turned from side to side, definitely liking what he saw: a tall dark man, slightly plump, but not bad for pushing thirty. Anyway, a touch of the portly suited a Psychaeologist, even allowing for all the behavioural gadgetry.

He pressed a button, and his clothes slowly moved across the rack. "The first day of the year," he mused. "What to wear?" He reached for a yellow one-piece. "This one will do, not too dull for me and not too bright for academia." Dressed, the Psychaeologist went to his auto-cook where he tapped out for real coffee with real toast and real eggs.

"Real food!" Alyssha reeled as if she were dizzy. "I'm so used to synthetics, I'll probably get high."

"Synthetics are cheaper." Jonan shrugged. "But you only live once."

They went onto the veranda, and although the Sunshine Coast had recently been regraded from subtropical to tropical, Jonan's garden was cool, thanks to the small solar-powered waterfalls that flowed over rocks and between clumps of miniature palms.

"It's so nice out here," Alyssha remarked, "even if those parrots do shriek like drunken students."

"Agreed." Jonan sipped his not-synthetic coffee. "I can't imagine leaving." A shadow passed over the garden, and he looked up. Surprised not to see any clouds, he returned to enjoying breakfast, but when the alarm beeped, he immediately rose. "Got to go. That damn thing'll only stop when I leave."

Jonan dumped their plates in the CompuKleen, collected his bag, and lead the way out. He locked the door and the alarm shut off. Then, clicking his remote, Jonan opened the mini-garage and watched with pride as a bright cylinder rolled out. He thumbed it, and the cylinder expanded into his much-prized solabub. "Beautiful, isn't she?" Jonan stroked the car. "I love the way it closes, but then, like a huge flower, blossoms open."

Alyssha's eyes shone. "It's a beauty. How old is it?"

"One year. Layer upon layer of paint gives it that deep, almost alive sheen."

"I wrote an essay once on the ancient Egyptians." Alyssha touched the bonnet. "They used to worship the beetle. I can understand why now. This colouring is just like the carapace of a huge red beetle."

The Psychaeologist grunted. He didn't like his prized possession being compared to a beetle, not even a sacred one. "Of course," he said, "the layers are tiny solar cells." He pressed the remote again, the doors opened, and they both entered.

"University," Jonan said clearly.

"University," a smooth female voice repeated.

"Check." He smiled. "I find it much easier to talk to my car than I ever did to my shower."

Satellite navigation took over, automatically keeping the speed to thirty. Enjoying the ride, Jonan pointed at a friend's car. "She paid almost as much for her bub, but it doesn't have anything like the lustre of mine."

"Why's that?" Alyssha asked.

"Some off-worlds specialise in smart paints, and a local mechanic finds them for me." Jonan looked thoughtful. "Actually, it might just be one off-world. He's a bit secretive about it."

"Is that legal?"

"A bit iffy." Jonan waggled a hand. "But sometimes that's what you have to do if you want the best."

They chugged along, standard distance apart, until the Hinterland Motorway where the autopilot gently accelerated to eighty. The University was their destination, most of it now in the hills around Mapleton. Jonan pointed behind them. "Did you know some of the University is still down on the coast?"

Alyssha shook her head. "I thought it had completely moved."

"The Marine Centre's there. Students dive down to it for their prac work."

"So it's not really the Marine Centre, just ruins."

"Your great grandparents might remember it." Jonan turned to the front again, the bub slowing as they reached Mapleton. Much of the town was taken up by the University. With its clusters of iridescent domes, towers, and manicured lawns, it formed a city within a city.

Alyssha gazed at the dense greenery. "I come from the bush and the long drought," she said. "I can't believe so much water is used just for grass."

"Native plants would've been cheaper," Jonan agreed. "But a nice lawn always impresses the off-worlders."

Alyssha shook her head. "We Terrans, we always know how to make our mark."

The solabub crossed the campus to arrive at the Applied Psychaeology Centre, stopping at a gleaming column. There, Jonan used his remote to collapse the bub and dial its parking coordinates.

"When I start work," Alyssha watched as the car was lifted up and put into its niche, "that'll be the first thing I buy."

Jonan didn't reply. He was imagining his vehicle among the many in the honeycomb parking space – shining like a ruby among rocks. Then he turned to his companion. "As I said before, this first week'll be very busy. So I don't know when I'll be able to see you again."

Alyssha stood on tiptoe and pecked him on the cheek. "Whenever." She walked toward the student library, turning to give him a wave.

Jonan didn't wave back. He was already heading for his own Department and to other adventures. At the entrance, however, he paused; his sense of anticipation was suddenly eclipsed by a huge wave of… of what? He looked around, expecting to see the trees bending in the wind and dust flying through the air. But there was no wind, not even a breeze. Not a leaf stirred.

# Chapter 2

Baffled, Jonan took one hesitant step, then another. Touching his little beard as if it were a good luck charm, he shook his head to clear it and was just entering his building when a familiar voice called out, "Jonan, Jonan, wait on a mo."

It was Evana, a fellow worker. In fact, he'd been the one to finally select her. An act for which she sometimes liked to show her appreciation – often after they'd run a group together. Mostly, though, theirs remained a casual connection.

She caught up with him. "Hi," she panted. "Nice morning."

The panting bothered Jonan. "I need to start exercising," he said, wondering if lack of breath explained the strange hurricane sensation.

"You say that at the beginning of every year."

Jonan grinned. "You're right, and it is a lovely day. Perhaps we won't have any cyclones this summer."

"Don't bet on it," Evana said. "Once in a hundred years has become once in a hundred days."

Jonan smiled, knowing she meant the students as much as the weather. Cyclones were unpredictable but student tempests were a constant. They entered the lift, and it smoothly took them to the second floor. Jonan stroked his beard. "Next time, I'll walk."

Evana lifted a sceptical eyebrow. "And next time, I'll fly. Talking of flying, was that your red solabub a few cars in front of me?"

The Psychaeologist pretended to be affronted. "Does any other shine as lustrely?"

"Lustrely, huh?" Evana smirked. "I thought I saw two heads?"

Jonan gave her a sly look. "Not two heads, it was one of

those rare occasions when I was in two minds."

They chuckled. Jonan knowing that Evana wasn't at all surprised to see him with a young woman. From the lift, they both stepped onto the glidewalk, reached their offices, and in a more or less simultaneous performance, they thumbed their doors.

*Not good,* Jonan thought. *Without even thinking about it, I used the glidewalk. Just walking more would up my exercise level. I'm doing things automatically, like a puppet on a string.*

At the word *puppet,* the Psychaeologist's vision darkened, and for a second time, a hurricane blew through his head. Jonan grabbed his desk for balance – yet nothing in his room moved. Puzzled, he looked out the window. The sun was shining and the clouds just drifted. He shook his head. *Vertigo,* he wondered, *that dizziness caused by the movement of crystals in the inner ear?* If it happened again, he'd make an appointment with the doctor. Giving his first sigh of the academic year, he pushed the incident out of his mind and consulted his calendar.

His Screen showed just two counselling sessions in the morning and a lecture in the afternoon. Good, he still had plenty of time to update his notes. But before looking at them, he went to the window. Students flowed along the paths and filled the glidewalks. In shorts and skirts, their glowing skins showed the benefit of the summer break. Jonan looked forward to meeting them.

He was anticipating adventures when a cough at the door interrupted him. His first appointment had arrived, a pimply postgrad studying space marketing. "Take a seat..." Jonan glanced at his computer, "...Tomas. How was your break?"

"Pretty good." The postgrad mumbled unenthusiastically about a family visit. "But I'm still stuck. My holos are supposed to encourage people to migrate to Sector 31, but I just can't do it. It's life-threatening, adventure stuff, but I just turn it into boring. Everything I do comes out boring, even to myself. How can I stop being so boring?"

Immediately irritated by the whiny voice, Jonan considered wild alternatives. "Have you ever tried drugs?" he asked.

Tomas blushed. "Only a few."

The Psychaeologist searched in a drawer. "I've got a litre of psychoactive drugs here. Fancy a swallow or two?"

The student shuddered. "Wish I could, but I'm too frightened."

Jonan held up a device. "How about a thousand volts of electrostim?"

Tomas frowned. "Space, you're kidding, aren't you?"

The Psychaeologist nodded. "That's an improvement. Last semester, you wouldn't have said boo to a mouse."

"Yes, you've definitely helped me. But I'm still boring."

*This needs some behavioural engineering,* Jonan thought. A light popped in his head. *Better still, how about a dash of mis-behavioural engineering?* Jonan leant forward with an earnest look on his face. Tomas gazed back expectantly. The oracle was going to speak.

"Yes," Jonan said heavily, "you are boring. Very, very boring." With that, he dropped his head onto the desk and began to snore. The effect was incredible, Tomas gaped and his eyes bulged. But Jonan's timing was perfect. He'd cut straight through the bullshit, and the student's expression of self-pity dissolved.

"That," Tomas burst into laughter, "is very very funny. Actually, that's the first good laugh I've had in ages."

Jonan rested his hands on his paunch. He was doing well, a breakthrough, and no artefacts required. "You're ready for a contract now, Tomas." The student gulped. "This is what you must do. Every day, you have to strike up one conversation with someone new, no matter how inane." Jonan stroked his beard. "In fact, the more inane the better. Out of every three chat ups, select the most inane as a base for a marketing holo.

Got it?"

Tomas gulped again. "The more inane, the better? Space!"

Jonan typed the contract onto his Screen, and they both touched an e-seal to sign it. The Psychaeologist was satisfied, no gizmos were needed to reinforce this student's behaviour, Jonan's authority would be enough. Growing up would do the rest. They shook hands.

"Show me your holo next week," Jonan said, shooing the student out.

When his Screen showed that Tomas had left the corridor, Jonan also left his office and went to the staff room. It had many cheap drinks, some synthetic, some imported from off-world, but he preferred his Terran-grown coffee and the ritual that he performed to make it, a little ritual designed to exorcise pimply postgrads.

The rich aroma brought Evana. "Going to share?" she enquired.

"Come to my room," Jonan replied with a mock leer, "and I will."

"Love to." And Evana meant it. "But I don't have the time. How about drink now, pay later?"

"That'll have to do." With a pretend sigh, he poured a cup, and Evana left, nose to the aroma. Shortly after, Jonan also left, returning to his office where he sat, sipped coffee, and once more contemplated his notes. Some were on the Screen, others were just hand written scribbles on his minScreen. These were the results of sudden inspirations. Strangely enough, his grand psychaeological inspirations tended to arrive just when he was trying to impress someone.

With a vain hope, Jonan put his scribbles to the scanner. His script came out as hieroglyphics. He wasn't surprised; even he had trouble deciphering it. That was the problem with inspiration. It never flowed neatly. He could, of course, type into his minScreen, but that just didn't have the seductive flow of writing by hand.

In an exercise in futility, Jonan closed his eyes and tried to mentally order his notes. But that was impossible. Instead of a conceptual framework, all he saw were images: glimpses of laughing students in short skirts. He gave up, took four steps to put his forehead on the glass and spent too long spying on the young folk down below.

Fortunately his second appointment was more interesting than the first. Pimple free, she was definitely more attractive.

"Please, sit." Jonan didn't need any notes to remember her name. "It's Mirena, isn't it?"

"Yes."

"What brings you here today?"

"Space," she replied.

"Yes?" Jonan already knew her background, but he wanted her to express it again in her own words. In a sympathetic tone, he added, "Go on, Mirena."

"I'm doing a postgrad thesis on tourism." Her words came out jerkily. "I was going to compare three off-world systems. It means interstellar travel but..."

"But?"

"The stars," she mumbled, "that terrible space. I look up, and instead of seeing the stars, I'm just aware of the immense spaces between them."

"The stars," Jonan echoed. "The immense spaces between them."

Mirena blushed. "You probably think I'm silly. It... it's not so much that, it... it's..."

"Yes?" He knew her problem, had encountered it many times before, and knowing it, he could sense her weakness, and his power over her.

"It's the way of getting there."

"Yes?"

"It's..."

"Yes?"

"It's the Probability Drive!"

"Of course, the Probability Drive."

There was an amazing power in those words. Even the hesitancy in using them spoke of their power. With some people, it took ages to get to that point. But in vocalising, Mirena had shown her potential, and Jonan knew that her problem would be a pushover. Nodding wisely, he stroked his beard. At twenty-three, the postgrad was open-faced and slim. She would be a nice person to work with, a nice person to work a space phobia with. A nice person.

Reaching out, Jonan took hold of a miniature Indo shadow puppet. About the same length as his hand, he could adjust its arms and legs into a variety of positions. This particular puppet, with its long nose, was one he used when he switched into lecture mode but didn't want to appear to be lecturing.

"Although it's been around for a while, most people still haven't come to terms with the Probability Drive." Jonan adjusted the puppet so that it held its head in its hands. "And no wonder. After all, how many people even try to understand quantum relativity? But once you've got quantum, you've got probability. And, somehow, this abstract concept has been turned into starships. The result means that travel across light-years takes hardly any time at all." He quickly walked the puppet across his desk. "And the price? Not much. Merely the security of being." He laid the puppet on its back.

Mirena smiled. "That's a very expressive puppet."

"He understands the physics of the Probability Drive better than I do. As far as I can judge," Jonan leant forward, "scientists discovered the Drive because of their frustration with Einstein. He said that nothing could travel faster than the speed of light. Apparently, physicists took this limit as a personal insult."

The Psychaeologist spread the puppet's arms in a *who-me?* gesture. "So these blokes looked for ways to step around

Einstein. The solution was..." Jonan did a ta-da. "...fractal orbitals. Don't ask, all I know is it involves three and half dimensions and more probability." The puppet scratched its head.

"So between our departure and our destination, we're probably both anywhere and everywhere. But not to worry because we're not in a real dimension, anyway, but only in a fractional one – which only makes us worry all the more."

Mirena giggled nervously. "And that explanation is supposed to make me feel better?"

"Well, relativity was explained to me in terms of dough that was kneaded, twisted, and folded. Just imagine if all those physicists had turned their hands to bread making. Our mouths would be here but our sandwiches would be light-years away."

Mirena giggled again, but this time without the nervousness. "And flavoured with a fractal probability spread."

"Ah." Jonan nodded the shadow puppet's head, "we have a mutual understanding. So fractal scientists handed this theory to fractal engineers to make starships. But fractal passengers found being a probability distribution was very fractualising." The puppet nodded. "Definitely scary, disturbingly scary."

"It really kills that sandwich," Mirena said.

"What made travelling even more scary was that, because of probability error, starships could only make smallish hops. It was a bit like skimming a stone across water. But to reassure us, scientists tell us not to worry because quantum entanglement keeps us connected... or corrected... or something." The puppet raised a hand. "What's that? What's quantum entanglement, you ask?"

Mirena nodded.

"Let's see." Jonan interlinked his fingers. "Basically, it's just a headache from trying to read the small print."

"Space!" Mirena's eyes grew big. "I never knew physics was

so weird."

Jonan spread his arms. "Anyway, the result for star travel was: getting there - one; sense of self-esteem - zero."

"I didn't want a sandwich, anyway." Mirena touched her stomach. "Honestly, just talking about it makes me feel sick."

"You're right. It is extremely unsettling. The real wonder is why everyone doesn't worry about being scrambled up and then being put together again." Jonan tugged his beard. "It's like Humpty Dumpty falling off his wall. But not to worry, Mirena, I've helped enough people to know I can help you."

"You can?" Her round face looked up at him with a mixture of fear and hope.

"Yes, definitely." Jonan had, in fact, worked on plenty of space phobias. With his psychaeological tools, he expected Mirena to perform in a world of imagery, a virtual world so vivid that her real world would pale before it, and she'd do things beyond her wildest fantasies. By the time he'd finished with her, she'd be ready to space jump in his bright red solabub. No, all that was straightforward. The probabilities that were really of interest to him now had more to do with their extra-curricular activities.

Mirena left, and she was smiling because his confidence had reduced her fears. Jonan however, was left to once more face his lecture notes. In a desultory fashion, he rewrote a few paragraphs. He might even have added a bit – who was he kidding? – when his Screen chimed. A click, and Evana's face appeared.

"A shemail," he said.

"You old he male," she countered. "You ready for lunch yet?"

"Already?" Jonan groaned. "I've still got to prepare a lecture."

"Use last year's."

"I already have."

She laughed. "They'll never notice."

"But I'm supposed to do research."

"Aren't we all?"

"Oh, hell." Jonan sighed. The first lecture was always the hardest. Yet once he knew his students the words just flowed. "I'll improvise. You're right, they'll never notice."

"Get onto your hobby horse. Tell them how and why the data age never led to downloading minds onto computers and all that cyberpunk crap. Then describe how the unfolding of space travel led the bright minds into other directions."

"Not all the bright minds!" Jonan objected.

"Not thee and me." Evana laughed.

Jonan brought up last year's notes on his Screen. "Yeah, people used to think that they'd just be able to hook up to a computer. It never happened. Mind isn't digital. Let's see, I've got something here, somewhere." He bent to look at his Screen. "From cyberpunk to cyber-bunk. Yeah, I can work on that. It'll be new and fabulous to these kids."

"Cyberpunk to cyber-bunk?" Evana echoed. "Meaning that while we can view the brain *as* a computer, it doesn't mean that it really *is* a computer? So the whole jacking-in business is impossible. Good, end of problem, the mind-body problem isn't solved by an act of data analysis. Does that make you ready to eat, then?"

"I guess." Pleased to leave his notes, Jonan joined Evana on the glidewalk that took them to the fourth floor of a neighbouring tower. The staff dining room was fairly full, mostly with Terrans, but also with a scattering of off-worlders. They sat in clusters: their clothing, their mannerisms, or maybe their skin colour enough to set them apart.

As usual, the dining room offered three main food alternatives. Jonan naturally went for the most expensive, the home grown. "Synthetics are for students," he said. "As for the off-world products, let the off-worlders stick to their own."

Evana, when with him, always did the same. They joined

their fellow Terrans for what turned into a long lunch.

"I went on a study trip," a Sociologist said. "Very interesting. The off-worlders really seem to believe that their planet is the centre of their solar system." The other academics laughed.

"I also went off-world," a Linguist said. "Not to study, but just to sit in the sun. After all, once the fare was paid, the food and accommodation were so much cheaper." She jabbed a fork into a piece of synthetic beef. "But I have to say, the food did have an odd flavour."

The others agreed. Off-worlds were barbaric, and it was good to return home. Jonan rubbed his belly, pleased he was single and could still afford to holiday on Terra.

The Psychaeologist listened for as long as he could justify then, with great reluctance, returned to his desk and his notes. Finally, after staring at his Screen, he copied last year's lecture onto his minScreen and eyeballed it, the ideas running through well-worn grooves. It would do, he thought. After all, it was only the first lecture of the year. For his next performance, he promised himself, he really would prepare.

He went over the salient points. Point one: Me. And aren't you lucky to have someone with my qualifications? Point two: Regurgitate his essay on *From Ancient Camel Routes to Modern Spaceways*. The motivations for trade in days past were the same as now: expansion, exploitation, and curiosity. Global warming and population explosion were just new varieties of old pressures. The need to find new countries had simply transformed into the need to find new planets – new Terras.

Once he reached the stars, he could then move into his specialty, space phobias. Jonan pressed a soft, well-manicured finger against his minScreen. To keep his lecture fresh, he could use Mirena as a case study. She would be cured by then, of course, but he would change her name and suggest it had happened a few years ago. With a few flourishes, he could tell her story and even she wouldn't recognise it.

On the way, he could also wax philosophical about the Probability Drive, reality, and Einstein's mysterious remark that quantum entanglement allowed for 'spooky action at a distance'. Jonan grinned. By asking questions about the probability of existence, by implication he insinuated the possibility of non-existence. He began to look forward to this class. Jauntily, and very sure of his own existence, he took the glidewalk to give a lecture for which he was quite unprepared.

# Chapter 3

After holidays, the lecture room always reminded Jonan of a medieval painting. It was the tiers and dais that did it, plus the multitude of scrubbed young faces. He saw there what he'd seen in so many ancient pictures. Young people who looked to the front of the room with eager anticipation. When he entered, all other activity stopped. Students who had been speaking hesitantly to new companions, or those who had been hiding behind their minScreens, faced to the front. They all wanted to assess their new teacher.

They'd see a man some ten to fifteen years older than themselves. They found him attractive – *they'd better* – self-assured, and charmingly archaic. For his part, he saw a blur of faces. Most of the students were Terran. A few, judging by their clothes or their unusual skin colour, were off-worlders. As was the custom, the men were smooth chinned. But they had a year in which to get to know each other, this group and Jonan, by which time he wouldn't be at all surprised to find that most of the men were sprouting trim little beards. Last year, so had one woman. Fortunately, hers had peeled off.

As usual, given a hundred faces, it was the unusual that stood out. As he introduced himself, "Dr Jonan Merize, Psychaeologist," he scanned the rows.

It was his greatest mistake.

It was his greatest good fortune.

From paintings and videos, Jonan knew people had changed through the ages, becoming taller, slimmer, and more graceful. That was the natural flow of evolution. But other changes had been forced on humanity. Wars had once been the main force for change. Now it was climate change.

Too many floods, too many droughts, and too many

bushfires had led to mass migrations. Waves of refugees had forced many closed borders to open. Not always, but enough so that even extremist groups had become more tolerant of differences in race, colour, or religion. Intermarriage was now the norm, leading to a glorious mix of traits that Jonan had never seen in old pictures. In his class, alone, he could find a black woman with naturally blonde hair, a yellow man with broad nostrils, or a white skin with slanted eyes. Terran evolution had wrought some bright and beautiful variations. Even so, it was still possible to guess who the off-worlders were.

As he scanned the rows, familiarity faded the Terrans into the background. His gaze stopped at one couple, marked out by the coarse fibre of their clothes and the awkward pride with which they wore them. A second group also caught his eye. Their skins had an odd blue tint that could've been taken for a trick of the light. But he knew the lighting wasn't the cause. The cause was trace elements; safe foods on safe planets that didn't kill, didn't harm, but over generations produced strange skin colorations. No wonder Terrans didn't eat off-world food.

His gaze moved on until one person alone caught his attention. After that, he couldn't have moved on if he'd wanted to. His vision tunnelled, fenced in, and a chasm opened. Jonan spiralled down, tumbling uncontrollably. For a terrifying and delightful moment, he was Alice falling down the hole into Wonderland. Falling… falling… falling… until at the other end of this tunnel sat a golden woman, a burnished copper statue, her face as imperially beautiful as an ancient Egyptian mask.

Impossibly, he saw her both up close and from far away. From up close, he saw skin of burnished copper, the tawny eyes of a lioness, and a glorious mane of golden hair. From afar, he saw the slender line of her body, the grace of her movements, and the music of her voice. In that moment of weird impossibilities, he could even see how she saw him.

Jonan didn't know how long that moment lasted. It only broke because the other students became restless. The break was like a knife across his brain, a knife with a blade of burning ice. The tunnel collapsed. The chasm closed, and he forced himself to resume his role. For the next two hours, words tripped out of him. He entertained, he challenged, he provoked. Yet he wasn't inside his words. He was a hollow man, a puppet whose strings jerked erratically.

Although convinced the girl had had the same impossible perception, she didn't react as he would've expected. He would've thought she'd be wide-eyed, questioning. Yet she only seemed mildly irritated, perhaps paying slightly more attention to his person than to his lecture.

As his inner turmoil reduced, Jonan hoped he seemed as controlled as she did. Had he had that strange perception because he'd met her before? No, he had absolutely no memory of a prior meeting. This was not some heightened déja vu. In those few moments between words, he came to only one conclusion: she came from Hebaron. Only trace elements from that planet gave skin that sort of copper colour, although never before had he seen it produce such radiance.

Eventually, to Jonan's great relief, his minScreen chimed: only ten minutes to go. He decided to cut the time even shorter. "I'll finish here." He started to pack up. "A reading list will be sent to your Screens."

The Psychaeologist then waited for the students to file out. He had two heartfelt pleas: that the golden girl would stay, and that no one else would. The God of Psychaeology was kind. The girl hung back, her expression a sign that something, indeed, had passed between them. Other students looked like they might stay, but the tension between the lecturer and the student was so obvious, they decided to pass.

While the others were still streaming out, the two remained silent. Jonan had time to see that her hair was not truly golden, but a deep red-brown with layers of different hues similar to his solabub. The result was that when light passed through her hair, individual strands appeared to be golden. In his tunnel perception of her, it was as if she'd been backlit. From close-up, however, her skin still reminded him of a well-burnished copper vessel.

The Psychaeologist couldn't stop staring. He desperately wanted to gaze into her eyes, touch the incredible gold of her hair, and embrace the grace of her movements. In contrast, she seemed no more than mildly amused, her only acknowledgement an enigmatic smile.

Jonan left the lecture room with her, deliberately walking slowly. When the distance between them and the other students was wide enough, he stopped and faced her.

"Did you… did you feel that incredible sensation?" he asked.

She pursed her lips, looking as if she didn't want to answer. Eventually she said, "Yes. Yes, I did."

Her voice was exactly as he'd seen it – heard it – evoking in him images of ancient monks, church bells, and dawn prayer. But he shook his head. He didn't want those kinds of religious images. Then Jonan did something that he couldn't remember ever doing before, he pulled nervously at his beard.

"Do you know…?" He forced his hand down, "D'you know what it was?"

"Well…" She hesitated, shrugged, "No, not exactly, not really."

Perplexed, the Psychaeologist said, "But you think you might know?"

"I… I'm not sure." She gave a brief laugh. "I think it was a mistake."

"A mistake?" Jonan stared at her. "A mistake? You mean something was done, but I was the wrong person for it."

The young woman shook her head. "No, maybe. I don't know. Really."

For the first time in years, Jonan questioned his sense of certainty. With an unusual awkwardness, almost with a sense of being forced, he asked, "What're you doing now? Would you like a drink? Can we discuss this? Talk about it?"

The answer was as reluctant as his question. "Yes?" She tilted her head as if she were asking a question and then had to wait for an answer. "Yes, that'd be fine." Her tone didn't convince him that it was fine. On the other hand, Jonan found it hard to believe that a student might actually refuse him. This was so weird. He was supposed to be self-assured and mature, yet here he was with a young woman, admittedly a beautiful one, and he was behaving like a kid on his first date. Like, and he shuddered, like Tomas, the pimply postgrad he was helping.

They walked on in silence and by unspoken consent entered the Astrobar. It was decorated with space ship memorabilia while the ceiling and walls were moving 3D starscapes. The girl studied them, probably searching for her home. Or, perhaps, she just didn't want to look at him.

Following her gaze, Jonan remarked, "There was a power failure here once. All the stars disappeared, and the owner said it was a local eclipse."

"Typically Terracentric."

Jonan grunted. He didn't want to argue about who was the centre of the universe. That sort of thinking should've gone out with Galileo. It hadn't but had only become worse when the spaceways had opened and some off-worlders had called themselves New Jerusalem or New Mecca or something equally religio-centric. Well, so much for wanting to appear in control.

With an irritable pull at his beard, Jonan said, "Coffee? Terran coffee?"

The girl waved her hands as if about to suggest something else then frowned and nodded. Then, as he dialled their order, she said, "Everything on Terra is pushbutton."

Rather than take affront, Jonan said, "Thus far and still no name?"

"Oh, yes. My name is Yerudit, and I'm from Hebaron."

"The where, I guessed: Hebaron. Settled by religious cults, if I remember correctly?"

She smiled. "By cults, you mean cranks?"

"No," he replied, too quickly. After a moment's thought, he added, "Well, yes."

Yerudit smiled again. "It was meant to be a new Garden of Eden."

"So were a lot of places. Zeus, Moses, and Shiva were also taken to the stars."

"Perhaps that's where they came from."

"Myths," Jonan waved a hand. "Projections from the unconscious onto the sky. You'd think in this day and age..." He stopped, her face had tightened. "You... you don't belong to a Clan, do you?"

Yerudit's smile faltered, then she burst into laughter. "You must think we're all cranky freaks! Well, perhaps to you we are. But a Clan? No, not that crazy."

"No, I didn't think you were," he said, pleased to see her laugh.

"I bet you did think it." Her eyes glowed with tiny gold flecks. "No, our people were wanderers rather than fanatics. They were searchers I suppose."

"Zennists, Kalinists, or Christenists?"

"No, none of those." She smiled slightly. "But some of the early settlers were, I admit, scientists – frustrated Obelisk hunters."

"I see," Jonan said, his tone colder than he'd intended. He wasn't in the habit of being teased, especially by someone young, female, and off-world.

Yerudit smiled again, like a not-quite domesticated cat. With a studied casualness, she added, "Of course, I do have my

Tsadkah."

"Your what?" Without knowing why, Jonan felt tiny prickles in his scalp.

"My Tsadkah," she repeated. "My instructor, my teacher."

"Tsadkah?" The hard sound tripped on his tongue. "A religious teacher?"

"He teaches us how to live."

So this beautiful woman was prey to the irrational, after all. She thought she was free, but really, she was tied to the old superstitions, a slave to the masks and symbols of her subconscious psyche. For the first time with her, Jonan felt superior, and a smug smile crept across his face. "I could teach you that."

"What?" She looked startled as if he'd suddenly changed the subject.

"I can teach you how to live," he repeated.

Her face flared. "How to live?" she snapped. "How to die is more like it!"

Jonan was shocked. Surely she didn't mean him, not him personally. How could she? She didn't know him. She didn't know how carefully he chose his foods, his wines, his clothes. She must mean Terra. Like so many off-worlders, she had a grudge. She was the primitive kicking against Terran sophistication. The barbarian was jealous of Earth culture. His sense of superiority returned.

"Cryptic," he said, "but your, er, Tsadkah, I suppose he makes a good living from teaching others how to live?"

"No," she said shortly, "he makes a living as a puppet maker. He is a puppet master."

"How appropriate," Jonan murmured.

Yerudit opened her mouth to reply when it happened again. Space distorted, a tunnel formed. Infinitely close and infinitely far, her face filled his vision. Her copper beauty. Her golden eyes. But the effect was so fast, so strong, that he flinched. So did she. The contact broke and he felt a deep sorrow, as if he'd broken a treasured vase.

"Why?" Jonan heard himself mumbling. "What?"

Yerudit's eyes were huge. "I thought it was a mistake." She frowned. "No, it is you."

*Mistake.* She'd said that for the second time. It echoed in the back of his mind. But him, a mistake? Forcing a chuckle, he said, "Of course it's me." The young woman smiled absent-mindedly, "But you were telling me about your, er, Tadkah..."

"Tsadkah."

"What was, er, is his name?"

The girl blinked and shook her gold copper mane. "Oh, Ariyeh," she said. "At least, that's what we call him. He says that it comes from one of the old languages. It means, well, it means a lion."

"A lion?" Jonan made a face. "Surely, he's a dragon." The young woman frowned. "A lion," he added hurriedly, "I've seen them in reserves, big lazy creatures like overgrown cats. D'you have them on Hebaron?"

"No. Not Terran lions. They're a symbol. Once they were proud creatures, bold."

"Yes." He could imagine the ancestors of those beasts, fierce and lean. Was her Tsadkah anything like that? Or, most likely, was he a big lazy cat and that was just the man's private fantasy? Sure of himself again, Jonan repeated, "What did happen before? How did you feel?"

She eyed him curiously. "Spoken like a Psychaeologist," she said. "How did *you* feel?"

A nice move, turning the question back on him. Despite himself, Jonan searched among his jumble of feelings. Finally, he said, "I felt that you alone existed." As the words left his mouth, he could've bitten his tongue. Total vulnerability. He waited breathlessly, expecting acid or, worse, non-recognition.

All she said was, "I felt the same."

Joy hit him like a bolt of lightning. Hardly able to contain himself, he asked, "D'you know why? How? Have you experienced it before?"

A smile fleetingly lit her face. "With my father, perhaps, otherwise, no."

"No?" Jonan wasn't convinced.

"Never."

"Not ever?" He thought she was too casual about the experience.

"Same as never." She smiled again, lighting his heart. But glancing at her watch, she added, "I must go. I'll see you at class next week."

"Yes, of course, next week," Jonan agreed. His voice sounded hollow; he'd hoped that they'd meet before then.

She rose, and he watched her go, a slim figure gleaming in the blue light of the Astrobar. He was convinced she could've told him more, much more. If he'd asked the correct questions. In the correct way. But what, in space, was correct?

Jonan returned to his room, hoping no more clients had been added to his afternoon. He was lucky, his Screen was blank. He went to the window and stared out. If Yerudit was going to be a new adventure then he couldn't have chosen anyone more beautiful. Yet he felt oddly disturbed, as if he hadn't chosen at all. He had the curious notion of treading in deep waters, sinking into deep space. Water and space? The deep and the high. Opposites, but not really. The seas had a bottom. But space? That had neither top nor bottom. Space went on and on and on, fold within fold – well, with some sort of probability.

An idea hit him, and he rushed to his Screen. Buttons flashed beneath his questing fingers. Incredibly, the response was a blank. He widened his enquiry. Still blank! In ten years of working with space phobias, he'd never had a case from Hebaron. And strangely, nor had anyone else.

# CHAPTER 4

Jonan felt discombobulated. A word fit for Tomas. But to apply to himself? Unthinkable. Today, however, it did apply. Irritated, he tidied up his desk then headed for the parking zone and summoned his solabub. It unfolded as usual, yet it didn't provide the usual satisfaction. Jonan returned home, but his house, usually his haven, now felt more like his prison. Unlike his normal self-satisfied serenity, moods played him like a badly-tuned instrument, and in a moment, he went from excitement to apathy.

The Psychaeologist decided to cook, normally his best self-therapy. Opening his fridge, he considered what to make. Most days, he would choose real food, but today, he selected a synthetic. No point in wasting the real stuff in his current mood.

An expensive choice, he cooked it with carefully selected herbs, and sat down to his meal with FreshSalad™ and a good Aussie White. Unfortunately, he just couldn't eat. He cut the synthetic but couldn't put it into his mouth. FreshSalad™, genetically enhanced to suit *your* taste buds, didn't taste. Eventually, he dished the whole lot in the recycler, went to his Screen and keyed in Hebaron. He desperately wanted to know about Hebaron, about its puppets and its puppet masters.

In contrast to the usual buffed-up tourist info, however, there was relatively little data. Although there were mentions of puppet masters, there was little mention of a Tsadkah. There were details of types of puppets: cloth ones that slipped over the hand, thin leather ones moved by sticks, or life-sized ones that were virtually exo-skeletons. To his annoyance, each type was demonstrated as if it were no more than a child's toy. Yet he knew how instructive a puppet could be from his own use, and the info certainly didn't explain why Yerudit respected a puppet master. Why even call him a master? The word had implications.

The Psychaeologist sat back and stared. An unlikely idea had hit him, sending tingles along his spine: data was deliberately being withheld. But who would or could be doing that? The Tsadkah and those under his influence was the obvious answer? But why? Were there no breakaways prepared to reveal all?

Jonan returned to his search, intrigued by the thin leather puppets with their mobile limbs. With faces that resembled dragons, when properly used, these puppets were not seen directly. Instead, with a light behind them, they projected their shadows onto a translucent screen. It was then the movements of the *shadows* that told their story. According to the info they were used to illustrate ancient myths. Perhaps they could also shine a light onto more personal stories? His? Yerudit's? The puppet master's? At the thought, Jonan felt a chill crawl along his spine.

Eventually, Jonan decided that the long-nosed creations were bizarre and sinister. So this was the twilight world that Yerudit inhabited.

Like his own puppet, the ones on Hebaron also had their origins in the old Indu Federation, a collection of countries just to the north of Australia. As toys, they were now a small part of Hebaron's export economy. But what the hell did the Tsadkah do with them? Jonan glared at the Screen. Religious groups with different origins lived in apparent harmony on this planet. Was that because it had been so easy to terraform, or was it because of the loose guidance of the Tsadkah?

Jonan clenched his jaws. The existence of this person infuriated him. Many of the villages and small towns on Hebaron had its teacher, the Tsadtun, and each teacher referred back to the Tsadkah. A few religions on Terra still worked like that, prompting Jonan to search for information on them. Pope or Chief Rabbi, he decided, were too autocratic a term for the Tsdakah. He was more like a Guru who led by example, but who wasn't necessarily followed by his followers. And the Tsadkah's example was pretty simple. Work with the hands was sacred, but a life where modern technology and science did all the work was a waste. Typical pre-Psychaeology hogwash. "Planetary politics!" Jonan growled. "Nothing to do with spirituality. Hebaron could easily be assisted with Terran know-how, but no, that would put them in her debt. Heavily. Which would then detract from the all-pervasive power of the Tsadkah. It's pure witch doctorism!" It was so easy for him to see this. Why couldn't Yerudit? Too conditioned by her environment?

Jonan snorted. Hebaron was enmeshed in the space age, yet its culture was so unscientific. In his next couple of lectures, Jonan would cover Tsadkah territory. Using his notes on Pythagoras, Mesmer, and Freud, he would show how magic, myth, and superstition arose from the needs of the primitive psyche.

Angry, he muttered, "It wasn't until Skinner, Rastikov, and Makato that neuroscience started to understand the psychaeological strata that underpins Psychaeology." Jonan simmered, yet he was also amused. He never spoke to his electronic gadgets, yet here he was, engaging them in intellectual debate, arguing with them.

Jonan stared at his Screen. What was he trying to get at, anyway? Something, he decided, to do with the abilities of a leader such as the Tsdakah. He tapped the arm of his chair thinking... thinking... until Mirena came to mind. Oh, how easily he would remove her space phobia, but he bet no Tsadkah would ever be able to help her.

"Okay," he admitted to the Screen, "perhaps I'm being contradictory. The ancient Egyptians with their potions and trances could remove a phobia so maybe the Tsadkah could as well." He poured a whiskey. What really niggled him though, and he hated to admit this, was that Yerudit with all her outward sophistication would probably prefer to seek out such a shaman – sham man, hah – rather than consult with him, a highly skilled Psychaeologist.

"Incredible," Jonan snarled. "I'm jealous, jealous of a witch doctor." It was absurd, yet true. It wouldn't matter if he hadn't wanted Yerudit, but he did. Wanted? No, not a want, much stronger, it was a force, a tremendous force. This was incredible, truly incredible. He couldn't get away from it. Although tired, Jonan returned to his Screen and again data-probed. But there was no more data to be wrung out. The Screen was as dry as an old sponge.

Frustrated, he forced himself to go to bed, setting the alarm to fade out with the lulling rhythm of waves, a rhythm attuned to his breathing. Gradually his tossing and turning eased, the sound sending him into a light trance. Picking up on his body's cues, the light changed, going from hazy pink to misty purple to velvet black. His sleep should've been restful, but it wasn't. Hamlet's words came to him, *To sleep, perchance to dream.* Dreams burst out of a screaming Screen. He dreamt dreams of puppets that controlled their manipulators. He dreamt of Hebaron, of sham men with shaman ways. He dreamt of entering the silent stretch of an endless tunnel, where noise and activity gave way to the sudden impact of silence. A tunnel of silence in which he saw Yerudit, saw her in detail. Saw her copper face, the long line of her body, the music of her manner. He saw a ten-sided triangle, a circle with no inside, a man with no shadow.

And so it began. A strange affair, if affair it was. It was the least consummated of all his affairs and yet the most compelling. A week later, after his second lecture, he went again with Yerudit to the Astrobar. As before, they were both awkward and defensive so when Yerudit rose to leave, he almost let her go. Yet he couldn't. Impelled, he reached out. Slowly, she stopped.

"Are you free," he began hesitantly. "Tonight? Would you like to come round for dinner?"

At his uncertain proposal, Yerudit shook her head. "No..." she began, but then her eyes glazed, and as once before, she tilted her head as if listening. "Well...Yes, all right, fine." She then hurried away.

That evening, before Jonan collected her, he ran about his house like an adolescent. He wanted everything to look right: the swords on the wall, the semi-antique vases, the few books of simulated ancient paper. Everything ready, he drove to the crystal spire around which the off-world dorms clustered.

At her door, Jonan adjusted his onepiece, silver grey and very dignified, then dialled and waited. She came very quickly, looking extremely beautiful, the quickness an indication that she was also nervous.

"You look lovely," Jonan said.

"You look... fine, too," she said politely. He had hoped for more enthusiasm. It only came when she saw his solabub, "What a lovely colour!" she cried. "I bet that was expensive."

Jonan was surprised. "You like it? Not too much of an indulgence?"

"Beautiful is beautiful."

"A special nano-crystalline finish. Totally self-powered." He put a hand on the vehicle. "It's an off-world product."

"I thought you preferred not to use off-world."

Jonan blushed. "It's the one area that's superior."

"It looks alive. But off-world, eh?" Yerudit grinned. Then she paused, bent, and peered more closely at the solabub's surface. "I wonder?" she said.

"What?"

"Oh, nothing." She waved a hand. "Just that it's off-world."

Jonan would recall that comment many events later. But now, just mildly puzzled, he put it aside as he used the remote to open the doors. They entered, and he dialled for home.

Yerudit jabbed her fingers at the air. "What's this? Is pushing buttons what Terrans do for exercise?"

"What do they do on Hebaron?" Jonan retorted. "Carry their cars on their backs?"

Yerudit grinned again, and Jonan's irritation faded. The bub began to move, and the young woman intently watched the road.

"Are you memorising the route?" Jonan asked.

"The Tsdakah says to always be aware."

The Psychaeologist spread his arms to indicate how harmless he was.

And so the fates mocked him.

When they arrived at his place, Jonan led her inside and then held his breath. He was surprised at his relief when Yerudit's expression was one of open admiration.

"So you really do like nice things?" she said.

"I like atmosphere." He almost scuffed his feet like a Tomas.

"It does have a good atmosphere." Yerudit smiled gently.

"Good, good. Would you like a drink?" Jonan asked.

"What've you got?"

"Terran martinis, lunar brandy, a Venusian shocker, and a..."

"You know how to make all those?" she asked.

"No," he admitted, "but this does." He indicated the Screen. "I'm famous for my menus."

"Your menus?"

"I worked with the programmer on them." Jonan could hear his defensiveness.

"But all you do is press buttons?"

"That's right."

"You don't chop, scrape, or peel?"

"That's right!" He felt himself getting irritated again. After all, he had done all the creative work. Why should he have to do the dirty physical stuff as well? He didn't subscribe to Hebaron philosophy, couldn't be expected to, didn't want to.

Then in what seemed to be a change of subject Yerudit said, "Do you play games?"

Still defensive, Jonan muttered, "What sort of games?"

"Physical ones."

That stopped him. Was this a come on? Despite the Tsadkah? Because of the Tsadkah? One could never tell with these off-worlders. Cautiously Jonan said, "Maybe."

"Then try and hold me down," the girl said.

Just what he'd expected! Out of reach of the Tsadkah and the superstitions quickly dropped away. The urge to touch her lighting his face, Jonan murmured, "Sounds fun."

"Could be? Try."

Smoothly, Yerudit lay on her back as Jonan stood over her. From here, she seemed so vulnerable that he felt like a bear above a gazelle. Yet when he sat down, he realised he had no idea what to do. With the belief it didn't much matter, he just spread his weight across hers. Her slim body gave, yielding a sweet scent. He'd almost forgotten why they were there when he heard a muffled voice

"Ready?"

"Ready," he replied.

He wasn't. Not ever. What he thought was going to be a harmless hug turned out to be a short sudden shock. In a trice, or less, Jonan flew up, crashed down, and was heavily sat upon. Her knee crushed his ribs. Her tone was infuriating.

"Um, are you sure you were ready?" Yerudit's voice quivered with suppressed laughter.

"Ugh, that hurts"

She shifted.

"Not quite what I expected," Jonan muttered.

"So I gather. Try again?"

"Okay." Anger – no, a competitiveness he usually hid – simmered inside Jonan. He wasn't going to be beaten. Not so easily. Not by a slip of a girl. He knelt, wrapped his arms around her, and squeezed. "Ready," he said and immediately increased the tension. Yerudit pushed. He pulled. She twisted. He turned. She rolled. He flew. Now he was definitely angry. "Okay," he snapped, "you try to hold me."

Yerudit nodded agreeably. He lay down. She stretched at his side, one hip pressed into his, and slipped one arm beneath his neck. "Ready," she called.

He'd show her. Jonan arched, wrapped both arms around her and rolled. Or tried to. It was like wrestling with a river. Or a rock. Whatever he did, she slid the other way. And however she did it, her slight weight always cut into his chest. Despite the unusual effort, he refused to give in. He tossed and writhed and bucked until his face was purple and his breath came in huge gusts, yet still he fought. Finally she released him. She just suddenly let go, and he was left panting for air like a stranded fish

With real concern, Yerudit rested a hand on his shoulder. "Jonan, are you all right?"

"Oh, yeah, yeah, sure I'm all right. A girl half my size glues me down, crushes me, robs me of breath, and then has the cheek to ask if I'm all right! Sure I'm all right. What else could I be?" He wiped his forehead. "Anyway, what about you?"

"I'm fine." She patted his chest, and amazingly, his tension dissolved.

Jonan smiled. "Right." He forced himself to breathe easily. "How in space did you do that?"

"Not in space."

"Pedant! On Hebaron, then. The gravity?"

"Oh, no. We're not grave." She smiled. "It's more a matter of energy."

Jonan sat up, still panting. It brought them so close together that their breath intermingled. He looked into her eyes, expecting to see amusement, perhaps contempt. Abashed, he looked away, towards his Screen. When he again faced her, she smiled.

Embarrassed, he said, "You ready for dinner?"

She nodded, and although it didn't turn out to be the night he'd hoped for, there was a curious intimacy in their being together. Yet despite the wrestling, or perhaps because of it, Yerudit kept him at arm's length for the rest of that evening.

Nonetheless their affair progressed. A week later, they became day tourists. Yerudit wanted to see the sights. The first stop was at the base of the awesome Himalayas. Despite the warming, the distant peaks still held some snow, the white layers reflecting shards of sunlight. Unfortunately for Jonan, Yerudit insisted that they climb. They did, for an hour. Making absolutely no difference to their distance from the peak, it merely turned Jonan's legs to jelly. Embarrassed again, he had to dial for a solabub to take them down.

The second stop was almost as bad, Egypt and the pyramids. It was hard to believe it used to be dry here. A wet blanket of heat beat down, and Jonan felt suffocated by it. There were also swarms of giant mosquitoes.

"Can't something be done about these?" Yerudit asked.

Jonan made a face. "They were genetically engineered to die. Thanks to engineering, they've mutated faster than we can get rid of them."

Beggars came out of the shade, demanding money. Yerudit stared at them in astonishment. "Why do they stay when Terra would pay them to migrate?"

Jonan pulled at his beard. "Fear of the unknown, I suppose."

Yerudit nodded sympathetically. "Can they get credit from my card?" she asked.

"Not a good idea," Jonan said.

But one of the men had a minScreen, and she put a small transaction through it.

The third stop was Jerusalem. The sun was low on their arrival, and the surrounding hills reflected a soft golden light. So did the ruins of the old city. What war hadn't accomplished, earthquake and climate change had.

Some ancient religious sites still stood. Men and women in a weird assortment of traditional costumes were their custodians. Jonan stopped by a wooden star that contained a sculpture of a male nude. A man in a loincloth stood by it.

"What are you?" Jonan asked.

"I follow Markel Angelo."

"What do you believe?"

"As outside, so inside. The Golden Mean without is the Golden Mean within."

Jonan frowned. "I don't understand."

"We have instruction. Give and you will understand."

Jonan nodded thoughtfully. Moving on, he whispered, "They send the money to off-world Cultists."

Yerudit shrugged. "Ask him for instruction one day. You may be surprised at what you might learn."

Jonan was surprised; he had automatically assumed that one Cult would deride another. But while the desolation of these ancient places unnerved Jonan, they fascinated Yerudit.

"I'd like to see more. Ariyeh, my Tsadkah, learnt from here," she said. "Maybe even from the Golden Mean man."

The Tsadkah. His enemy. Yet rather than let her return alone to Egypt or to Isralistine, Jonan again went with her. This time, they spent a whole day.

"The cities are virtually empty," Yerudit remarked.

"The air is humid, but the rivers have dried out."

"But they could be Terraformed."

"Terraform Terra?" Jonan chuckled. "They could, I suppose."

"But?"

"I guess WorldGov would rather reduce the Terran population."

She gave him a cool look. "Of the darker Terrans, no doubt."

Jonan shrugged and they continued the tour, travelling in shuttles between the remnants of tombs and sphinxes. In the desert, Yerudit touched the worn stone of a sculpture as if in search of its heart. Then from above, they spotted the dry course of what had once been the Nile.

Jonan found these remains unexpectedly moving. Of course, he'd brought women here before and aired his historical knowledge. But with Yerudit, it was different. Perhaps because her copper skin was so similar to the burning sand, she seemed to belong there more than he ever did. Instead of stating facts, he quarried his Screen for information about Nefertiti and Cleopatra. Through Yerudit's eyes, he regressed to student mode and questioned the value of progress. Humanity had advanced technologically. They also pushed for continual growth. But why? There didn't seem to be any satisfying answers. Hence, he supposed, the existence of people like the Tsadkah. Not a welcome thought for Jonan.

They stood by The Great Pyramid, an ancient monument that had been eroded first by intense dryness, then humidity, then savage cyclones. "These buildings," he indicated the ruins, "were built by kings to honour their gods, but really, they built them for their own glory."

"True," Yerudit agreed. "But didn't they also build them because they strove? To say: I am here and I want to be eternal?"

Jonan stroked his beard, this was a familiar ground. He'd gone over it with, oh, so many students. "From the viewpoint of eternity, a stone pyramid endures only a little longer than drying bones. They looked outwards by mistake."

"Where should they look?" Yerudit's face was serious, with

no hint of amusement.

"Inside."

"To look inside?" Yerudit smiled. "Do you?"

"I'm a Psychaeologist," Jonan said smugly.

"But maybe Psychaeology doesn't go deep enough."

She turned from the sterile sands and approached a mobile stall. Portable solar units powered the air-conditioning. Shards of pottery and fragments of jewellery were on display. Although they were probably fakes, Jonan was still moved by these symbols of an ancient civilization. Holding hands, they moved from stall to stall, and for once, Jonan was almost sorry to leave Egypt and to return home. Yet this was the one time he should have been delighted, for on landing, Yerudit gazed dreamily into the depths of his iridescent solabub. Jonan waited, not knowing where her thoughts were going.

After a long moment, she murmured, "Take me to my place, I want to show you something." He took her to the university. She ran in and moments later came running out with a thin wafer. "For your Screen," she explained.

"Isn't it on aethernet?" Jonan asked.

She shook her head. "Not this."

Back in his lounge, she slid the wafer into the Screen. Music began and Jonan froze. The haunting sound sent electric tingles along his spine and penetrated deep into his bones. "What instrument is that?" he asked.

"A flute."

"What an incredible synthesizer!"

"It's not from a synthesiser, it's from real wood."

"Wood? But we no longer use woods for making musical instruments. "

"It wasn't made on Terra. On Hebaron, we have instrument makers who experiment with materials."

Jonan listened intently to the sound. "Could I buy one?"

"We only sell these to neighbouring off-worlders."

Yerudit put a finger to her lips, and the incredible music played with silences, silences as rich as the harmonies. As the haunting sound continued, Yerudit's face smoothed out so that she seemed almost asleep. Suddenly, when Jonan thought she must be in a trance, she rose, slid out of her tunic and stood almost naked. Moving to the centre of the room, she stood completely still. Light glinted from her copper skin, and she could have been a magnificent statue, a burnished statue drawn from the sands of ancient Egypt.

When he was expecting to do no more than to drink in her beauty, she moved. No, moved would be too strong a word. There was the tiniest of movements. No, that was also wrong. It was not a movement but a tremor, a shiver. Her whole body quivered, a wave ran from her calves to her thighs to her arms, a wave as slow as the advance of the desert sands, as indeterminate as the shimmer of desert heat. Her stomach, her shoulders, and her breasts joined in this slow undulation. Individual muscle fibres moved hypnotically.

Jonan was drawn into a fantastic world, seeing her simultaneously as part and as whole. In ultraslow motion, she lifted an arm, raised a leg, turned her head. She danced a dance that painted pictures of the infinitesimally small and the enormously vast, from the deepest outside to the deepest inside.

Finally, music and movement stopped, but the room remained energized, filled with the power of creation. The copper figure stood in the centre and glistened. Jonan was afraid to move, yet when he could, there was only one conclusion. Like powerful magnets, they flew together: licking, caressing, stroking. Drawn into a vortex, their bodies rolled and arched and tumbled. Giant forces crashed around them, used them, emptied them. This was the love-making of the gods, an impersonal and explosive love.

It came to an abrupt climax. For a moment, they clung

together, then like two halves of a crushed walnut, they fell apart and silence lay between them. Words could not follow that explosion.

Still without speaking, Jonan took Yerudit home. Kissing her gently, he watched as her slim figure disappeared among the crystal buildings. He sighed deeply, and it was almost too much of an effort to press the button that took him home. Yet once returned, he was too overwhelmed to sleep and went instead into the garden. There he gazed into the stars and wondered at the force that had impelled them.

The stars, those tiny points. It was so hard to believe that men and women actually walked out there. Not even there, but on the invisible specks which circled them. Yet that, too, was an illusion. What he was seeing was light that was old before humanity had even left for the stars. Strange to think that in coming here, Yerudit had travelled through her own past. Though again, even that was not true. The Probability Drive took one out of the normal dimensions.

Jonan shook his head. Nothing was true. Everything had become contradiction, even her dance. Though physical, it had gone straight to the metaphysical. He remembered how he'd once searched for meaning. He'd gone to lectures, read all the books. He'd sought out gurus, imams, all the renowned teachers. Coming out none the wiser, he'd turned to indulgence. This dance, however, had penetrated to the secret recesses of his mind and touched on forgotten yearnings.

*But did he want that?* he wondered. *The yearning? The striving? Or were they being forced upon him?*

# Chapter 5

"Fly me to the moon." Yerudit was looking out the window at the evening sky.

Jonan regarded her quizzically.

She turned. "Literally."

"I'd rather metaphorically but..." Jonan did a search on his Screen. "There's a shuttle every hour."

"Saturday?"

"Good for me." Jonan would've made any time good for him.

Accordingly, on the next Saturday morning, they left for the domestic terminal. They arrived in time to see a slim needle glitter briefly on a column of fire and shrink into the blue sky, leaving only a black afterimage.

With time to spare before the next shuttle, Jonan gave Yerudit a mini tour. The terminal boasted all kinds of sleek gadgets, but what mostly held her attention was the Zen-type waterfall, made of a wooden wheel, so old it was burnished. As it turned, it carried sparkling water and shiny pebbles, both as bright as jewels. When it was their time to queue, Jonan had to drag her away from it.

As they pushed through the throngs, they passed a group of towelpackers, Terrans who sought alien adventures. Carrying *The Hitchhikers Guide to the Galaxy* in hi-tech towels, they greeted each other with, "Forty-two's the answer. What's the question?" The very variety of their clothing marked them with a kind of bizarre homogeneity.

Yerudit smiled at them, then her interest shifted to at a rarer sight. A non-human was in their queue. She nudged Jonan. "We are not alone," she intoned.

Jonan rolled his eyes. "Those old time holos with the mad

scientist staring into space."

"Yes." Yerudit sniffed. "Silly, wasn't it?"

Jonan nodded. "Looking outward rather than inward."

"Not that we've found many higher intelligences. Though there are some lower ones that might yet evolve." Yerudit poked him with her elbow.

"Me?" Jonan tugged at his beard. "I don't want to evolve. I've always been fascinated by ancient civilizations."

"As long as you don't have to walk among them."

"True. I don't think primitive life would suit me," Jonan glanced upwards as a shadow seemed to pass over him. Seeing no cause, he added, "But I do like ancient architecture."

"On Terra, you mean?"

"Everywhere."

Yerudit looked sideways at Jonan. "Does that include the Obelisk?"

"I'm interested in the Obelisks. Although, we know so little about them, we actually can't say if they're ancient or not. In fact, I have the impression WorldGov has blocked data about the Obelisks."

*"The Obelisk,"* Yerudit repeated.

"Yes, them." Jonan indicated the non-human, as it shuffled forward. "We haven't a clue about the Obelisks, and nor do they." He again indicated the Ziranian. "First contact with the Zirs was a buzz. For a while, anyway, but because they breathe a different atmosphere, we found we had very little in common. Ironic, really, in the end, it was just..." He waved a hand, "an exchange of baubles. We'd gone to the stars in search of angels. Finding mere mortals, we spurned them."

"Very poetic." Yerudit motioned with her chin. "So, not many non-humans on Terra?"

"No." Jonan pulled at his beard. "You certainly don't expect to be in a queue with one."

"You think it's a he or a she?"

Jonan made a face. “Let’s call him a he until we know differently, and I guess he’s some sort of social scientist. They wouldn’t study our physical sciences, they’re way in front of us there.”

“Do we study theirs?”

Jonan shook his head. “We try to but can’t make the jumps. We have to go through a few more hoops before we get there.” Jonan consulted his minScreen. “He’s probably a descendant of what we used to call a Watcher. They’ve been observing Terra for ages.”

“I remember.” Yerudit laughed. “The little green men stories.”

“Well, that’s what they look like.” Through the Zirenian’s transparent Suit, they could see he was half Jonan’s height, wore a floor-length tunic over his mottled green skin, and had a pair of saucer-sized eyes. “He looks like a wise and compassionate frog,” Jonan whispered. He then slapped his thigh. “Of course! Myths and legends of princesses who kissed frogs that turned into princes. Maybe there were prior encounters.”

Yerudit looked at him admiringly. “What a good idea! You think if I kiss him, he’ll turn into a prince?”

“From our point of view, he’s probably as rich as a prince.”

The Zirenian’s Suit had picked up their speech, and so he turned to speak to them, his wide lips making curious shapes. His words, however, were clearly translated. “We are not little green men,” he said, “nor little green women. We are little green multispores.”

“Multispores?” Jonan echoed, pleased at being addressed by the non-human. “A group thing?”

“Yes, no,” the Zirenian replied. “Difficult to explain. Look for explanation in your minScreen.” He paused. “Kisses, unfortunately, do not make us princes.”

The Zirenian’s skin showing flashes of yellow, Jonan

checked his minScreen. "I believe he's now laughing."

They'd reached the head of the queue, and a stocky man held out his hand. "Tickets, please." The Zirenian handed his across. The man turned it this way and that. "Where's your visa, mate? Don't wanna put yer in a detention centre, do we?" The non-human dug in his bag and brought out a stamped plasheet. "Right. You go that away."

Yerudit waved. The Zirenian, in return, waggled his long-fingered hand. "Isn't it strange," she mused, "in the old holos, aliens never wore clothes."

Jonan chuckled. "He wore a rather nice silver tunic. Went well with the green."

"In the holos, they also fly space ships with claws too thick to use the controls."

Jonan tilted his head up to properly gaze down his nose at her. "You don't think we'd show aliens in a good light, do you?"

Smiling, they went to their seats and gazed out the window. On silent power, the shuttle rose, and they were soon high above Terra. Below them, they saw blues and greens, interspersed with ugly swirls of grey.

"What a pity," Yerudit said.

"This planet's a goner," Jonan said off-handedly. "The Climate Scientists warned the pollies, but, you know, too many of them had their hands in the pockets of fossil fuels."

A light flashed, indicating people were free to move.

"Drink?" Jonan suggested.

They went to the bar and found the Zirenian already there. He waggled his flexible fingers at them. Yerudit waved back. Jonan consulted his minScreen. "The finger-tentacles are actually called fingatules," he read. "Hmm, maybe that should be pronounced finger-tools." He took a closer look at the Zirenian. "And he, I can't call him *it,* is still wearing his clothes. Good ones, too." Jonan bristled with pretend indignation. "Space, I think he goes to a better tailor than I do."

Jonan also noted the thin tubes running through the transparent Suit. "There's his atmosphere," he said, "and there's probably some sort of anti-grav in there as well to adjust his weight up or down. I imagine," Jonan said dryly, "he also carries his own Terra belly pills."

"But he wouldn't eat our food!" Yerudit protested.

"No, but you know what travellers are like."

"I do, indeed." Yerudit dipped into her bag and dangled a small packet. "How off-worlders deal with synthetics." She nudged him. "The Zirenian could just use a force field," she said, "but I guess the Suit makes it easier for him to talk with the local natives." She giggled. "Hey, that's us. Well, you, anyway. You're a local native."

"Native?" Jonan harrumphed. "I am Doctor Merize, Psychaeologist."

Terra was now a blue-green plate beneath them, as luminous as Ming china on a velvet cushion. "It's beautiful," she murmured, "truly beautiful. Even with the grey."

The Zirenian moved closer. "It is beautiful," he agreed, "and was more beautiful before the pollution. We tried to warn you, but the human race has strange tendency for self-immolation. This is guilt, perhaps?"

"Guilt?" Jonan nodded. "Maybe? It's there, in the old religions."

"Yes, old-man-with-beard-in-sky. Now, no religion. We, too, once. Next stage, very interesting."

"The next stage?" Yerudit queried.

"The next stage. Evolution of religion does not stop." The green skin flickered. Jonan looked at his minScreen; more alien humour.

When the Zirenian moved closer to the window, Jonan thought about their common history. The E-Ts had been watching Terra from before the industrial revolution, right through the fossil fuel period and on until the water wars.

What message of theirs would, could, have got through? Only a nuclear blast. Thank space the Zirenians had been peaceful. Or maybe the non-humans had recognised that Terra was too difficult to Zir-form. Even after the drama of first contact, Terrans had continued to fight and to pollute. No wonder, there had always been Clans eager to leave. Maybe the Zirenians had helped them. Out there, the Clans could create their own utopias. Although Jonan had always doubted the new societies would stay utopian for long. He glanced sideways. Now, though, because of Yerudit, he was beginning to reconsider.

She was still gazing in fascination at the Zirenian. Jonan was surprised to experience an odd stab of jealousy. He tapped her shoulder. "Try a Luna Crescent," he said, leading her back to the bar. Their drinks arrived, and he led her to a different window. "There's Luna." He pointed at the shadowed disc.

Yerudit smiled. "I wasn't really thinking of kissing him." She turned to the window. "Lovely, truly lovely, even though so stark and pock-marked. A planet with acne."

A bell chimed, time for the passengers to resume their seats. They strapped in, and the shuttle slowly settled beside a silver tunnel. Connecting to an airlock, it prevented travellers from getting outside. Suicide was too easy that way. In theory, it was still possible but so difficult, the depressed gave up while the demented became confused. It kept Terran statistics from looking too bad when compared to other planets. *Lunatic* was back to being a word not a state of mind.

Fortunately within the domes, there was an excellent system of glidewalks and sliptubes. Jonan, feeling confident, said, "I've been Lunaside many times, so you choose where you'd like to start."

"That's easy," Yerudit replied, "where men first landed."

Jonan waved a hand. "All roads lead to Brisbane," he said. "On Luna, two places are easy to get to and Luna Foundation is one, the place of first landing." He paused. "The *alleged* place of first landing."

"It isn't?"

"I'm not sure. Politics and real estate have made their mark even on space history."

"You mean?"

"Oh, who claims what. Where it's easiest to build. What looks best on the brochures."

"Space, you are a cynic."

"You think?"

They had entered a vast and busy dome. At a doorway, a large sign read: *Central One.* A clock that gave Terran time read: *Luna Tick*.

Yerudit groaned. "Do they have to?"

"And you thought I was cynical? It's for the honeymooners. To put them in the mood."

"There's more like that?"

"You'll see."

The sliptube arrived, another silver cylinder that glided noiselessly above a silver ribbon. They entered, a warning light flashed, and the doors closed. With a gentle acceleration, the tube glided out of Central.

"Best not to look out yet," Jonan said. "There's no atmosphere so everything glares." Not quite fast enough, the smart-glass dimmed. "Now's okay."

Yerudit squinted through the window. As her vision adjusted, she turned to Jonan shocked at the huge multi-coloured signs that covered whole mountain sides. "Ads!" she exclaimed. "Here? Can't Terrans leave anything alone?"

Jonan stroked his beard, then found he was tugging it. He usually found these signs amusing. "Man's message to the stars?" he suggested.

"You really think Zirenians want Luna toothpaste?"

Jonan shrugged, but fortunately, the neon signs were soon

left behind. The sliptube slowed as they slid into another dome, the famed Luna Foundation where Jonan bought two tickets.

"It's a show?" Yerudit exclaimed. "What sort?"

"A sound and light re-enactment." Jonan was again apologetic. "It's educational. For, er, children."

Yerudit shook her head in amazement. "Are all Terrans, children? They are Luna Ticks!" She laughed – but not with humour.

They sat and waited. The main lights dimmed and the vastness of space made itself apparent. A few people gasped, they'd never been exposed like this before. Then the effects began. Living ghosts filled the spaces. A hologram of a rocket roared out of the sky and landed on a sheet of fire. A space-suited man bounced in slow motion across the rocks and planted a flag.

"One small step for man..." he began.

"One big yawn for women," Yerudit said.

The spaceman's speech echoed between people and the stars, a drama that Jonan enjoyed but did not believe. This site was too photogenic to be authentic. Yet he buzzed with the excitement of the performance, and it amused him that machines could create such an illusion. He looked sideways at his companion. Burnished copper. It would be easy to think she was an illusion, too.

She caught his eye and grinned. "For the children, you said? Obviously for the big children." Once she'd accepted Luna as a theme park, Yerudit obviously enjoyed it. Even the lunch, although she winced at the menu: Luna burgers, Galileo crunch, and Tyche coffee. "They don't let up, do they?" she remarked.

Fortunately, the cooking was a thousand times better than the names, and so in an agreeable mood, they went on to Contact Crater, the place where Zirenians had first shown themselves to humans. Here they booked into another drama, one that replayed three times a day, more on school holidays. As before, Yerudit shook her head in wonder, fascinated by the holo of a Zirenian flying saucer. The sleek disc was totally silent. They could well understand the shock as it landed virtually at the feet of the early astronauts. Towards the end of the show, a buzz at their side disturbed them.

"Hello," said the Zirenian. "Remember me?"

"No. Who are you?" Yerudit giggled.

Jonan laughed. "Of course, we remember you. But how do you recognise one human from another?"

"I total sense you," the Zirenian replied.

"You what?"

"Total sense. Sight-smell-taste-other."

"Oh." Jonan consulted his minScreen. The Zirenian had more acute senses, other senses. Although, obviously, he hadn't tasted or smelt them through his protective suit. Anecdotes even suggested the E-Ts were telepathic. Not everyone had given up the idea of angels in the sky.

The Zirenian, his skin colouring with humour, asked, "You like this show?"

Evasively, Jonan replied, "It has its moments."

The Zirenian made a sound that came out as white noise – Jonan guessed at laughter – then he added, "Meeting big shock for you. Big funny for us."

"Funny?" Yerudit pounced on the word.

"So much dignity. Like now on holoshow."

"Wasn't there dignity?" Yerudit said.

"Yes, but..." The Zirenian puffed out his Suit and flapped his arms. Jonan and Yerudit laughed out loud. The nonhuman, however, waved a webbed hand. "See, me now funny to you. You were funny to us, but no one dare laugh. You too frightened."

Jonan indicated the stark exterior. "That alone frightened us. Add you and we were terrified."

Yerudit wiggled her fingers for attention. "Why did you wait till they were on Luna?"

"If land on Terra, we would have to go on talk shows, reality shows." The Zirenian's skin changed rapidly, indicating more laughter. "If land on Terra, too much politics, too much near to nuclear strife."

"Is Zirenia like Terra?" Yerudit asked.

"Not like. You more like."

"Me? Hebaron?"

"I think."

"How?"

"One day, you see, perhaps. But excuse, talking make tired. Perhaps speak later."

The Zirenian walk-hopped towards the station. Yerudit watched him. "How are we more alike?" she wondered.

"Not we," Jonan said pointedly. "You."

"Us? Us off-worlders?"

"No, off-worlders differ too much. He meant you specifically."

"Hmm." Yerudit frowned.

"But not me."

"Hmm," she repeated and touched his cheek in a rare gesture of affection, "you're different again."

They followed the Zirenian and caught a sliptube to *Moonbeams*. As a restaurant, it was almost too much, too open. The walls were muted to vanishing point, giving the impression they were in the restaurant at the edge of the universe. As *Moonbeams* was in shadow, the effect was overwhelming. Nearby rocks gleamed in silver-black, and above them, the stars shone, a thick soup of a galaxy.

"Unearthly," Jonan murmured.

"Unearthly," Yerudit agreed. "Lunarly."

"And beautiful. But not as beautiful as you." Jonan smiled. He had said that before to other women, to many other women, but this time he meant it. The starlight illumined Yerudit as if she shone from within.

With a gentle smile, she said, "The stars are our infinity."

"Yes?"

She indicated the vastness around them. "I mean, it's what the Tsadkah said. The stars are within us."

Ariyeh the Tsadkah, her teacher. The world turned and Jonan felt another pang of jealousy. The Tsadkah and his mysterious sayings. This wasn't going to be just a happy-go-lucky weekend, after all. Well, he hadn't really expected it to be. With Yerudit, nothing was ever just happy-go-lucky. There was always philosophy.

In a quiet mood, they went on to their hotel. The building, like so many on Luna, was a honeymoon trap with pink and pearly decorations. Tired from traveling, Jonan lay on the bed and idly pressed a button. A panel demisted and showed the icy beauty of the stars. Hopefully, he turned to Yerudit.

"Join me?" he said.

She shook her head. "Not yet." She sat and gazed upwards, homewards he guessed, then closed her eyes. In moments, she became immobile, her copper skin turning her into an ancient golden fresco. In contrast, Jonan became restless. He touched buttons here and there; the bed changed, the light changed. Yerudit, however, did not change. Then when she did open her eyes, she gave a distant smile.

"Good?" Jonan asked, feeling ignored.

She nodded and smiled again. But this time she really saw him, and at that, his mood immediately lifted. He wanted to reach out, to touch her, to lay with her. But not wanting to risk a direct refusal he only said, "Show me your dance."

A mischievous expression lit her face, and Jonan knew that whatever she did, it wouldn't be the same as before. It wasn't. Yerudit took a wafer from her bag and put it into the Screen. As he'd guessed, a quite different sort of music came out, staccato and martial so that even the silences were jerky. Yerudit began to move in synch with the music, bending into spine-breaking positions and holding them during the long silences. She twisted, arched, and punched. Sometimes she moved faster than he could see, sometimes slowly, although still with a dynamic tension. There was tremendous strength in this dance. Though it was as hypnotic as the first time, it was totally lacking in sexuality. The music and Yerudit stopped at the same moment.

"You like?" she asked, the grin returning.

"Fascinating. Like a rabbit with a snake."

She laughed. "Which of us is which?"

Her tone was so friendly that Jonan ached to touch her, but yet again, he approached indirectly. "Teach it to me?" he asked.

She frowned, again tilting her head to listen inwards. "Yes," she said hesitantly. "I can but…"

"But what?"

"First you must learn the individual postures."

"Then show me." Jonan spoke more curtly than he'd intended, but a competitive streak, long dormant, had again stirred within him.

In reaction, Yerudit studied his face. Smiling as if she actually liked what she saw there, she dropped to the floor and balanced just on her fingers and toes. "Do this," she commanded.

As she held the position, Jonan slowly knelt on all fours, put his weight on his fingers then stretched out his legs. In a few moments, his arms began to tremble.

"Hold. Hold. Hold. Change."

In one movement, Yerudit span onto her right elbow. Relieved to get the weight off his arms, Jonan also attempted to spin, but only managed to bang his hip on the floor. Muttering, he pushed up again and took the new posture. Laughing now, Yerudit used her hands to turn his shoulders, her knee to straighten his back, and her fingers to lift his chin. At his lack of success, Jonan scowled.

"Space jelly," she murmured.

"It hurts," he complained, struggling to hold the position.

"Is that a reason to stop?"

"When better?"

"When I say so."

Jonan groaned.

"All right," she laughed. "Stop!"

As floppy as a released spring, Jonan slumped on the floor. He was beginning to see the playfulness that lay beneath her copper gravity. And the challenge. From his prone position, he growled, "Show me more."

Yerudit assessed him. "You sure?"

"I'm sure. Definitely. Well, maybe."

"But are you sure, you're sure…?" She laughed at his expression. "Okay, copy me."

Then for an eternity of pain, the payment for being obstinate, Yerudit demonstrated movement after movement. Jonan creaked and groaned in imitation. Now he understood why it had been so hard to pin her down. She was as fit as an athlete.

Eventually, an exhausted Jonan crawled onto the bed. Yerudit sat on the edge and smiled. "Once you've mastered those then you can learn the dance."

"That'll take forever," he complained, though in his heart, he determined it wouldn't.

Her hand rested on the bed. Cautiously, Jonan reached for it. At the contact, she looked down as if surprised. "I was thinking," she said, "of the Zirenian. It was quite a coincidence to meet him. The Ariyeh speaks well of them." Then with a casual grace, she undressed and slipped into bed. With a peck on his cheek, she moved to one side and promptly fell asleep. Jonan listened to the rhythm of her breath, angry and disappointed. They might never meet the Zirenian again but Jonan was jealous of him.

Jealous of an *it,* he thought savagely, a space-warped-it that Ariyeh the Tsadkah had spoken well of. He mentally groaned. But if he was jealous of that he might just as well leap into the vacuum of space and give up. His hand hovered to touch her. That vacuum, however, was not to be filled that night.

# Chapter 6

With Yerudit so close, Jonan had a restless night; his hormones rat-a-tatting chaotically against his skin whilst all his muscles ached. It didn't help that Yerudit slept so soundly. Didn't she have hormones? Wasn't she a woman? Well, he knew she was. Wasn't he a man? Obviously not. When the early morning found him bleary eyed, she awoke bright-eyed, bushy-tailed, and ready for anything. As long as anything was the climb up to Lunar IV.

This lookout, one of the special places, was garish free: no holoshows, no ads. Near the summit, even the artificial light and gravity were faded out. It was all natural, at least as natural as life within a dome on an airless planet could be. And it was stunning. Undimmed, the stars were awesome. Myriad diamonds shone out of a solid blackness, a blackness so total it somehow seemed alive. The stars were the glittering eyes of a fathomless beast.

Yerudit gripped his arm excitedly, and they stayed long after Jonan was ready to leave. Insofar as Luna had any noise and bustle, Jonan wanted to get back to it. In fact, after the void of Lunar IV, Luna Central felt almost like home. There, as he gradually unwound, Jonan gazed around in the hope of spotting the Zirenian. But they entered the shuttle without seeing him.

"Humans and Zirenians don't mix that much," he remarked, "although we're not so different. Just scientifically behind."

"Ariyeh says we can't accept that they're a thousand tech years ahead of us."

*Ariyeh*, Jonan bridled. "An expert, is he? What else does he say?"

At his tone, Yerudit's expression became distant. "He also

says they advance slower than us because they put more emphasis on…" She paused and grinned, "wisdom."

"I understand that," Jonan said stiffly. "After all, I am a Psychaeologist." She nodded. Surprised at her agreement, he asked, "Does he means the sort of wisdom that relates to your puppets?"

It was Yerudit's turn to be surprised. "You know about the shadow puppets?"

"I Screened Hebaron."

She smiled. "Why?"

Jonan blushed and pulled furiously at his beard. "After I met you."

"Flattered." She grinned again . "So what did you learn?"

"That you use puppets to tell your myths and superstitions."

"Myths and superstitions?" She raised an eyebrow of fine-spun copper. "Perhaps. But we see them as part of our life."

"Some sort of psychodrama?"

"Some sort of spirituo-drama."

Uncertain if she were teasing, Jonan said, "I'm not sure I understand."

She laughed. "Well, that's a start. It is hard to understand. Perhaps you should come to Hebaron and see for yourself." The invitation, put so casually, made Jonan tingle with anticipation. Yerudit, too, became excited. "Hebaron," she echoed. "On the way back, there are a few places I just have to visit. Look." She rummaged through her bag. Jonan expected her to pull out her minScreen. Instead she held a plastibook with pages that actually turned. The book described out-of-the-way planets with words on the left side and holos on the right.

"They're very well done," Jonan observed. "Who did them?"

"The Tsadkah, of course."

"Of course." A bitter taste arose in Jonan's mouth.

"He made it. At home, I even have paper books with glorious illustrations in gold leaf."

"Seems he can do about anything," Jonan said in a tone that would've soured honey.

"It seems." Yerudit's tone was wistful. "I made some as well."

"Why go to all the trouble? Why not use Screens like everyone else?"

"Why not?" Yerudit tilted her head as she did so often when she spoke of home, once more giving the impression of hearing the inaudible. "A paper book," she said, "is something you can feel and smell as well as just look at. You can practically taste it, eat your words. It's organic, close to the earth. Surely even you must know that to make something with your hands is to feed your soul."

"A Tsadkah aphorism?"

"An off-world attitude."

"I've never made anything with my hands. Only with my head."

Yerudit inspected his soft palms. "You're still unfinished, but hands with this shape, they're crafty."

Jonan studied his hands, thinking to joke, *I'm not crafty*, but he said nothing as Yerudit returned to the book and slowly turned its pages. Despite himself, Jonan was drawn in. Reading together, their shoulders touched, and he was all too aware of her heady perfume. Too soon, the Luna shuttle touched down.

Encouraged by their closeness, Jonan said, "Come on to my place?"

Yerudit moved away. "Not now, I want to make notes."

Held at bay, Jonan went home alone. Although now, alone meant lonely. He roamed the house in search of something to do, wondering about using his hands. But except for parts of his gourmet cooking, all he could find were buttons to press. One minor way to use his hands would be to Screen Evana, but that felt wrong, felt unfaithful. Faith? In this day and age? All the same, he held back and decided to do Yerudit's exercises instead, pushing his muscles until they screamed. After that, he took a long hot shower, adding oils intended to relieve his muscles. When he went to bed, it wasn't because he was tired, but because he'd exhausted all the other possibilities. Nor was he at all surprised by the dreams that sleep dredged out of his psyche. They were of the reaching out, never attaining sort, of swimming in deep space after an ever-receding starship.

That weekend should have cemented their affair but didn't. It only registered as a marker and after it they simply accepted they were somehow being thrust together. But it was a very unsatisfying state of affairs. Jonan would put himself out for Yerudit; she would become distant. He would be casual; she would want to be friendly. In all, he began to fear she would've preferred not to see him. Yet neither of them could escape the web that bound them.

Nor, no matter how much he tried, could Jonan overcome his jealousy of the Tsadkah. Even Yerudit's most casual mention would infuriate him, and she quickly learnt to speak casually of her teacher when with Jonan. The Ariyeh was a part of her in a way that Jonan wasn't. Yet wanted to be. But wasn't allowed to be, an experience he found new and unsettling. To compensate, he pushed himself into his work. Two and a bit projects were at hand. The bit was Tomas.

"Show me your latest holo," Jonan said. The student handed across a cube, and the Psychaeologist inserted it into his Screen. After a rush of brilliant colours, a suave couple in designer clothes entered a high-class restaurant. A caption read: Making it in Sector 31. "Excellent," Jonan said. "No more rugged miners digging up dirt. A lot more inference." He gazed at the postgrad. "You look different, too."

Tomas beamed. "I've started using SkinGlow, and I've taken up hover skating. It's great for bumping into people."

"Good work, Tomas." Jonan returned the holo. "You don't need to see me anymore."

Tomas made a face. "And I was just beginning to enjoy it."

Then he grinned, shook Jonan's hand, and left.

The Psychaeologist experienced a little pang. It was, he surmised, the same little grief as when a parent takes a child to school for the first time. But it was such a small tug, he easily smothered it by turning his attention to his two other projects.

One concerned Mirena. The other was the Enhancer Group, an event led by both Jonan and Evana. These two projects were going to interweave because Mirena, under his care, was doing so very well. In a couple of sessions, they'd probed the details of her space phobia, her family relationships, and her current affairs. After that, he'd started to record her brain waves in response to different tranquillisers. By the fifth session, they were really ready to go, and so on the sixth session, Jonan used an electro-sedative to put Mirena into a Delta-4 state. A feedback loop kept her there. In that deep relaxation, Jonan used the Electro-Image Enhancer to stimulate her senses.

In his own imagination, Jonan the artist-scientist held a paintbrush in one hand, a test-tube in the other. The science was to use the Enhancer to feed phobia-related images to Mirena. At the lowest level, she had no fear of a multi-sensory construct of a distant starship. But when Jonan took her closer, the negative reactions began. The art was then to know whether to take her closer while increasing the relaxant or else to back off.

The more techie-minded Psychaeologists preferred to back off, but that took too long for Jonan. He liked to skate closer to the edge, knowing he could do this as he'd taken the time to build up a relationship. Consequently, he could push Mirena where others feared to tread. So when the Enhancer showed her fear, Jonan guided her to go closer, and with the feedback, her muscles felt as if she was actually walking. Simultaneously, she smelt the actinic odour associated with the Drive, and as the scene developed, her fear reactions increased – as did her doubts about her sense of being.

Jonan cracked his knuckles like a pianist ready to tackle a difficult concerto. His province was Psychaeology not Philosophy, so Mirena could intellectually *doubt* as much as she liked – as long as she didn't actually angst about it. So for her fears, he used the Enhancer to dampen down her *to-be-or-not-to-be* doubts. In this way, she lived in the images but hardly worried about them. Since the student responded so well to his direction, Jonan was confident that in two more sessions she would be able to face the most vivid images without any phobic reaction.

Jonan was confident because he had performed this many times before. Once, he had philosophised about it, grappling with questions of consciousness and probability space. But not anymore, his motivation had changed and instead of trying to understand mind, he'd turned to how best to manipulate it.

Yet now he seemed to be changing again. On his second session with Mirena, the old questions resurfaced. Less to do with her, he decided, but much more to do with Yerudit. The attraction between them was such a puzzle as to be almost occult. In fact, when Jonan should've been planning the last sessions for Mirena, his thoughts kept drifting away. He continually Screened Hebaron in search of its secrets. The distant planet haunted him. In particular, he wanted to know about the shadow puppets. He frequently replayed the holos, hoping to see more, even stared at his own little indo-puppet, trying to see through it. He had the strangest impression that the shadow puppets held the key to the workings of the mind – at least his mind.

Mirena, of course, was never aware of his self-doubts. To the student, he remained the trim-bearded, suave, and slightly plump figure of supreme self-confidence. With that confidence in him fixed in her mind, she approached her final ordeal: facing the real thing, Probability Space itself. A commercial run would've been ideal, but to save costs, they used the University's starship. This put an extra strain on Mirena, for not only was the vessel old, but many of the other passengers had similar problems to hers.

When they came to entering the starship, Jonan murmured, "Any worries?"

"No, not at all," she replied. "Excited, if anything."

There was certainly a lot of hustle and bustle. Not only were therapists and their clients on board but so were student officers and stewards. Inevitably, one group was led by Evana, who waved as she shepherded her charges to the bar.

"Drink," she urged them. "It's a good friend of the phobic."

More people trooped into the starship and the whole lot milled around excitedly. When a light flashed and a voice announced take-off, many passengers gasped. Take-off was a reality. A muted roar from the ship produced an intense silence, followed by an excited buzz. At an increase in pressure, Jonan knew they were lifting off. He checked Mirena. In response, she laid a hand on his arm.

"Don't worry," she said cheerfully. "I think, therefore I probably am."

"Descartes," he said.

"Probably. Not that it helps. After a while, it becomes I emote therefore I probably am not."

Jonan relaxed, enjoying his superiority in a way he never could with Yerudit. Feeling good, he gazed out at the green-blue glow of Terra. Around them, the student stewards practiced their services. It was all quite relaxed. Then the interior pulsated in a warm pink, the windows opaqued, and without any further tremors, the starship moved into Probability Space.

Now there were only small windows that could be opened, and it took nerve to do so. Jonan could. Could Mirena? He led her to a window, put a finger to the button and said, "Ready?"

Though pale, she nodded. Jonan pressed the button, the window irised opened, and Mirena gasped. No wonder, for Probability Space was by no means empty. It contained layers upon layers of stars. Yet focus on an individual cluster and it was no longer there. The stars were as mobile as a shifting shoal of silver fish, moving first in one direction, then abruptly changing pace. Even the Electro-Image Enhancer couldn't match this reality, so it was no wonder Mirena gasped, but more with wonder than with fear.

The starship skimmed through Space, through an ever-changing kaleidoscope, sometimes sharp, sometimes blurring. Mirena watched wide-eyed while Jonan kept one finger on the auto-sooth. She had a temporary implant but it was never needed. She soared with the ship.

For lunch, they entered norm space at a distant solar system. The captain had chosen well, and they circled a misty planet with a rainbow of rings. Mirena raised her glass in a toast.

"Well done," she said. "I knew you'd help me."

"You made it very easy," Jonan replied, the words sliding smoothly from his tongue. They clinked glasses, fingers touched and momentarily stayed together.

Effectively, the remainder of the trip was just for the trainee stewards. The therapy was over and for the rest of the day, they could just enjoy themselves. They ate and drank and the air between them grew intimate. When the starship returned in the evening, it was all too easy for Jonan to say, "My place?"

"Love to," Mirena murmured.

"My solabub awaits."

Jonan pressed the button for them to enter, the button to adjust the seats, the button to take them home. There was no unspoken criticism. Nor was there any when he pressed the button for drinks.

"To therapy," Jonan toasted.

"Its benefits."

Their eyes met, here were his old adventures. They entered the lounge, and he flipped the master button. Now only the direst emergency from outside could disturb them. He poured more drinks. Then, at the time that he had promised to contact Yerudit, his lips were sliding down Mirena's smooth and naked belly.

# CHAPTER 7

The next day, Jonan felt unusually unsure of himself. He didn't think sex with Mirena was wrong. He just didn't feel that it was right. And that made him irritable. Why should he feel guilty? That sort of morality went out ages ago. Even so, he felt defensive when, as previously arranged, Yerudit came to his house.

"I called you twice yesterday," she said, an edge to her voice.

"I was, er, working late."

"That's not like you."

"It was a client. She had a Probability phobia, and I had to take her into Probability Space."

"Was that the only space you took her to?" Her eyes scanned his face, her own face growing tight with tension.

"I had to keep her with me. To, er, make sure."

"To debrief her, no doubt."

Yerudit was now icy, his hesitations confirming her doubts. Yet multiple partners were no big deal by Terran standards, at least, Jonan's version of them. Still, he found himself groping for words. Finally, he burst out, "It wasn't like that. At least, it wasn't meant to be like that. It just happened."

"Just happened? I thought you were the giver of choices. Did you, then, not have a choice?"

Jonan slumped into a chair, becoming more agitated when the programmed seat tried to adjust for his comfort. Yerudit loomed above him, her words falling on Jonan like bricks. When he made no defence, she whirled and plunged out the door. He struggled for words, but still hadn't found any when he stumbled after her. Nor did he have any words to call her back.

But Jonan did want her back, more than anything, and her

departure dug holes into his heart. He cursed himself for being such a fool. Cursed himself for wanting her so much and cursed himself for indulging with Mirena. For it was just an indulgence, no more satisfying than scratching a passing itch. Yet at the same time, he was angry. The copper-skinned off-worlder was not blameless, her unpredictable affection and her unpredictable sexuality had unsettled him. That as much as anything had caused him to wander.

Over the weekend, Jonan tried to contact Yerudit, but her Screen wouldn't answer him. He waited for her at his lecture but she didn't arrive. Finally, he left a note by her door. That brought a reply. His Screen read, "I'll see you at your next lecture. Otherwise please don't try to contact me. Please."

Jonan stared at the message. Although negative, he took it as a sign that he *was* important to her. With little hope, he sent her a bunch of flowers, expensive genetically modified flowers. Yet, as expected, there was no reply.

So, the next lecture it was to be. Jonan arrived early and fiddled with his notes. He hoped she might already be there. He feared she mightn't come at all. The other students came, sat quietly, and gazed expectantly. When everyone else was seated, Yerudit finally arrived, but clearly didn't want to talk. Worse still, she chose a distant seat, and although he tried not to stare, he was all too aware of her slim, copper figure.

Jonan faced the class and the familiar words trickled out, but they seemed to him to have no meaning. It was as if he was looking at his own hand and had no idea what it did. Desperately, he tried not to look at her, but his gaze skittered in every direction. When it did happen to go to her, she either looked down or looked through him. His emptiness turned to ache, and he knew their brief affair was now over.

During the lecture, while poised between emptiness and ache, Jonan felt a curious sensation, an electric tingle at the base of his spine that spiralled up and into a peculiar buzz at the top of his head. Instinctively, he looked at Yerudit. At the same moment, she looked directly at him. The electric tingle suddenly exploded, whooshing up from the soles of his feet to the top of his head, and as at their first meeting, his vision tunnelled as if only the two of them existed. The moment was so intense, he could not only taste the copper gold of her skin, and hear the pounding of her heart, but he could also sense her deep, deep sadness.

As swiftly as summer lightning, the vision passed, as did the tingling and the buzzes. Jonan found himself stopped in mid-sentence and had to struggle to continue. Once more, he had the overwhelming sense that the two of them were being thrust together. And although he didn't like the idea that he was a puppet to external forces, he didn't object to its goal. Nor, it seemed, could Yerudit. At the end of the class, she was the last to leave.

"It seems," she said, "that we must try again."

Although this was what Jonan longed to hear, her flatness infuriated him. "I've already said I'm sorry," he muttered. "We don't have to go on."

"No, we don't." Head down, Yerudit slowly walked away.

Even though his mind told him to let her go, his feet moved to keep up with her. As she kept in step, he was prompted to say, "Perhaps we can just be friends?"

She gave a wintery smile. "With us, that may be even harder than being lovers."

Jonan made a face; that sounded like another Tsadkah aphorism. "Well, we could try. D'you want to meet for a drink tonight?"

Yerudit smiled wanly. "All right, Jonan, we'll try. I'll try."

So because of that strange force, they met again, although both remained polite and wary. Yet because he couldn't refrain from talking about it, Jonan asked, "D'you have any idea what happened?"

Yerudit looked sad. "Ask the Tsadkah," she replied. "He knows."

The Tsadkah! Jonan didn't want to think about the man let alone speak to him. Thinking of the Tsadkah made Jonan broody, and their desultory conversation fell into silence. Shortly after, he took her home. At the door, however, they found that they couldn't just part, but unwillingly arranged to meet again. And again and again. Jonan was strongly attracted to Yerudit and just about accepted the idea that they were being thrust together. Yerudit was not as attracted to Jonan but was more willing to accept the idea they were being thrust together. And so they kept meeting.

On one of their friendlier days, Jonan took Yerudit to the Flinders Ranges of South Australia. The desert light was intoxicating in its intensity. In a bout of pure pleasure, they clambered up orange slopes so barren that no sign of human habitation was visible. Jonan panted at the climb but was determined to do better that he had done those weeks ago in Egypt.

It made for an exhausting day. Returned to Jonan's place, Yerudit asked, "Do your legs ache?"

Jonan wobbled his knees. "Heaps!"

"You've kept up with the exercises?"

"Yes."

"Do they really ache?"

"A bit. Not as much as last time."

Yerudit gave a rare smile, a warm smile that made her copper skin glow like embers. In a much less guarded manner, she said, "Show me what you can do."

Ah, but that was a difficult one. If he backed out, she'd be critical. If he performed with wobbly knees, she'd be critical. Yet the same obstinacy that had kept him doing the exercises now prompted him to demonstrate. With a grunt, he stretched up and then bent down. Bottom in the air, his weight rested on just hands and feet. After a long while, he slowly raised one arm, put it down, one arm and one leg, put them down, and on and on from posture to posture until he was trembling with the effort.

"Superb," Yerudit said. "I'm really surprised." She paused, put her head to one side and thought. Or listened. "Well, perhaps not," she said eventually. "I'm not surprised."

"I am," Jonan said grinning wildly. "I thought you'd say what about this, what about that, what about everything."

"Am I that dreadful?" She laughed. "What about… what about linking the movements together?"

"As in your dance?" Jonan's body was trembling. Not just with muscle ache, but also with excitement.

"Watch." Yerudit bent back into an arch then, in a few flowing movements, reversed herself into a bridge. "Now you."

"Show me again."

She repeated the movement but at high speed so that they both laughed at the sheer impossibility of it. Then Jonan tried. He bent and with the grace of an arthritic tortoise toppled onto his back. He tried again. Again and again. For five… ten… twenty minutes… determination pushed him. Finally, he sank into the carpet. "I'll creak if I go on," Jonan panted.

"I'm still surprised," Yerudit said, "even though I'm not." She crawled over to him and rested her head in the crook of his arm. Her fingers stroked his cheek. With a sigh, she reached inside his shirt. This was so unexpected, a surprise, and yet not a surprise. By exercising, he had evidently given her a gift, a gift that she really appreciated. Gently, they uncovered their bodies. He saw again the copper glint of her skin, felt the soft-hard touch of her, and tasted her sweet-saltiness. Jonan moved inside her with the slow steady movement of classical music reaching for its climax. Yet even beyond, they remained as one, unwilling to ever pull apart.

When they did, the contact remained. Yerudit stayed that

night, and Jonan sensed a subtle change. The barriers that had kept her aloof had at last crumbled.

Fortunately, Mirena wasn't a problem. That one night with her was just her way of thanking him. Shortly afterwards, she went into space and completed her thesis without any phobia. Evana, however, did prove to be a problem. She had grown used to their irregular intimacies. Having other partners had not interrupted them before, and she couldn't see why it should do so now. Although not demanding, she did drop hints. And these increased as the day of their Enhancer Group drew closer.

The Electro-Image Enhancer was normally used only with individuals, with brain scans and tranq levels finely adjusted to the one person. Physiological parameters, however, were fairly similar for similar personalities. This meant that a carefully selected group could be hooked up together. So Jonan chose people with no serious problems, but those who wanted to expand their awareness, perhaps to push it to an extreme – an extreme of tactile awareness.

Perhaps in earlier times, this had not been such a problem. People who tilled the earth and baked their own bread received plenty of tactile stimulation. Yet in this generation, so much was done at the press of a button. Even sex was easily entered into, but making a simple show of affection had become more difficult. It was Jonan's pleasure, through the Enhancer Group, to facilitate such displays.

In June, at the end of the semester, their first combined group was finally ready. They met on a bright winter's morn when birds, which once migrated, were singing as though it were spring. With such perfect weather, as soon as they'd hooked the students into the Enhancer, Jonan one-wayed the walls; no one could see in but they could see out. More than just see. Through the Enhancer, the twinkling sky could be tasted as a rich and heady wine. The waving trees could be smelt as the subtlest of perfumes. The flight of the multi-coloured rosellas was the soaring towards freedom of every student.

Jonan and Evana both played the Enhancer, feedback turning them into gods as they gradually harmonised the group's brain waves. With random variations pulled into synchrony, the students spontaneously moved into a circle. By the end of the morning, they were holding hands, hugging, and stroking.

In the afternoon, Jonan introduced them to his theories, making the young ones both excited and apprehensive. But with their trust in the two adults, it was easy to Enhance the excitement, tranq down the apprehension, and bring them all back into synch. Then they paired off. Jonan had already made eye contact with a female, Evana with a male. In their pairs, they took turns at controlling the Enhancer. The walls opaqued, the lights dimmed, and finally each couple separated into its own little room.

Subliminal visuals suggested touch, subliminal aurals induced relaxation. The temperature within each room gradually increased. Encouraged by these cues, it became all too easy to touch. All too easy to touch, to explore, to remove. And Jonan's partner was willing, so very very willing. With her hands, her mouth, and her legs, she reached the climax he had so very carefully orchestrated. And, no doubt, Evana and the others had reached the same conclusion.

Eventually, a warning bell chimed, rang a second time, and then a third, giving them time to adjust. The lights rose, the partitions disappeared, and Jonan glanced around at faces flushed with intimacy. Evana sent him a great big wink. The group had been a success, barriers and taboos victoriously transcended.

Jonan talked the students down from the haze of unreality to their everyday and then sent them out into it. Although most would've preferred to remain. But only two people remained, Evana and Jonan. Evana of the slow-fuse smile, of the seductive approach. Her clothes fell away, and light turned into shadow. Half seen, half hidden, she tantalised. In the ritual ending of their groups, their flesh confirmed their self-congratulation.

Although even as he participated, Jonan knew it was a great mistake.

# Chapter 8

With the morning alarm, Jonan stretched luxuriously; memories of yesterday still washing pleasantly over him. But the mood wasn't to last. The Screen chimed. It was Yerudit, her copper face a metal wrought to breaking point.

"I rang you last night," she said.

His euphoria evaporated. "I was working," he muttered.

She tried to speak again but her face contorted, the nearest he'd seen her to tears. Eventually, she squeezed out, "That's what you said the last time. This time, I had pains. Stabbing pains in my stomach."

"Last night?"

She spoke bitterly. "In the afternoon."

Jonan shivered. "D'you still have them?"

"No, they went very quickly."

He paled. The afternoon was when he'd been with Evana and hadn't given a thought to Yerudit. No, that wasn't true, he had thought of her all the time, each and every moment. Yet each and every moment, he'd fought to push the thoughts into the background. Thought and fought. Now she was on the Screen, staring accusingly, and there was nowhere to hide. Jonan sagged, guilt written all over him. Without a word, Yerudit's face disappeared; she'd cut the connection. Jonan immediately called back but his code was rejected.

He stared at the Screen, at 3D fractal patterns playing a meaningless dance of pixels. And it was as if he'd been punched in the guts. Mentally frozen, he went onto the veranda and stared into his garden. His chime sounded, he had to get to work. He had clients to help and students to teach. He couldn't let them think the supreme and confident Psychaeologist had descended into self-pity. He did what he had to do, but it was an effort.

Whenever he could, he Screened Yerudit. He also tried her minScreen, but to no avail, he'd been blocked out of both. In the evening, he went to the crystal spire where she lived, but with no reply to his ringing, he paced around the dome, hoping to see her on the grass. Plenty of students were there, but she wasn't one of them. He went back to her place, but had the curious feeling that it was as empty as himself.

Unwilling to go home, Jonan went into town, avoiding the glidewalks and walking instead. He stopped at a bar. Warmth and chatter filled the air, but he was a rock, and the vibrant atmosphere just flowed around him. Late in the night, with a humid wind blowing, he searched for his solabub, but he couldn't recall where he had left it. For the first time ever, he had to use the minScreen to locate it. It was the first time he'd lost it, and the first time its bright red sheen failed to cheer him. He pressed its buttons for home, a mockery at his fingertips.

Once there, he slotted the bub into its place and approached the front door. As he put his finger to the entry button, the light flashed on his mailbox. It opened to his fingerprint. Inside was a bundle, but even as he reached for it, an icy shiver ran along his spine. He unwrapped it and found a puppet, a long-nosed, dragon-faced shadow puppet. He held it up, posing the dragon silhouette against the crescent moon.

It was made of some primitive material, a form of leather, dyed in blue. For a brief moment, he wondered why it wasn't made of copper. He immediately Screened Hebaron and discovered this was a farewell not a greeting. He stared at the puppet, fascinated by its ugliness; then pulling at its rods, he twisted it from one contorted position into another. On an impulse, he bent it into one of the postures he'd learnt from Yerudit, and then he adopted the same pose. Gradually he worked through her dance; the puppet moving and Jonan following. In those crazed hours, he danced with the puppet, and when he slept it rested on his pillow.

For the few hours left of the night, Jonan tossed and turned. In the morning, he Screened the students' residence, but he was too late.

"Yerudit left yesterday," the receptionist said.

"Where to?" Jonan croaked.

"A tour."

"A tour? Where?"

"Off-world."

*Off-world?* Jonan gazed blankly at the receptionist's face. "Thanks," he said at last and Screened off. He now knew where Yerudit was. She was following in the footsteps of Ariyeh her Tsadkah. She was star travelling. For once, Jonan felt no jealousy of the Tsadkah; he just felt the emptiness of being without her. Somehow the day passed. His mouth made noises and his body performed, but he was not in the sounds or in the gestures. Only at night, when he pushed himself through the exercises did a spark of life return, a pain to counter pain.

It was a few more days before Jonan again touched down on the land of the living, mainly by telling himself Yerudit didn't matter. There were other women equally exotic, plus Evana was always ready to comfort. For three, four, five weeks he continued with the business of life. Then one evening after a heavily perfumed shower, he saw himself in the mirror. Really saw. And it was a shock.

Jonan fingered his little beard. How carefully he'd nurtured it, thinking it gave him the aura of a wild buccaneer. A buccaneer? Wild? Him? He was a petty teacher in a secured position. He did nothing that wasn't safe. His beard was an anachronism. Savagely, he rubbed cream into his cheeks. The hairs came away, and he stared again at the mirror. How changed. His body had lost weight; his eyes had gained it. No buccaneer, he simply looked miserable.

Jonan went to his Screen. He was to meet someone tonight,

a female someone, but he'd forgotten whom. The Screen told him, but the name meant nothing. He sent a message; he wouldn't be going out tonight. Another night? Yes, that would be nice. But he knew there wouldn't be another night. He was sick of nights.

Wearing only shorts, Jonan entered his small back garden. Thick clouds rolled in a sky still recovering from an overdose of carbon dioxide. In the gaps, stars appeared and disappeared. Strange to think that Yerudit was up there. As strange as wondering how many angels could dance on the head of a pin.

Above his head, a fruit bat swooped noiselessly between dark branches. Jonan approached a tree and touched its bark. It felt so rough after all the buttons. A thick branch extended above him. Drawn to it, he reached up, took hold, and pulled. With straining muscles, he slowly rose: something he'd never been able to do before. He hung there, a human bat, until his strength gave out.

Standing again on the earth, Jonan touched his cheeks. It was unexpected to feel skin after so many years of beard. He touched the grass, and that too was odd after the buttons. It was dry, dry enough for him to balance his weight on hands and feet. He began the routine he'd learnt a year ago, a century ago, using pain to counter the emptiness.

For two more weeks, Jonan avoided any more affairs, any complications. Instead, he began to dream of Yerudit. Not romantically, he was too numb for that, but he sensed a contact, saw silver lines of force running from star to star to join the two of them in the shiny velvet of deep space.

The shadow puppet had found a permanent position on the edge of his Screen. He'd had it for several weeks now, the weeks since he'd last seen Yerudit. He found its bulging dragon face ugly, ugly but fascinating. Even though he'd once danced with it, he still couldn't see why anyone would want to tell their life by it. Yet as the nights drew on, it had become his only companion. He gazed at it, and through it, tried to see her.

One evening, he was taken by surprise. A voice entered his head – or so he imagined – and said, "Come to Hebaron. Come."

Jonan startled. Had the puppet moved? Had it spoken? No. It remained just a thing. Yet once again he heard, "Come to Hebaron. Come."

Those words beat inside his skull, driving away all thoughts of sleep. For it hadn't been her voice, a female voice, it had been a man's. A man's voice! Surely, he told himself, it was just a projection: himself telling himself. Yet he wasn't convinced, and although the words were spoken without great emotion, Jonan just couldn't ignore them. Instead he started doing calculations. How long to the end of the year? How much leave did he have? How much money?

In that time, Evana turned out to be a true friend, covering for his frequent lapses as well as occasionally taking over his lectures. In return, though, he had to tell her why.

Her reaction surprised him. "You must really love her," she said, her expression wistful.

"Love?" Jonan echoed. "Yes, but also like a force." He waved a hand. "But really, I just don't know."

Evana raised an eyebrow, but he couldn't explain. Words weren't there, and he couldn't be bothered to dig for them.

Evana kissed him, a chaste kiss. "Take a holiday," she said. "I'll fill in for you. You need the break; I need the money." When he looked doubtful, she added, "If you don't go, I'll start spreading rumours."

"Thanks, mum," he said and attempted to smile.

So with Evana pushing, Jonan applied for leave. She probably did spread rumours, for his application was speedily approved. Probably, it also helped that he looked so haunted. A look that lightened, once he actually put in his application, for the decision to travel proved to be a pointer. If his request had been refused, he would have resigned and gone space-about as a towelpacker. An act, on Terra, that approached blasphemy.

Shortly after approval came through, Jonan went in person to book his ticket. On that day, the shadow puppet went with him for luck. Some luck. For that was the day the attacks began.

# Chapter 9

Yerudit had been fascinated by the Tsadkah's travel book, frequently taking it out to look at. Or maybe to look through, towards the planets it represented: primitive places. She was a primitive fascinated by the primitive. Jonan wasn't, but he was fascinated by her, so if that was the way she'd gone then that was the way he also had to go. If she lingered on the first or second planet, he might even catch up with her. A needle in a haystack? Only if the haystack was as big as a solar system. He didn't care, destiny would bring them together.

But would she visit all the places she'd dreamt about? On the one hand, she'd left the university early so that gave her time in hand. On the other hand, by not completing the course, she might have to pay some debt. Or her penalty might be she wasn't allowed to leave Hebaron again. Who knew how these basic societies operated? Taken all together, it was likely she'd be selective in her visits, especially as his gut feeling said that Yerudit was on a pilgrimage.

So Jonan would copy her. As it was, he wasn't mentally prepared to go straight to Hebaron. If she was there, he wasn't yet ready to face her with the Tsadkah present. If she wasn't, he couldn't bear the humiliation of waiting for her in the other's presence. He needed to prepare. If he caught up with her, good, but if not then this would also be his pilgrimage. He would prove to her that he could suffer on her behalf.

With that decision made, Jonan consulted the Screen for routes. He fed the travel data into a smart program, and the Screen silently applied its heuristics – which were, he knew, just another use of probability calculations. Probabilities in virtual space were calculating probabilities in real space – whatever real meant. As the Screen presented alternatives, the shadow puppet sat and watched. Jonan even had the curious idea that it was guiding him, and he wasn't sure if he liked that idea or not.

He could've arranged everything through the Screen, but thought it would be more symbolic to go to the University travel office in person. A big mistake; the Terrans there had frequent dealings with off-worlders and had acquired an unpleasant veneer of superiority.

"G'day," said a sleek figure with a self-satisfied smile, "My name is Beruce. Are you looking for a pleasure cruise?"

"Not exactly," Jonan passed across his list of names. "I want to go to these places. Some anyway."

Beruce looked at the list. "Oh, you're a religious."

"No, I'm a Psychaeologist."

"Ah, I understand, a study trip. I studied Psychaeology myself." Bruce preened. "As a student, I was particularly interested in that person… Um, archie types… What was his name? Oh, ages ago."

"Jung," Jonan supplied.

"Yes, Yung. He went all over the place studying natives."

Jonan felt an increasing dislike for Beruce, even though he was only voicing the Psychaeologist's own prejudices.

"So, you'll be another Yung."

"I don't exactly subscribe to his ideas."

"Of course not," the other said smoothly. "Who would in this day and age?"

Who would? Yerudit would.

"Now what hotels would you like? I'm afraid there are very few decent ones." The man showed Jonan his Screen. "Only at the terminals, I'm afraid."

"I won't book accommodation, I'll take my chances."

Beruce looked shocked. "Are you sure? They can be very basic, you know."

"I'm sure."

"Towelpacking, eh?"

Beruce shrugged elegantly; if this customer thought roughing it would be romantic, let him find out the hard way. For Jonan's part, he was glad to be finished with the travel agent. He understood now why off-worlders thought Terrans were fools. And why they felt oppressed by them. Jonan the mediator-conciliator felt like leaning forward and punching the travel agent in the nose.

Although it wasn't late, it was storm dark when Jonan reached home. Blue clouds swirled as if stirred in the cup of the sky, and a blustery wind fought against him as he struggled to reach his door. He pressed for entry but nothing happened. Unusual, the wind must've reduced his thumb pressure. He pressed again. Still nothing. The door would neither slide nor iris. Impossible. The storm air was electric, and the hairs on Jonan's neck stood on end.

Below the normal touchpad was an emergency panel. Jonan slid it open and used his minScreen to enter today's programmed release code. He gripped the handle, allowed a moment for DNA analysis, and then pulled. The door moved a fraction, then shut again. Bewildered, Jonan stepped back. This was terrible! Locked out of his own house! Angrily, he leant against the door, intending to push it, but that was when he detected a shadowy figure through the permaglass. Hell, someone was in his house and holding the door shut!

Jonan started to dial for emergency services then stopped; he'd deal with this himself. Anger rising, the Psychaeologist gripped the door and strained. It slid just enough to encourage him to tug even harder, but when he paused for breath, the bloody thing slid shut again!

Red-faced and panting, he braced his foot and tried for a third time, putting all his strength into it. Nothing… nothing… Ah, something! Something… Everything! The door flew open, and Jonan crashed to the side. With a deep chuckle, the shadowy figure, no more substantial than the blustery wind, blew past him. By the time Jonan had struggled up, he/she/it was nowhere to be seen.

Completely disoriented, Jonan slowly edged through the open door and fearfully entered every room. Feeling foolish, he also checked the garden while holding the sharpest kitchen knife in his hand. No one was out there, nor had anything been touched. He put on the outside light and searched for footprints. The air oozed with moisture, but he couldn't find any marks in the mud or on the grass. Inside again, the Psychaeologist locked all the doors and once more went through the house. He was now convinced: no one could've broken in, not without setting off the alarms.

The event was so unusual that Jonan began to think he'd imagined it. Not all, of course, his back and muscles told him that. But a man inside his house? Impossible. No one could've entered. Jonan poured a stiff whiskey. Putting down the empty glass, he noticed that the shadow puppet was grinning – or so it seemed.

Soothed by the whiskey, he thought of making supper. But he didn't, his appetite had vanished. For something to do, he sat down with the current issue of *The Australian Psychaeologist* and tried to dismiss the whole business. Very quickly, however, he began to tremble. A stranger really had broken into his house. His house! He shivered with the shame of violation.

It seemed like an incident that Jonan would never forget, and even the next day, in the familiar surrounds of the University, he felt disconnected. He was making his real coffee when Evana, tracking the aroma, joined him.

"Some for me?" she asked.

"Sorry?" Jonan was gazing out of a window.

"Any coffee for me?"

"Yeah, sure." Jonan waved vaguely in the direction of his coffee machine.

Evana turned him to face her. "What's wrong, Jonan?"

"What?" And Jonan, the Psychaeologist who believed it was necessary to voice one's every concern, merely said, "Oh nothing, just busy, busy arranging my trip."

Although unconvinced, Evana obviously realised that this was one time when it was better not to delve. As it was, *busy* created its own truth. In the business of arranging his trip, even being blocked from entering his own house became a dim memory. Leave forms were filled out, students were graded, and bags were packed then unpacked until there was just one. Over a number of hectic weeks, the Psychaeologist resolved a hundred details, reaching a point where he just wanted to slink away.

Evana, however, was persistent. "You're acting as if you're guilty of something," she said

"Doing a tour of primitive off-worlds?" Jonan spoke without his usual energy. "It's generally considered to be slumming."

"You know better, Jonan." She squeezed his hand. "I know better."

With a natural compassion, Evana helped where she could until, on his day of departure, she took him to the terminal. They arrived just in time to see a great starship lift off, an incredible sight. On anti-grav, the huge shiny cylinder rose in complete silence, dwindled to a tiny speck, then vanished. Somewhere out in space, it would shift into Probability Space. Moments later, it would be probability-years away.

"Awesome, isn't it?" Evana murmured, her face still turned upwards. "You frightened?"

"Of travelling?"

"Of arriving?"

"I try not to think about that."

"No angst?"

Jonan shrugged. "It wasn't as if I decided to go."

"An undecided decision."

"More like an impelled one."

Evana turned her face from the sky. "You're changing, Jonan. You're becoming more mysterious. Harder, too." After a while, she added, "Harder but softer."

"How d'you mean?"

"I don't know. Perhaps that's what's making you more mysterious."

With time to spare, they went to the bar. A few Terran business people were there, looking important in their austere suits. There were many more off-worlders, their clothing reflecting the primitive places on the starship's route. Some of them had already discarded all pretence of Terran dress and wore fleecy tunics or robes. There was also a sprinkling of towelpackers. One man even wore his hi-tech towel as a kilt.

Evana indicated him with her glass. "I hope you keep your dress sense, kiddo."

Jonan smiled. "Don't worry, I will."

"I wonder."

A voice announced flight numbers and Jonan's heart raced. It was his turn to board. He rose.

"See you in two months." Evana hugged him. "Maybe."

"Maybe?" Jonan echoed. "Why not? It's all the leave I've got."

"You never know. If you didn't choose to go, you might also not-choose to not come back."

"Not-choose to not come back?"

"Whatever."

Jonan pursed his lips. "I don't think so. I mean… no, I really don't know."

"That's exactly what I mean."

With a final hug, Jonan stepped onto the glidewalk for the first security check. One machine scanned his body, others his luggage. With a final wave to Evana, he was checked yet again, this time for souvenirs. Terra didn't like off-worlders avoiding their tax. Towelpackers were asked to open supposedly hidden compartments.

Beyond security, another glidewalk sloped into the starship. Looking at it, Jonan was vaguely aware that a man had stepped in front of him. Still focused on the ship, Jonan paused to let the other go ahead. Peripheral vision informed him, however, that the man was still in his path.

"Excuse me," Jonan said, beginning to walk around.

The man shifted slightly, lowering his head so all Jonan could see was a wild mop of red-brown hair and a stance suggesting the stranger wasn't going to move. Bemused, the Psychaeologist realised this was just like a schoolyard conflict, and feeling silly, Jonan reached for the other man's shoulder. Yet just as his hand rose, the man turned sideways and simply slid past. Jonan lowered his hand thinking this was the second attack against him. Attack! As the word hit him, he whirled around. Yet as before, the man had simply disappeared.

*What in space did these attacks mean?* Although many people knew of Jonan's departure, none had reason to prevent it. He wasn't halfway through therapy with anyone, and he certainly didn't owe anyone any money. Not that this attacker was like anyone he knew, anyway. There was a certain aura about him. If he'd ever met him before, he'd certainly have recognised him.

Once on board, Jonan ordered a drink. He sipped it and gazed around. A physical attack, he mused, or just the intention of an attack. He really hadn't faced one of those since school. In fact, most of his life he'd been learning how to avoid physical fights. Wasn't that what being civilised meant?

He stared out a window into the bright blue of the sky. Out there, hidden, were a million stars in a million galaxies. It then hit him, really hit him: he truly was leaving civilisation. Overwhelmed, Jonan glanced at a young traveller. Perhaps he, the smooth Psychaeologist, should also have brought a hi-tech towel. It contained many more gadgets that his minScreen did.

An electronic bell chimed; the ship was departing. Excited passengers rushed to the windows. But Jonan stayed where he was. Through a window, he caught glimpses of green, then as the ship rose, he saw an exquisite turquoise globe resting on a velvet background. Jonan's heart skipped a beat. He'd forgotten how beautiful Terra was. Yet even as he murmured a soft farewell, the view changed to an indeterminate silver-blue; they were now skimming through Probability Space.

Hours later, the shifting blur changed into the hard blackness of norm space; they'd completed the first jump. The ship was now within the probability distribution of a star. Computers would find out where they were then plot another Probability dive which, with a high probability, would take them closer to their destination. Probably... probably... probably... And so the probabilities built up. Although Jonan thought he was immune to Probability phobias even he began to have doubts. Most of him was probably connected as before, but there was that tiny, infinitesimal probability that a tiny, infinitesimal part of him was somewhere else. A tiny, infinitesimal, important part. How could he be sure he would be properly reconstituted?

Reconstituted... reconstituted... He remembered a childhood song. *The head bone is connected to the neck bone. The neck bone is connected to the chest bone. The chest bone is connected to the knee bone. The knee bone is connected to the nose bone.*

His head bouncing against his chest, Jonan awoke and gazed around. He'd been dreaming. He'd dreamt he'd been smeared out in space as if he'd become the milky-way. Then he'd been put into a glass, water added, and reconstituted. It seemed he was becoming phobic. It seemed he was starting to have fears about non-existence. As Jonan shook his head to clear it, he saw his reflection in the window. He looked so dark and gaunt, he could hardly identify with the comfortable face he'd worn for so long.

Not wanting to deal with those doubts right now, Jonan called the steward and ordered a tranq: to sleep and perchance not to dream. Yet when the pill came, he didn't take it. He needed to stay clear-headed for Yerudit. Instead, he hooked into a Screen and tried to read.

As the hours passed and the starship alternated between probability and norm space, Jonan read himself into exhaustion. His eyes blurred from pictures and his ears buzzed from sounds. He closed the Screen, went to his cabin, and drifted into a restless sleep.

He dreamt again of being reconstituted. Then he was running... running... running along an endless tunnel. Not getting anywhere, he fragmented. He was the Big Bang, the exploding universe. Multiple ribbons of him unfolded through space. Ribbons... strings... superstrings An eon later, they would fold up once more, be reconstituted. Eyes gritty, Jonan rose and went to the dining room. The atmosphere had changed, the off-worlders much louder now, more at ease and eating with gusto. Jonan ordered a Terran meal and ate by himself. Not able to taste anything, he felt he was on a futile chase, a mistake of a pilgrimage.

Two hours later, the bell chimed. First landfall and Jonan's stomach churned. What, who, would he find here? On impulse, he went to his room and took out the shadow puppet. For some reason, it reminded Jonan of the man who had attacked him. Then a flash of brilliant green made him turn to the window. So this was the first planet Ariyeh the Tsadkah had visited. Jonan gazed at the rotating sphere and for the first time wondered what had motivated the Tsadkah to come here, to this particular place.

***

A stocky man with a wild mat of hair stood before a pillar. From his point of view, frozen light reached up to treble his height. From his point of view, it also touched the furthermost stars. He concentrated, let everything go, and stepping forward, let his mind reach out.

# Chapter 10

Star travel confirmed the age-old belief of two universal constants: death and taxes. The latter became apparent when the Psychaeologist had to pass through customs at Varli, his first destination. Jonan supposed the current ritual hardly varied from that of ancient times. It was easy to imagine an ancient Greek stepping onshore at Egypt.

*Egyptian Customs officer: Name?*

*Pythagoras: Pythagoras.*

*Egyptian: So what've you got here?*

*Pythagoras: Er, just some triangles.*

*Egyptian: Triangles, eh. This lot looks pretty sharp.*

*Pythagoras: They're, um, isosceles.*

*Egyptian: Isoscel-knees, eh. Look dodgy t' me. Terrarists could definitely use 'em as a weapon. Wottabout these funny ones?*

*Pythagoras: They're right-angle triangles. The sum of the squares...*

*Egyptian: Is equal ta the right amount of taxes. Wotta they for?*

*Pythagoras: The pyramids.*

*Egyptian: We've got enough pyramids, thank you. We don't want no foreign ones. There y'are, two weeks. Next, please.*

Jonan smiled at his daydreaming. Except for brief moments with Yerudit, it had been a long time since he'd felt playful.

He waited in the queue as customs officers dealt with tax and security. Jonan thought that by now there must be a gene for it, a customs gene, plus a corresponding passenger gene. How else to explain why, despite the buzz of excitement, the travellers simply shuffled forward?

After a delay, long by Terran standards, the exit doors opened and glidewalks connected the travellers to a large dome. It was a sign, Jonan hoped, that this first stop wouldn't be too primitive. Carried forward, he collected his bag and went through more security. The officers behind their windows eyed him curiously. The why was obvious, Jonan was the only Terran without a business suit. Tough tachyons! Jonan ignored the officers and scanned the waiting crowd. He had the strange hope Yerudit would be waiting for him, although he knew his hope was foolish. There was no Yerudit here and no reason why there should be.

Totally alone, he began to feel sorry for himself, regretting he hadn't booked a hotel. That at least would've taken one decision away from him. He searched the terminal for a public Screen. Not seeing one, he briefly thought to go back on board. At least he knew where he was on the starship. Luckily, he recognised the return-to-the-womb symptoms, and forcing himself to stay calm, kept looking until he spotted the sign:

*WELCOME TO VARLI*

Below the sign was a tiny cubicle containing a smiling woman. She had a chocolate brown skin that might have originated on Terra but her olive eyes matched the colour of the jungle he'd glimpsed from above. That unusual colouring reflected generations of local trace elements.

Stopping at the open doorway, Jonan hesitated. "I'd like to book a room. Can you help?"

"Yes, of course." The woman indicated a Screen.

"Oh," he exclaimed, "so you do have them here."

"Yes, of course," she repeated.

"Then if you've got one," Jonan said, using irritation to mask his loneliness, "why aren't they available to everyone?"

Her green gaze went over his clothing. It was obviously synthet while hers was natural. "You're from Terra, het?" Her gaze lingered on him. "Not too many Terrans just drop in here, other than towelpackers, of course. Too basic, I guess." She grinned.

Her obvious interest in Jonan lifted his flagging spirit, and so he persisted with his question. "And the lack of Screens?"

"To use machines less and relate to people more. Het."

"Not very cost-effective."

"No, but a lot more fun." Her grin became cheekier, and Jonan couldn't help but smile back. A polite smile, he noted. Not long ago and he would've leapt the counter and carried her away with his charm. After all, he was a Terran and in this backwater that should've been charm enough. Yet he suddenly had a glimpse of himself from outside. Dark, intense, and surprisingly, untempted.

"Have you any particular interest?" the woman asked.

Jonan took out his minScreen. He did have a particular interest. The Tsadkah had followed a zigzag path among the stars in search of Obelisks. Shrivite communities had grown around some sites, groups that were the guardians, perhaps even the worshippers, of the Obelisks. The data wasn't clear, but it seemed some of these groups expected the original makers to return. These groups were so close to being Cultists, Jonan wasn't sure how to reply. Should he admit to an interest in Obelisks and Shrivites? No, he was too embarrassed. He looked up. "A place near water would be good."

"Water? Varli Main has a river. Kunsi is a bit further on, on the coast. That's a nice place, het."

"Okay, that sounds fine."

"Let's see." She studied her Screen. "Something off the beaten track? Hotel Suldie will do. Suldie is the owner. She's used to towelpackers."

"I'm not..."

"I know." The woman gave a friendly smile. "But Suldie is the one. I'll book you in."

"Okay, thanks. I appreciate it."

Jonan headed for the exit. To his dismay, that was where civilization ended. Light from the dome fell only a short distance. Night had fallen, and with little public lighting, the area outside was dark. The heat of the day remained, however, a thick and musty blanket that threatened to smother him. The air was filled with the rich odours of overripe flowers, sweaty animals, and pungent spices. Like a wine, Jonan thought, this was an air with body.

Spotting a waiting solabub, he guessed it was a taxi and hurried towards it. A smiling brown man waited by its door. Jonan hesitated. Taxis on Terra didn't require a driver.

"Where're you going, friend?" the man asked.

"What's that to you?" Jonan replied.

The smile didn't waver. "You're Terran, het? We don't automate much here. I'm the driver."

"Driver?" The man looked too casual.

"That's it. You say where you want to go, I take you. Het? Then you pay me."

"I see." Jonan looked around. In the dark, people were climbing in and out of vehicles. He had no idea what was usual, and no other taxi was approaching him. "It's not very economical," he grunted, wondering what to do. "You should get Terra Trading out here."

"No thanks." The man opened the passenger door. "We like it this way. Het?"

Jonan shrugged, but although uncomfortable, he entered the solabub. "Do you know Hotel Suldie?" The man lifted an eyebrow, and Jonan realized that he had been shouting. "Hotel Suldie?" he repeated in a quieter tone.

"Sure, I know Mama Suldie. Let's go." The man lifted a lever to float the bub and angled another to point it. Jonan expected a rough ride but it turned out to be pretty smooth, though not nearly as smooth as an automatic. It was probably also used for off-track driving, Jonan guessed. Perhaps to allow Pythagoras to smuggle triangles?

It wasn't long before they came to a town, the centre such a maze of crowded streets, an autopilot would've burnt its fuses sorting through its complexities. The human pilot, however, was unfazed as he negotiated a way through this busy rabbit warren. At the same time, Jonan took in the streetlights falling on non-synthet clothes, all too aware of that he was actually off-world. He'd been so orientated towards Yerudit and Hebaron that he hadn't taken much account of the steps in between. Yet here he was in Varli, a culture he would normally avoid, and he had yet to adjust to its reality.

At a turn in the road, they left the busy streets and drove along the sea front, its dark mass heaving like a huge animal getting ready to rise. The driver, however, spoke enthusiastically. "Hear that sea, het? Smell it?" He took a deep breath.

Jonan nodded but didn't reply. Whilst he did speak to his solabub, he wasn't in the habit of chatting with it. Also that heaving mass of water made him uncomfortable: heaving oceans on Terra had a habit of dumping on the unwary. His discomfort went up a notch when the driver, stopping at a modest looking hotel, grimaced at Jonan's minScreen.

"Plascash, het? Let's go in, get us some real money."

"You don't have any sort of scanner?"

"No friend, just my eyeballs." The driver led the way through a small but dense garden to a highly polished counter. "Need some cash, Suldie," he called. "How's it going, het?"

A dark woman smiled at him then at Jonan. "You're Jonan, het? The terminus Screened you were coming." She reached out. "You'd better give me your minScreen so I can pay this lazy man."

"Het, I'm not lazy Mamma Suldie."

"You too lazy to get a scanner."

The driver grinned. "I don't get a scanner because that's a good excuse for me to come in and see you."

"Go on with you." Suldie scanned Jonan's minScreen then counted out notes. The driver took them, puckered his lips for a distant kiss, and left. The hotel manager, smiling broadly turned back to Jonan. "Bring your bag, and I'll show you to your room."

They left the foyer and entered another garden. Without artificial lights, it was so dark that Jonan could just make out the vague outlines of the local trees. Used to domes and spires, the amorphous landscape felt threatening, and he kept turning as if someone might jump out at him. His unease increased when a shadow suddenly moved, but it was just an ornament swinging on a branch. His heart still pounding, he was relieved when Suldie entered a small cottage. Jonan reached for a light button to press, but Suldie twisted a switch. An electric bulb, familiar to Jonan through historical holos, came on and illuminated a small, green tinged room. Jonan touched one wall.

"Rock?" It felt completely different to his polymerised house. On tip toe, he touched the low ceiling. "Branches?"

"It's called thatching. Cosy, het?"

Jonan tapped the rock, it was softer than he'd expected. "Does this last?"

"It's not meant to. It gives work."

"Oh yes, physical work." Jonan reached up to touch the thatching. "Is this indigenous?"

"Varli had to be heavily terraformed so everything here is part native, part Terran." Suldie waved vaguely towards the stars. "Terra was not supposed to modify planets with highly evolved plants and insects."

"It kept to that rule, didn't it?"

Suldie made a face. "Some multi-planetary companies could afford to make Terra look the other way."

"I never knew."

"Terrans don't."

Not knowing what to say, Jonan touched the wall again. Rocks certainly rendered the work ethic of Ariyeh the Tsadkah concrete, he thought wryly. But it was so different from Terran ideals – and Jonan's. He wondered if this ethic was common to all off-worlds or was it a result of the Tsadkah's influence, or even that of an Obelisk? He suddenly felt hemmed in. Reading about an ideology was one thing, but finding himself in it was like being a fly in an alien web.

The Psychaeologist unpacked his bag then wondered what to do next. He took out his minScreen, but there was nothing there he wanted to view. Searching further in his bag, he found a torch and went outside. Following the sound of the sea, he took a path that led down, and when his feet scrunched on sand, he increased the torch's beam. The light showed a shore tinged a similar green to the walls of his room. Collecting a handful of sand, he let the particles drift through his fingers. Copper oxide or copper something, he thought. He switched off the light and allowed the night to close in on him. The darkness was warm and moist and full of quiet sounds. A small creature flew towards him, chirruped then disappeared. After that, there was just the murmur of the sea.

Or was there?

The back of Jonan's neck prickled. He sensed a presence and heard the rustle of a branch. But there were no other sounds. Jonan held his breath. Someone was watching him! Was this the prelude to another attack? He tensed his muscles, this time he was going hit back.

Pushing down his fear, Jonan let anger bubble up, and then he whirled. There, amongst the trees, was a silhouette. He switched on the torch and rushed forward. Space, no one there! In a cold sweat, he swung the torch around but found nothing, not even a footprint. Still swinging the torch, he returned to his cabin. Hand on the door, he hesitated. Was someone inside? Was there? He flung the door open. There was a dark shape. A person? No, just the shadow puppet. But was it where he'd left it? No! Yes? He wasn't sure. He'd have to be more aware of it in future, in fact more aware of everything. He prowled the inside of the cabin, his torch on its highest level. When finished, he was surprised. His restlessness had gone. He laughed aloud; while increasing his alertness, adrenaline had also calmed him down.

Jonan slid the old-fashioned bolt home, then tapped on a window. It didn't seem very strong, but if someone did try to break in, the noise would surely wake him. Feeling more secure, he entered the little cubicle that served as his bathroom and wrinkled his nose in distaste; it obviously didn't have a disintegrator. He went to the sink to wash and jumped on seeing his reflection. His eyes were deep sunk and burnt with an inner fire. He looked wild or mad. Perhaps that explained the attacker. He was just a figment of Jonan's madness.

The Psychaeologist snorted, if this were madness then part of him was starting to enjoy it. He collapsed on the bed and let exhaustion take over. So many changes in such a short time. As vague images of dark shapes among trees merged with those of starships that winked in and out of existence, Jonan surrendered to sleep.

The next morning, he was ravenous. Dressing quickly, he looked for a button to press, then remembered, there were no buttons here. He would probably have to toll a gigantic bell or beat a resonant drum. Jonan threw out his arms, not knowing whether to laugh or to groan. He stepped outside; on the narrow veranda were a chair and table that took his breath away. Made of pure wood, back home they could pass as priceless antiques. He remembered now that this sort of furniture was imported into Terra. Yet since it came from off-worlds, and was marked as such, it wasn't held in high regard. Hmm, he liked it. His sense of taste must be changing.

Jonan's attention shifted to a basket on the table that exuded a delicious smell. Real coffee, more real than the brand he used at home. When he lifted the basket lid, he found a pot inside, along with several hot rolls. He poured the coffee into an elliptical cup. Its aroma was mouth-watering but its colour was unusual. Jonan fished out a few bean particles. As he'd guessed, there was a hint of olive-green in the brown. The bread was the same, and he hoped it wasn't copper oxide, copper sulphate or... copper wheat. Unwanted trace elements were one reason he'd always avoided non-Terran planets. Yet here he was and he had a choice: get used to it or go home. Go home? Well, if that was what his figment-of-an attacker wanted then he'd show him. Jonan took a sip then a bite. If this stuff didn't kill him, it would probably do his bowels no *end* of good. Very punny, he thought.

Finished eating, Jonan took more interest in his surroundings. The garden which had been so threatening last night now displayed a glorious range of colours. The green was more vibrant than he'd ever seen on Terra, and the reds were more contrasting. It made the huge flowers look like living flames. His room was even more appealing by day, too. Unlike the smooth cool plastiment sheen of his own house, these rough-hewn walls gave the impression of warmth. All right, their softness meant decay, but decay also implied being alive. Probably a Tsadkah aphorism, Jonan thought, *You're only alive when you decay*. Huh.

Next, he searched his minScreen for data about Varli. With little Terran trade, it didn't warrant a big entry. There were a few places on the planet where Yerudit might be, but one seemed the most likely. Jonan had the distinct impression, however, that she'd already left. Varli felt empty of her, a curious notion to have about a whole planet.

Although early, the day was already hot. In reaction, the broad leaves of the trees had turned and reduced the area they presented to the sun, the reduction in shade increasing the heat. The only relief was a breeze coming in from the sea, tempting Jonan to follow the path to the beach where he watched the swimmers. Noting that loin clothes were the custom, he hired one from Suldie and immersed himself. The water had an odd taste, more metallic than salt. He thought if he stayed long enough, his children would acquire the green eyes of Varli. If he stayed long enough, *he* would acquire the green eyes of Varli

Refreshed, he was returning to his room when, at a faint sound, he whirled. But it was only Suldie, lighting a candle on a small stone altar. As he watched, she murmured a prayer and waved her hands through the aromatic smoke. Then she sprinkled petals around the altar, a serene expression on her face. Jonan scowled. Suldie belonged on Varli, he didn't.

Nonetheless, there was one place he had to visit, and so Jonan towelled down and changed into his onepiece. Its indestructible sheen settled against his skin, marking him as the outsider. Next, he showed his minScreen to Suldie.

"You want to visit Shriva?" Her tone changed from polite friendliness to real enthusiasm. "The spiritual centre?" she said. "Why didn't you tell me earlier? Are you going to stay there?"

"I'm not sure," Jonan replied. "I'm looking for someone."

"Terrans don't usually stay there." Suldie laughed. "Too basic."

"If she's there, I'll stay."

"Oh?" Suldie studied Jonan with a new curiosity. "Yes," she said slowly, "I do believe you would." Suldie keyed directions into his minScreen. "You'll have to get a bub into town and another from there."

"Will it take long?"

"No, one or two hours, it depends on the connection, het."

"Two hours! Isn't there a shuttle?"

Suldie waved a finger at Jonan. "We don't like to burn up our air if we can help it. Het?"

*Het? Het, indeed!*

When the vehicle arrived, Jonan reluctantly returned the

driver's cheery greeting. They hadn't gone far when the man stopped to collect another passenger. "Alon," the driver called. "This is the man from Terra."

Alon put out a calloused hand. "Pleased to meet you."

"Ah, pleased to meet you, too." Jonan pried his fingers from the iron grip.

"We don't usually have businessmen out here," Alon said.

"I'm not a businessman."

"Oh, a towelpacker."

"Not quite." As the man continued to gaze at him, Jonan felt forced to add, "I'm looking for someone."

The bub collected more people. They glanced at Jonan then gabbled away in non-Standard. Every so often, Alon would surface and ask him another question, the locals looking at Jonan with increasing warmth. As one woman left the bub, she took a flower from her hair and pressed it into Jonan's hands.

Squashed between people and bounced between seat and roof, Jonan could just about totter out when they entered the capital, Varli Main. To smooth out the kinks, he decided on a short walk and found himself in streets that were more green jungle than concrete. This, he thought, was how it must've been a thousand years ago in Terra.

Feeling bold, he sat at a café and bought a local drink. Other than having a green tinge, it tasted fine. He looked around. Busy, busy, busy. One group was pulling down a house and carting it away. Further along, a second group was putting up a house. He wouldn't have been at all surprised to see one side of a building being built while the other side was being removed. And despite the mess of brick and thatching, the work was carried out mostly with smiles. Jonan was puzzled, unused to seeing people enjoy having strained bodies. He was used to seeing machines doing the labour while office workers wore strained faces.

Being in the capital, he saw a few other Terrans. They stood out in their synthet clothes, passing Jonan with just a curt nod. Probably local administrators for Terra; Jonan was glad his papers were all in order. They looked as if they'd make life difficult for a traveller. Especially one who verged on being a towelpacker.

Finishing his drink, Jonan lingered for a while longer. When he decided his stomach didn't need a toilet, he rose and flagged down a public solabub.

"Yes, friend?" the driver said.

"Can you take me to Shriva?" Jonan asked.

The driver gave him an appraising look. "I can take you. But do you want to go, het?"

"Why not?"

"Terrans in synthet suits are not usually interested"

"I am."

The man smiled. "Then jump in."

Jonan entered the bub and straightaway took out his minScreen. Why didn't Terrans go to Shriva? No reason. He shrugged. At most, he guessed the place was merely an item he would one day discuss with Yerudit. He put the minScreen back in his pocket and the bolder locals began to direct their questions at him

For another hour, they took country tracks through thick jungle. Jonan had always thought it was impossible for a bub to have a truly bumpy ride, but this one proved him wrong. Cynically, he thought perhaps these were made especially for off-worlds to reinforce their frontier mentality.

On the way, they passed a few villages. As in the main town, the people there were busy hewing and planting, although they often stopped to smile and wave. Sometimes they flagged the bub down just to have a chat. Sometimes there was a bit of good-natured haggling and a bundle of fresh vegetables changed hands. At irregular points, people got on or off, each newcomer eying Jonan curiously. Further from the main town, they were less inhibited and asked: *What're you doing on Varli, het? Where are you from? How many kids you got?* They found it hard to believe a man his age had no children. Even Jonan began to feel it was unnatural. Pioneer mentality. He'd have to defend against it, adjust somehow.

The questions took some edge off the journey's physical discomfort, but it was a relief when the bub bounced out of the jungle and the sea with its breezes came into sight again. They descended a winding cliff road with the sea on one side and rock face on the other, both tinged with green. Below them, fishermen worked on their nets, and beyond them, a small village clustered around a twinkling bay.

Jonan was beginning to think this could be the place for some genuine R & R when a fierce looking man caught his attention. Strongly built, his hair was shaved back from his forehead while the rest of it was tied into a topknot. Also, instead of the local two-piece of loose trousers and shirt, he wore a short-sleeved robe. It was green, of course, and his dark muscles gleamed against it. Jonan gazed at him: buccaneer or samurai? Or was this for a period costume martial arts movie.

Suddenly, however, a more sinister notion popped into his head. This was his attacker! The thought was completely illogical yet Jonan gaped at the man with astonishment. The Psychaeologist even jumped when the driver tapped him on the shoulder.

"See the wooden gateway." The driver pointed. "That's the entry to the Shriva."

Jonan exited the bub, paid, and watched the vehicle wheeze into the air and jounce away. Suddenly, though, his heart began to pound. The sight of the fierce man reminded him that Yerudit might still be here, after all. But there could also be another reason for the excitement: one of the mysterious Obelisks might be near.

# Chapter 11

There was a gateway, but there were no gates, simply posts like an ancient Shinto temple. They led into rows of thick bushes with large, red-tinged flowers, providing a striking contrast to the pervasive green. Jonan approached the entrance carefully. This was just the place for a stalker attack.

His hesitation caught the attention of the samurai. "Hey, you," the big man boomed. "Do you seek entry?" He balanced on his toes like a prize fighter so that Jonan realised why this particular gateway didn't need a gate. This man's muscles were gate enough.

Wary of him, Jonan said, "I'm looking for someone."

"Looking?" The samurai stepped closer.

"Searching."

"Ah, searching." The man relaxed. "We are all searching." Then as if he'd made a great joke, his wrestler's face broke into a huge grin, and his palm, broad as a tropical leaf, clapped Jonan on the shoulder. "Come." He turned. "I will take you." He strode through the gateway only to stop at a low, flowered-bedecked building. "Ah." He inhaled deeply. "Dinner."

Jonan, still reeling from his welcome, peered through the doorway. Men and women were cutting, slicing, and washing. Without thinking, Jonan said, "Don't they have autoslicers?"

"Yes."

"Then?"

"When?" Solemnly, the man held up a hand to display his fingernails. "We believe that a little bit of under-the-nail dirt adds to the flavour."

Jonan grimaced, then he saw the other's shoulders heaving with suppressed laughter. This was definitely Yerudit-Tsadkah territory.

A little further on, they came to a small stone cottage. "Enter!" The big man gestured in what was part invitation, part order, and Jonan found himself in a room that clearly served as both office and library. A woman, as tiny as his escort was big, sat in front of a Screen, books in both paper and plasti towered above her. When she looked up, Jonan was struck by the intelligence that lit up her face.

The big man touched his right hand to his heart. "Thera." His voice made the walls of books tremble. "A visitor."

"Good." A gentle smile warmed the creases of her face. "You are very welcome here."

Jonan had expected her to ask him who he was and what he wanted. Thrown by this ready acceptance, he said, "Even though you don't know who I am."

Jonan's escort dropped a big hand on his shoulder. "Do you know who you are? Ha!" He roared with laughter. "I have much work. I will return when he knows." He looked Jonan up and down. "That should give me plenty of time."

"Vulcan!" Thera admonished, but he merely touched his hand to his heart again and departed, leaving behind a wake of deep chuckles. "A good boy," she said of the giant, "but always joking."

"His Standard is very stilted," Jonan said a little sourly.

"He refused to learn it when he was young, now he makes a bit of a show of it. Many off-worlders are, well, anti-Terran." She motioned for Jonan to sit. "What has brought you here?"

"I'm looking for someone." Jonan leant forward, finding that he wanted to explain. "On Terra, I'm a Psychaeologist, and I met someone."

"And he or she sent you here?"

"Indirectly."

Thera waved a hand. "They're probably details we don't need to know."

"But you are in charge here?"

She smiled that gentle smile again. “I’m just the librarian.” She waved a hand to indicate the books. “Since I don’t have the brawn of a Vulcan, they act as if I have the brain.”

“Which you obviously do have.”

“No, I’m just good at books.” She touched the pile. “I’d better put in your name, then we know how many to feed.”

Jonan took out his minScreen. “You can import my data directly.”

“Data.” Thera tut-tutted. “Oh, how we do like to encode people.” She plugged his small machine into her larger one. “But there, all done.”

Jonan took back his minScreen. “I’m looking for a young woman called Yerudit. Has she been here? Have you seen her?” He showed an image to Thera. But when she didn’t reply, he repeated, “Have you seen her?”

For answer, Thera turned the minScreen and studied it from different angles. “Such a marvellous device.” She put it on the table. “And yet...” She handed him a book made of rough paper, the pages having a slight green tinge. “You can really feel history in these.” She stroked the text. “You can sense the searching of the ages.”

She passed the book across. It wasn’t the first paper book Jonan had handled, but it wasn’t often he had the chance to hold one. He found it curiously... alive. Like the wall made of rock. He remembered years ago, when he’d first thought of himself as a buccaneer, he had trained intensively with swords. His hands had blistered and hardened. He could’ve avoided the roughness with creams, but he’d been proud of those calluses. Now, the paper reminded him of that, the rare hand of a working person or craftsperson. Its warmth was curiously comforting, too.

The tiny woman watched as he stroked the cover. “Yes,” she said quietly, “Yerudit was here.”

Jonan suddenly found it hard to breathe. He leant forward,

gripping the book. "When? How long for? When did she leave?"

Thera's hands pushed at the air as if to press him back. As he straightened, she smiled her wonderful smile. "It's hard to say, Jonan. Our days are slightly longer than yours but our weeks are shorter. How can we say how long? Time is a riddle."

"I don't want riddles. Roughly, how long?"

"Perhaps Yerudit is your riddle," she said gently. "But if you want to use this Screen, you can work out when she left by Terra time."

Jonan shook his head. "No, I'm sorry." He brushed back his hair. "That doesn't really matter. D'you know where she went?"

"To Haja."

Jonan pressed buttons on his minScreen. The optimiser agreed, the next probable step was Haja. He showed the route to Thera. "Do you think this is correct? Is there an Obelisk there?"

"Possibly, it was part of the Tsadkah's journey."

"What else could lead him to going there?"

"He wasn't just going to." Thera smiled her smile again, and though she was tiny, he felt like a little boy. Then, resting her wrinkled hand on his, she added, "He was also going from."

"From?"

"Yes. From Terra."

"Ariyeh? The Tsadkah?" Jonan stuttered. "He's from Terra?"

This time, Thera grinned. "That's right, he's one of you terrible Terrans."

Jonan sucked in his breath. That was a surprise. Though it shouldn't have been, people were always leaving Terra, especially idealists. Why not the Tsadkah? Yet in Jonan's mind, Ariyeh was so much Hebaron, so much the off-worlder that he was actually shocked.

"You see," Thera was saying, "life is full of riddles. Time and space. Yerudit and Ariyeh. And, of course, travel and probability."

"Probability?" Jonan echoed. "Surely we understand that now. And why link that with them?"

This time, Thera's ancient face lit up with a truly childish delight. "There," she said, "we all have our riddle, if only we could but see it. Yours, I'm sure, is Yerudit. Yerudit and Ariyeh. Ariyeh and probability."

Yerudit? Yes, that Jonan could understand. And Ariyeh? Maybe he, too, had a place. But probability, what had that to do with anything? Sure, he'd worked on probability space phobias but somehow Jonan didn't think that was what she meant. But then, perhaps, she meant nothing. Maybe in this out of way place, she merely maintained her position by creating mysteries. On the other hand, perhaps all this travelling was clouding his mind.

Jonan rubbed his face. "I don't follow you."

Thera twinkled. "Don't follow me. Follow him."

"Him!" Jonan shook his head. "No. Just her. Not him."

Thera gently patted his hand and rose. "Come, it's time to eat." She led the way back to the flower-bedecked kitchen. Twenty or thirty people were in a queue, some wearing the same green robes as Vulcan. As Jonan studied them, he discovered the clothes had subtle patterns woven into them: stylised lions, or dragons, or sphinxes.

"Are they symbols of your beliefs?" Jonan asked. "Or of the Shriva?"

"Ah, the Shriva," Thera replied. "It is Ariyeh's word, from the Indus, Shiva, the god of dance. Yet the same word from the Semitics means to sit in study. It's perfect, het? The same word means absolute motion and absolute stillness."

Jonan grunted. This Ariyeh was just too clever by half. He inched forward. Reaching the head of the queue, Thera took a wooden tray and gave herself small helpings from larger bowls.

"I only eat plant protein," she said. She pointed to other bowls. "For visitors."

But Jonan didn't dare and only selected what she had. Thera then led him to a bench under a tree. As they sat, Vulcan passed. Seeing him, Jonan tilted his plate to see if it really did have under-the-nail additions.

"What're you doing?" Thera asked.

Jonan blushed. "Just checking it was clean."

"And why shouldn't it be, het?"

"Oh, something Vulcan said."

Thera burst out laughing. "You Terrans! So serious and yet so innocent!"

"I thought he was joking but..."

"But who knows with an off-worlder?" Thera smiled, unaffected by his prejudice.

Relieved, Jonan remarked, "He looks very strong. What does he do here, cut down trees?"

"Oh, no. We try to keep the old forests and their habitats. No, when here Vulcan works much more on metals, hence his name." She grinned. "Though names can vary here."

"Vary? An odd idea. How often? By the week or by the month?"

"By the personality."

Jonan grunted. "In my experience, personality change requires geologic time spans."

"For most," she agreed. "Which is why some people believe in reincarnation."

"Reincarnation!" Jonan tried to pull on his now non-existent beard, then slowly lifted a spoonful of soup to give himself time to think. "I suppose," he said after a while, "one could imply the other."

"Yes, change takes time, maybe more than one lifetime. Who knows?" Thera waved her spoon. "What d'you think of the soup?"

Jonan sipped again. "Hmm, strong body. A hint of naughtiness in the middle of the tongue. Rough but highly palatable."

Thera chuckled. "A few lifetimes here and we'd call you Soup Buff."

Amused, Jonan swirled his spoon in the soup then, despite any dirt-under-the-fingernail spices, he cleaned out the bowl. He next inspected the other foods, finding only beans or vegetables. "Does anyone here eat meat?" he asked.

"Only visitors, and only if the cook is prepared to make it."

"Not even fish?" Jonan indicated the green ocean at the end of the path.

"Not here, maybe in town."

"Vulcan, too?"

"You think if he lives on *greens,* he should be more *weedy*?" Thera laughed

"Well..." Jonan waved his hands vaguely. "I know gorillas were mainly vegetarian so why not Vulcan? Oops!" He looked around furtively. "I didn't mean he's a gorilla."

"Don't worry, he'd be flattered. Beautiful animals." Thera frowned. "I believe they're extinct now on Terra."

"Some have been DNA regenerated."

"But those are sterile." She gazed upwards. "There are some planets where they've managed to breed."

Jonan nodded. Like most children, he'd been fascinated by big animals, but climate change had greatly reduced their numbers, one reason why Terrans relied so much on synthetics instead of on cows and pigs. Jonan, however, had organised his life so that he could eat real meat when he wanted to. He had no desire to live just on lettuce leaves. Although Yerudit had, he remembered. She was always very careful of what she ate, and though she'd never tried to stop him eating meat, she'd physically, or just mentally, move away when he did.

Thera was watching him with bright eyes. "What're you thinking, Soup Buff?"

"Did geologic time just pass?" Jonan responded.

"In thinking time, yes."

"Oh, I was thinking about Yerudit and food." He shrugged. "We'll see."

He looked around. So far, he hadn't really taken in the setting. Although it was possible to eat inside, everyone was outside but in an inside sort of way. Benches were positioned beneath spreading umbrella trees so that wherever one sat, there would be shade. Even in the rain the cover would be thick enough to provide shelter. Only wind might be a problem. A nice way to live, Jonan thought, comfortable, a little rough but not too hard. At least on the surface.

"Before, you said something about a riddle. Do you have one?"

Thera looked at him with olive bright eyes. "My riddle?" she echoed.

"Yours."

"Do you know why the Tsadkah came here?" she asked. "Why he then went on?"

Jonan shrugged and again tried to pull at his beard, but only found itchy stubble. "I assume he was looking for the perfect planet, a genuine utopia." There was something else as well but his mind was cloudy and he couldn't quite dredge it up.

"Ye-es. But the Tsadkah is more mystical than metaphysical."

"They're not the same?"

"He was concrete not abstract."

Jonan snorted.

"No, truly. He doesn't go much for philosophy, he wants concrete results." For once, Thera looked irritated. Rising with a smoothness that made the Psychaeologist feel like a dinosaur despite his new exercise regime, she said, "Come, I'll show you."

He went after her, expecting nothing more than a provincial version of Psychaeology. Nor did he change his mind when Thera led him towards a small temple. The grey stone with its sloping roof and pillars reminded him of ancient sites on Terra.

"Is this why the Ariyeh stopped here?" Jonan asked.

"Why do you say *the* Ariyeh?"

"Tsadkah is too much." He shrugged. "So is Ariyeh."

"Another riddle," Thera said. "Nearly there." She stepped into the temple, but Jonan hesitated. There were enough pillars and statues here to hide someone, lots of someones. But sensing no danger, he went inside. The light immediately felt different: a cool green that sparkled as if with hidden lights and that gave Jonan the feeling of swimming under crystal waters.

In this dreamy translucent light, he floated past carvings of dragons and lions and unicorns. In contrast, a simple black pillar stood in the middle of the space. It could have been the knitting needle for a stone-age giant. Yet closer and he stopped. His vision tunnelled. *Yerudit,* he thought in shock. But it wasn't. It wasn't a person, it was a towering pillar of black stone. Except it wasn't black and it wasn't stone and it didn't tower. It was a black hole, a space, an endlessness, the result of an equation where the probability of existence was absolute, or zero, or both. His head span. He stumbled and would've fallen, but an unexpectedly strong Thera held him.

Jonan studied the unnerving stone with the statues around it. Hoping it was just a projection, he searched the area for a projector. He didn't find one, although he desperately wanted to. It was one thing to have a weird experience with a live person, it was quite another to have it with a block of stone.

"So this is why he came here," Jonan said eventually.

"Yes."

"It was here or he put it here?" Jonan didn't think the question made sense, but his mind was still clouded.

"No."

"You did?"

"No."

"Who then? Vulcan?"

Thera shook her head. "That is the riddle."

"You won't tell me?"

"No one knows."

"No one?"

"Go closer. Look at it carefully. Try to touch it."

"Touch it? Or try to touch it?"

"Try."

His senses alert, Jonan approached the pillar. It was much like the stone of the building. Yet nothing like the stone of the building. It was like layers and layers of frozen light with difficult-to-see carvings on the outermost layer. In fact, they seemed to move as if not quite there, as if the pillar was continually being brought into existence.

With an effort, he focussed long enough to see just how unusual were the shapes. With Thera closely watching him Jonan said, "It's from ancient Terra?"

"Try to touch it," she repeated. Jonan put out his hand. It tingled. Startled, he pulled back. "Closer," Thera urged. He tried again, reaching further. The strange tingling increased and he couldn't get any closer. No matter how hard he struggled, the pillar refused his grasp.

"No one has ever got close," Thera said.

Jonan, sweating and scowling took a local coin from his pocket. Holding it tightly, he tried to scrape it along the surface, but there was still no contact. He just rubbed air.

"Here." Thera handed him an old phaser gun. "Sometimes I have to stun large animals. Try it." Jonan played a weak beam along the stone, not a mark. Gradually, he increased the power. Still no effect, yet when he ran it across the coin that neatly split into two.

"Impossible!" Jonan gasped. "It should've made some mark!"

"It didn't," Thera said dryly, "and clearly, it doesn't even reflect the power."

"Of course!" Jonan's jaw dropped. "If it did, it would've cut me in pieces."

"It absorbed the power."

"What in space is it made from?"

"Is it in space? Who knows?" Thera shrugged. "That is the riddle. Look closer. D'you recognise any of those symbols?"

Jonan squinted at the carvings. Again he had the impression of movement, along with an enormous power. "They're not familiar." He shook his head in awe. "But they remind me of things. Should I know them? Did Yerudit and I visit them on Terra?"

Thera shook her head. "Apparently not, I've searched all the texts, nothing"

"Nothing?" Jonan searched for alternatives. "What about the Zirenians?"

"They know as little as us."

"Impossible!" He again shook his head. "Doesn't anyone know anything? How long has it been here? What does it do? Why?"

The tiny woman put out her palms as if to warm them. "Nothing is known about it. We are fools to even call it stone. Perhaps it is a machine. Perhaps it is an animal. Terran scientists have studied it but learnt nothing. They haven't interpreted a single symbol. Their most powerful machines couldn't take a single atom out of it."

"I don't understand." Jonan felt breathless. "How can there be such a thing? How come I've even heard nothing about a pillar here?"

Thera turned to him, her face glowing as if the object had energised her. "How many people on Terra think about the sphinxes? Or the pyramids? Or the many other great wonders? Few, because no one there cares. Here, Terrans stopped wanting to know because they couldn't understand. True, there was enormous excitement at first, but since they couldn't understand it, Terrans slunk away with their tails between their legs. Nor did they want to advertise their failure. Beaten by an off-world unknown? No. But we of the Shriva believe there must be a way, a non-physical way, to understand them."

"Them?" Jonan echoed. "You mean there are more?"

"Yes, there are more. Wherever Ariyeh visited that's where they are."

"The… this Ariyeh, does he know what they're for?"

"Perhaps? He has told us to meditate on them, and he knows more than we, so we do. You felt the warmth yourself. Meditate and you will feel the fire. Not everyone responds to the stone, but you did. You felt something more than warmth. Few do that. Meditate and I'm sure you will also feel more than fire."

Images of fire sprang into Jonan's mind, bright and beautiful flames that burnt through the haze of his mind. A clear memory also burst through. Travelling an ancient desert with Yerudit, the sun had set on a horizon streaked with purple and gold. Yerudit had gripped his arm.

"And a pillar of fire shall lead them," she had murmured. "Look, Jonan, a pillar for us."

And here was another pillar. He stretched out his hand once more. Yes, no doubt of it, a tremendous power was there.

"Have you decided, Jonan?" Thera was asking. "Do you want to stay?"

But he shook my head. "I came for Yerudit, not for fire."

She nodded. "Yet perhaps they are the same. Once you feel the stone, you can feel it from afar."

That he could believe.

Thera pulled at his arm. "This is enough. Some become ill."

That, too, Jonan could believe. Walking away, he was as awkward as a puppet on tangled strings. But once outside he asked, "D'you have a name for it?"

"Stone, pillar, needle. Whatever. Names are for the familiar. This never becomes familiar."

*He, she, it,* Jonan mentally added. Then at a sudden realisation, he staggered: the object was an Obelisk, he'd just encountered an Obelisk. Despite his reading about them, he'd just never realised how magical it would be. Then he clicked his fingers. Why hadn't he guessed what it was? After all, they were the point of the Tsadkah's journey. His mind awhirl, Jonan knew – was absolutely certain – this Obelisk, whether animate or even inanimate, had clouded his thinking so that its presence had dramatically enhanced its impact.

His legs still wobbly, Jonan wondered how best to describe this astonishing structure. Obelisk wasn't enough. Obelisk of Frozen Light was better or, better still, Pillar of Frozen Light. Awestruck, he followed Thera back to the kitchen and collapsed onto a chair. She made a drink which he gratefully accepted, guessing it was a sedative because after a few sips, he could almost stop struggling against the Obelisk's impact.

With the light fading, Thera again said, "You may stay at this Shriva if you wish."

Fully recovered, Jonan said, "I thank you, but no. The Obelisk is incredible, but Yerudit is that and still more."

"I understand." Thera smiled her smile. "That is the riddle."

She walked with him to the gateway, a gateway with no gate, if one discounted Vulcan. The big man stood there, a strong guardian with a peaceful expression, wearing a faint smile as if listening to an inner music. *Listening to the Obelisk,* Jonan thought.

Vulcan nodded, beaming as they passed. "Does he know who he is now?" he asked.

"He knows enough," Thera answered.

The man's gaze remained on him as Jonan waited for a solabub, and the Psychaeologist had the vague unease of being measured, causing him to glance sideways at the other. If he was the attacker, Jonan didn't stand a chance. Of course, his opponent might only have meant to frighten him, and if so, he'd definitely succeeded in that. But he'd also made him angry, and that had made him much more alert.

Jonan was still watching Vulcan when, with a twinkling of lights, a solabub arrived, full of brown-skinned, olive-eyed Varlinese, all chatting gaily. He wondered if they knew about the Obelisk. Or cared. Probably not, if they did, they would all live at the Shriva. Or perhaps it was a matter of degree for as the solabub moved away, the locals put their palms briefly to their hearts.

Both exhausted and excited, Jonan returned to his room and took out his minScreen to send a message to Evana.

> *Do you remember the pillars or obelisks discovered on a few planets? I visited one today. Strange, and electrifying. My minScreen is limited. I wonder, can you find out anything about them? Greetings from Varli, Jonan.*

He sent the message then stood in the doorway, wondering if he could see his words bounce from star to star. He stood on the threshold of his room and looked back in. The shadow puppet was sitting on a chair. Too tired to exercise with it, he collected his torch and headed to the beach. Listening to the waves, he felt the silken crunch of the sand beneath his feet and began to relax. But then, Jonan heard a faint sound. He whirled, his torch lancing out, but no one was there.

Made more vigilant, Jonan headed back to his room. But on the way, he had the distinct impression that a shadow flitted across the veranda. Anger overcame caution, and he drove forward while shining the torch over the bushes. Although he saw no one, his senses remained on alert as he gripped the handle and threw his door open. At first, he thought that nothing had changed. Then he didn't know whether to laugh or to cry. The shadow puppet balanced on its head.

# Chapter 12

Bemused, Jonan gazed at the puppet. Had it moved by itself? No, impossible, someone must have moved it. With a sudden surge of fury, Jonan darted outside and searched the bushes. A shadow moved. He shone the torch on it, but no one was there.

The Psychaeologist stomped back into his room, but this time on seeing the puppet, he understood and burst into laughter. The puppet was Jonan, and the Shriva had turned him on his head. How very symbolic. Yet when the Psychaeologist went to turn the puppet the correct side up, what he saw was even more striking: the puppet wasn't upside-down at all, only the shadows had made it seem so. Or, stranger still, only his thinking had made it seem so.

Jonan sat on his bed, rubbing his chin. Was there an intruder, someone who was following him? Or had someone, Vulcan say, provided the information? Jonan thumped the bed. Or was he misreading the whole thing and the situation with the puppet was just his imagination? Briefly, he considered that the green food had psychedelic side effects. But no, if that were the case then the planet would be swarming with towelpackers. Jonan pursed his lips. There *was* an attacker. There had been too many signs. He growled; he had to fight back.

Too restless to do nothing, Jonan searched through his minScreen and found one of Yerudit's music pieces. Perfect. He stretched along the floor, supporting himself on hands and toes. Slowly, he shifted the weight onto his fingers and held that position until he was quivering. With further exercises, he felt sufficiently energised to try Yerudit's dance routine. Then, sweat flying, he followed the actions of a holo programmed with fighting techniques.

Bouncing on his toes, Jonan realised he was now literally

fighting fit. How ironic. Terrans never fought; they litigated or embargoed. The hell with that! Those things were too intangible. Jonan studied his fists with the joy of discovery. Yet even as he did so, a new idea formed: perhaps what he faced was even more intangible than signs and shadows. In which case, fists and fitness meant nothing. That idea was even more ironic… or contradictory… or something.

Still, fists and fitness was what he had. Stripping his bed, Jonan stood his mattress upright and tied belts around it to make a body. Two towels tucked into the belts served as arms. Then, copying the fight holo, Jonan twisted its arm, punched its nose, and threw the whole caboodle onto the ground. Reaching to pick it up, he saw himself in a mirror. He was brown and fit, and for the first time in months, he was laughing, really laughing.

He slept well that night. The only letdown was that in order to follow Yerudit, he had to wait three days for the next lift-off, unheard of on Terra where ships left nearly every hour. But the delay was a reminder that he was in the backwaters, and the wait was lightened by a reply from Evana.

> *The Government restricts all mention of mysterious objects found on other planets. I'm told there are plenty of conspiracy theories on 'dark' sites but I'm no computer expert and don't know how to find them. Mirena was asking about you. Keep well and see you soon, Love, Evana.*

The reply cheered Jonan even though it didn't provide further information. He was also pleased to hear about Mirena. Her name disturbed him, however, and at first he couldn't work out why. Then he realised, she reminded him of Probability phobias, and the reminder brought with it a slight aversion. He, the curer of space phobias, was reluctant to recall that eye-wrenching, mind-stirring blur. No, he wanted to go through norm-space to his next destination. A ridiculous idea, of course; the distance was so vast he would have to reincarnate a hundred times to cover the distance.

So this was Probability Space phobia. Jonan had been so superior about it, but now he felt slightly nauseous just contemplating it. Away from the scientific rationalism of Terra, it was too easy to imagine himself coming out of Probability Space with his toes as his nose, his teeth as eyelashes, his guts as a turban. As far as he knew, such distortions had never happened – theoretically, couldn't happen – but out here, on the edge of civilization, it seemed all too likely that it did happen, but was hushed up. Space, he was starting to think like an off-worlder.

Despite his fears, when it came, the star travel passed easily. But the arrival at Haja didn't. The air outside the starship was as wet and humid as a tropical jungle. Even inside the spaceport, despite the struggling air-conditioning, it was as hot and steamy as a sick dragon's breath. This planet, Jonan realised, was Varli *down*. Or maybe *up* by the Ariyeh's thinking, for Haja was even more sparsely populated than Varli, the waiting solabubs no more than open aircars that barely managed to hover.

Jonan wandered the excuse-for-a dome until he found an untidy tourist office. "Is there a Shriva settlement here?" he asked.

The woman behind the desk eyed his clothes with amazement. "You're from Terra?" she asked.

"Yes." Jonan looked around the dome. Clearly, he was the only Terran in the spaceport. "A Shriva settlement?" he repeated.

The woman pointed to a counter. "A shuttle will be leaving shortly for Kandi. Just buy a ticket over there."

Nodding his thanks, Jonan joined a small queue. Most of the vehicles were pitted, suggesting they did the impossible and also hopped into space to mine meteorites. On one a dent was so large it had been painted to resemble a monster's eye. On another, the pitting acted as the centre of a bullseye. A sign alongside the shuttle read:

*Verging Spaceways*

*Pay before leaving.*

*You might not have the chance to pay afterwards.*

Jonan sighed, hoping the message was just off-world humour. He waited in the queue, the other people eyeing him and whispering in much the same way as he had on first seeing the Zirenian. Here, although he was human, he was also the alien.

Sitting in the shuttle, Jonan half-expected the vehicle to be launched by elastic bands. To his relief, it clawed itself into the air then flew in a low arc over dense forest, its noise causing bird-like creatures to zoom out of the trees. Jonan kept flinching, desperately hoping there wouldn't be a collision.

When his eyes were open, he spotted clearings where small villages were set along a blue coastline. Obviously, the Ariyeh went for the rural. Or maybe, Jonan thought, that was the choice of the Obelisks. Maybe they had been deliberately placed to create a contrast: futuristic, hi-tech sentinels set against lo-tech countryside. A paradox. Or as Thera would say, a riddle.

The shuttle touched down in a small town with wide streets. The people here were lighter skinned than on Varli and burlier. Though friendly, they eyed Jonan with curiosity. Clearly, while the Probability Drive rendered everywhere virtually equidistant from Terra, some places were still less equal than others.

The dusty terminus was just a collection of sheds. Outside it, Jonan found a vehicle that looked much like an upside down cooking pot, one that had cooked a lot yet washed but little. A man beside it watched him for a moment then shambled over.

"Zalman, zamir," he called. "You want to hop in?"

Jonan tensed at the approach, but relaxed when the man kept his distance. "I want to go to the Shriva community. Does your, er…" Jonan paused, not knowing what to call the battered vehicle.

"Solabus."

"Solabus? Does your solabus go there?"

"Yes, zamir, my bus goes wherever it's paid to go. As to the Shriva, it's a long walk otherwise."

The man strolled back to his vehicle and patted it affectionately. Jonan sighed. He really didn't want to get into that battered pot. But when he did, the other passengers nodded equably. And he didn't feel too uncomfortable. Although his clothes still marked him out as Terran, his tan made him almost as weathered as them.

Once inside, the solabus lurched into the air and wheezed along a wide track, the driver beeping for people and animals to move away. On the side of the road, Jonan saw curious plants with such thin trunks and branches, it seemed impossible they could support their huge blossoms.

He also saw log houses made, he guessed, from stripped down tree trunks. The houses had doors but none were closed. Frontier honesty, or was it that everyone owned the same, so what to steal?

Occasionally, the solabus left the track to drop people, producing a great deal of hugging and kissing. Their natural exuberance, he thought. Natural here, but very unnatural on Terra. This laughing and chattering would be considered most undignified back home. Home? Hmm, was Terra still home? It seemed a minute thing, viewed from afar by a telescope in reverse.

One by one, the others were dropped until Jonan alone remained. He began to get uneasy again and glanced suspiciously at the driver, who noticed, grinned and then called out, "Not long now, zamir. Not long."

Jonan tried to relax. Fortunately, on the next bend, he caught sight of a glorious stretch of blue sea and a line of wooden houses hugging its shore. As Jonan gazed at them, the driver made a leisurely sweep of his hand as if to say, "See, I told you so." This must be the Shrivite community.

On the ground, Jonan dug into his bag and took out a handful of coins. The driver selected some, gave a casual wave, and drove on. When Jonan did a quick currency conversion, it was so little he almost ran after the bus to offer more. Then he shrugged. The driver must know his business.

As Jonan approached the sea, the fishermen, busy at their nets, waved. He waved back as he continued on towards the Shriva. There was no gateway here and no muscular Vulcan acting as guardian. In fact, the approach was deserted, and so Jonan walked on towards the largest building. Made of wood, it also stood out by having curved eaves on the roof. Just before reaching the large building, he came to a smaller one with *Office* written on it. As the door was closed, he stood where an autoeye could see him. When it didn't open, he slapped his thigh. This door didn't even have a handle. Of course, it wasn't automated. He pushed and the door flew open.

At the noise, an extraordinarily tall thin man turned and peered at Jonan, while Jonan gaped at him. For some reason, this bony person had strange bits attached to his nose and ears.

But the man smiled. "Zalman, zamir," he said. "Please come in." When Jonan entered, still staring, the man touched at his face. "Something wrong?" His fingers found the bits. "Oh, my glasses."

"Glasses?"

"Spectacles." As Jonan still looked blank, he added, "They correct my vision."

"Oh." Jonan took a step closer. "I've seen those in historical holos. Are you in a play?"

"No, zamir. As I said, these are to correct my vision."

"But..." Jonan was stumped. "You could have treatment."

"I know. You are indeed correct," the man agreed. "But an emphasis on that seeing might, perhaps, undermine the true seeing."

Ah, Jonan understood, another example of the Ariyeh's back-to-the-basics teaching.

"You are a stranger," the man said.

"Yes," Jonan replied.

"To yourself?" Tall bony chuckled.

Another maker of riddles. "That, too."

"You want to stay here?"

"I'm looking for someone."

"Ah!" The tall man's eyes widened. "Yerudit."

"How did you know?" Jonan gasped.

The tall man again chuckled. "The whole galaxy knows."

"The whole galaxy?" Jonan echoed.

At his expression, the other waved his hands. "No, no, not really. I was joking. You are not the centre of cosmic conspiracy rumours." He frowned. "Cosmic rumours that the big bang was a big fart are grossly over-rated. Sorry." His bony face lit up. "I should tie a superstring around my finger to remind me of that." His grin rearranged itself into a serious expression. "Yes, Yerudit was here some weeks ago, and we don't have many visitors so a young man searching for someone...?" He shrugged.

Excitement gripped Jonan. "D'you know where she went, where she is now?"

The man nodded. "She was going on to Probos, but there are not many starships that plough that route, zamir. You will have to wait, but here you are most welcome."

Jonan consulted his minScreen. Yes, Probos was the next most likely destination. He tapped his fingers on the wooden desk. "Stay here? I don't seem to have much choice."

The man grinned. "Then you are lucky, a choiceless choice

is the best choice." Jonan grunted but the other just peered at him over his strange lenses. "My name is Tipal," he said. "Come with me and I'll show you where you can stay."

Outside the office, the tall thin man turned his head left and right. "Ah, choices," he muttered then pointed away from the large building and towards a crooked path bordered by trees. He strode along it, reaching a hut made of branches. Although clean, it only contained two wooden boxes. Tipal patted one of them. "Aha," he said, "a good bed." He pulled a flat bag from inside the other box. "And a good mattress."

Jonan gazed at the two items. "Is that all?"

"All? Tut, tut, they are enough."

"Tut, tut?" Jonan echoed. "I've never heard anyone say that before."

Tipal bowed. "Welcome to the planet of Polite Anachronisms." So saying, he threw the flat bag onto the wooden bed and dropped onto it. With a whoosh, a flurry of leaves flew into the air. Unconcerned, he wriggled until he was comfortable. "There," he said, all bones and angles, "Now I'm comfortable."

Jonan shook his head. He was on a search, the echo of a pilgrimage, and all he found were clowns and riddles, riddles and clowns. He thought of Terra with all its comforts. It wasn't too late, he could go back. He could contact Evana and say he was coming back. But to actually go back? Face again the laconic driver? Sense the eyes of the fishermen on him? Show his failure? No, he couldn't go back, not yet, anyway. With a sigh, Jonan put down his bag.

Tipal rose. "Leave that here," he said. "I'll show you around."

"But the doors don't have locks," Jonan objected.

Tipal gazed sadly at the door. "You're right, zamir. Someone has stolen the lock and filled in the hole." His bony face became melancholy and his lips twitched with a muttered incantation. "There, now," he said, "that should keep out all those superstitious Shrivites." He looked gravely at Jonan.

Jonan couldn't help smiling. "All right," he said, "I don't carry anything of value to a Shrivite community."

Tipal graciously waved a hand. "Other places, other values."

They went towards the sea. Despite Tipal's long legs, Jonan's impatience kept putting him in front. As they tripped over each other, Tipal stretched out a long arm. "Relax, zamir, relax."

Jonan slowed, noting that half the fishermen weren't fishermen at all, they were fisherwomen. His prejudice surprised him, but that wasn't the only surprise for their catch was not fish. It was seaweed.

"Very tasty." Tipal smacked his lips. "Especially when fried."

"Even for a Terran?"

"For a hungry Terran? Yes." Tipal stopped and looked at Jonan. "Although your hunger, I think, will not be filled by food."

"No." Jonan nodded. "Yerudit."

"Yet she is but a measure."

"What d'you mean? A measure of what?"

Tipal stared at the sparkling sea. "I'm sorry, zamir, but this you must find out for yourself."

Jonan eyed him, thinking Tipal knew more than he was saying. An electric tingle ran along his spine; he was on the edge of an understanding. Just as they stood at the edge of the sea, so he stood at the edge of something as deep. But the moment passed. Tipal waved to the fishermen – who never caught fish and weren't all men – then moved on. Jonan hurried to catch up, and together they walked to the large building with the curved roof.

"This," Tipal said, "is our place of zindance."

"Zindance?" Jonan echoed.

Tipal laughed and scratched at the stubble that served as his hair. "Sorry, zamir, I forget. In our dialect, it means to sing and to dance."

"But this is a temple, isn't it?"

"Yes, zamir?"

"You sing and dance in a temple?"

"Yes, zamir, a regular orgy." He laughed but then, like a clown, stretched his long face even longer. Jonan, smiling, entered the temple. As on Varli, there were many pillars and statues set amidst flowers and bushes. Jonan wandered among them, inhaling deeply. Tipal watched with amusement. "Ah, zamir!" he exclaimed. "Are you really from Terra?"

"I'm beginning to wonder." Jonan held out his arms. "I was. Now, maybe, only my clothes are."

Tipal laughed. "We can change that, too. But, zamir, I will tell you. What you seek is not here. We must take you to it."

Jonan, guessing he meant an Obelisk, asked, "Is one here?"

"Not far, but underwater. Tomorrow I will take you, after the zindance, but now you must earn your keep."

Jonan frowned. "What do you want me to do?"

"Choose. Books or food?"

Jonan held out his hands. "My fingernails are too clean for food so it'll have to be books."

Tipal laughed. "But you must always be clean for food."

"A muscle man told me it was under-the-nails-dirt that gave flavour."

"Ah, Vulcan. He likes to joke."

Jonan was surprised. "You know him?"

"Like you, he is the talk of the cosmos." Tipal clapped his hands to his mouth. "No, no, not like you. He alone is the talk of the cosmos."

Jonan shook his head. More clown. "Take me to your books," he ordered.

He thought he knew what he was in for, but he wasn't. Used to e-reading, Jonan found the paper books heavy and cumbersome. Before long, Tipal was bringing them down faster than the Psychaeologist could stack them. Jonan was sweating when his companion tapped him with a bony finger. "This is part of the zindance," Tipal said.

"Space, and I thought you were on nano-steroids!"

Tipal grinned. "Watch."

Jonan did so and gradually realised that Tipal worked to a rhythm. Not a be-bop-de-do but a coordinated absence of friction. Loosening his muscles, Jonan made the task much easier by becoming the medium in which the work was the message.

A century or two later, Tipal stretched. "Time to eat," he said.

Jonan also stretched. He creaked. "What's the time?"

Tipal patted his stomach. "Eating time."

"How d'you know?" He couldn't see any clocks.

"My stomach is aligned with the cosmic lines of eating." Tipal replied. Jonan laughed, and Tipal pretended to be hurt. "But truly. Drop me anywhere and my nose will twitch on the dot of dinner." He frowned. "Although a dot for dinner is a small dinner, indeed."

His eyes still twinkling, the tall bony man nodded in confirmation when he entered the communal kitchen and saw the cook reaching for a bell.

The cook turned and grinned. "I thought I'd try a bit later today," he said, "and see if you came too early."

"He's new," Tipal said, "and thinks he can trick me." His long face became mournful. "And by the time they learn, someone else is in charge."

He led Jonan to a table, and they began to eat. Eventually, Tipal leant forward and asked, "What d'you think of it, zamir?"

"Good," Jonan replied. "Tastes like fish."

"Fish, never!" Tipal looked pained. "Seaweed! Very nutritious."

"Seaweed?" Jonan took a closer look. It was true, he was

eating seaweed, roasted seaweed. He chewed thoughtfully. He'd always prided himself on his palate, hence his preference for Terran food. But had it been as tasty as this? Was Terran food really that good or were his taste buds changing? He'd have to look into that when he got back.

When he got back? A strange notion. Terra now seemed so far away, a fantasy away. The Probability Drive really had turned substance into insubstantiality, as if home was too smooth and only in these rough worlds was there enough friction to create reality. Home. Jonan tried to work out how far he was from home, but hours of shifting books had shown him just how heavy words were. Exhausted, he yawned. Although early by local time, he yawned again. Fatigue shuttered his eyes, and the other people grew hazy.

A bony finger prodded him. "Go to your room, zamir, and sleep. Soon we will zindance, then again when the sun rises. The zindance will show you how to make work easy. Sleep now, and I will wake you then."

"Yes," Jonan mumbled, his words melting into his chin. "Sleep now. Zindance tomorrow." With an effort, he rose, and a soft murmur of goodnights went with him. He thought dimly of the intruder and tried to rouse himself, but couldn't. He lay down on a mattress suitable only for a fakir yet instantly fell asleep.

Sleep, perchance to dream? Or, on the other hand, perhaps not, for Jonan's first thought on waking was how much he'd enjoyed it. His muscles still ached, yet that only accentuated the pleasure of just lying there. It was dark outside but for his body time, it was already morning. Not to get up now was an indulgence. Him, indulge? He did, and for the first time in ages, he rolled onto his side, and simply let his thoughts and images come and go as they pleased.

Too soon there was a soft knock on the door. Cautiously, Jonan sat up and watched it creep open. His hair prickled and his muscles tensed, but it was only a long lean head, the leading edge of Tipal.

"You are awake, zamir," he whispered. "That is good. Come, the zindance will start soon."

"The zindance?" Jonan mumbled.

"To greet the dawn."

"Oh, yes, the dawn. Gotta greet the dawn."

He pulled on shorts and shirt then dribbled water over his face. It would be interesting to watch a primitive ritual at first hand. Every Psychaeologist should do it. He joined Tipal, finding the predawn air warm but the shadows cast by twin moons disorientating. Bright against a plethora of stars, the double shadows went ahead of them as dark horns. For once, Tipal moved quickly, yet the temple was already full with men and women in loose clothes sitting cross-legged on the ground. As they entered, Tipal handed Jonan a coarse mat.

"For your ankles," he whispered. "The floor is hard."

They slipped in, and Jonan put the mat beneath him. In the complete silence, he surreptitiously looked around. Most people had their eyes closed and emanated an aura of peace. He also closed his eyes, but despite the mat, his ankles were beginning to hurt when a subtle change occurred. At first, he couldn't tell what it was. Then another change came, and this time he identified it: a hum, a deep and powerful resonance. The sound came from the people around him, a double or treble, glottal vibration that coursed through his body. The volume increased and it became like the sea, wave after wave of tremendous power.

There were currents and counter-currents. Although Jonan could only discern the harmonics, the effect evoked an intense yearning. An image of Yerudit, vivid as a holo, leapt into his mind. Her copper hue had a golden lustre, and he ached to touch her, ached with a pain that was physical. The pain grew and grew as the sound went on. Yearning became tangible.

Lines of force connected him to her image.

When it seemed the sound was a bubble that just had to burst, a woman rose and began to dance. Within a slow strong rhythm, she became the focus; the waves of sound moving into her and giving her shape, yet they also flowed out of her. The hum became solid, and the pain of the yearning turned into daggers of sound.

In an atmosphere as charged as a phion-beam, the woman stopped. Instantly, so did the hum. In the intense non-sound that followed, silence rushed in, the silence of an unstruck sound. At an unspoken signal, everyone rose. Tipal signalled, and Jonan followed. In the dark, they crossed the sand and stood at the edge of the sea. In ones and twos, people slid into small boats and paddled away.

"Come," Tipal murmured and lifted one long leg into a small canoe. He paused. "Do you have a torch?" When Jonan shook his head, Tipal stroked his long chin. "Better if we have one. Wait, zamir, and I will bring light." He drew his leg back and walked back along the sand, and moments later, his long shape merged into the forest.

Jonan waited, listening to the soft sound of the boats as they paddled away. At a noise behind him, he turned expecting to see Tipal. But it was a shorter man with head down, holding out a torch.

"Tipal sent me with this," he said. "Let us go."

Jonan nodded and turned to enter the canoe, then hesitated. "But what about Tipal?" he asked.

"He's busy. Come."

Tipal had never used a tone of command. "No," Jonan protested, his unease growing. "I said I'd wait. I'd better go and see him."

The man gripped his arm. "Come," he repeated.

The strength of the grip cut through Jonan's relaxed state. Suddenly he knew that in some mysterious way, the attacker had found him. With a shout, he tried to snatch his arm away, but the man began to drag him towards the sea.

"No!" he shouted. "Tipal, Tipal, help!"

As Jonan shouted, he began to push back. Yet with astonishing speed, the attacker slid around Jonan and began to drag him backwards. Jonan snapped. So far, he'd been passive, assertive not aggressive. Well, bugger assertion. Now for some aggression! He ducked and weaved; kicked and punched; fell down, leapt up; pushed and pulled. In ankle deep water, the two men slammed each other. Yet all this must've happened in seconds for Jonan heard a door bang and feet pound along the path. He renewed his efforts when the man twisted inside Jonan's defence and threw him into the water. As Jonan surfaced, his attacker darted across the sand and into the trees. Jonan rose but he only saw Tipal.

"What is it, zamir?"

"I was attacked." Panting, Jonan pointed into the bushes.

"Here? Surely, not!" Tipal looked to where Jonan pointed, his voice suggesting doubt. "Such a thing has never happened before."

"Didn't you hear anyone?" Jonan asked.

"I heard you shout."

"Dreck!" Jonan swore, using a word from his childhood.

Tipal shook his long head and shone the torch he'd brought into the trees. No one. Jonan took it and shone the light at the wet sand, but any marks were already washed away.

"You did not imagine it?" Tipal asked.

"No! Never!" Jonan held out his wrist, expecting to show marks, yet none were visible by torchlight. Also, to his surprise, his outstretched hand was rock steady.

Tipal shrugged. "Come, zamir," he said, "we will look into this later. Now we must go."

He stepped into the canoe and swung the light for Jonan to follow. Moving with care, the Psychaeologist lowered himself onto a narrow seat. Once settled, he was surprised to see the vessel had an engine when he'd expected only paddles.

"So you don't do everything by hand," he said.

"At rare times, zamir, there are storms."

"And this old-fashioned motor propels the canoe through the water."

"No, zamir." Tipal smiled. "This old-fashioned motor will hover."

"An antigrav unit!"

"Yes, zamir. It pollutes little. Though this way is even less." And with a slow rhythm, Tipal began to paddle.

As they slid through the water, Jonan wondered if Tipal was correct. Had he only imagined the attacker? With everything around him so different, his whole sense of reality was undermined. As the green-red colours of the rising sun transformed the surface of the sea, he even began to wonder if all this was merely a dream. He would wake and find himself in a programmed bed with his routine set out before him. Or perhaps, this was real and all that other was simply a dream, a dream of indulgence. He remembered an old, old story. A butterfly dreamt it was Confucius only to awake to find it was Chaos Theory.

Mentally, Jonan shrugged. Right now, metaphysics was a void, a black hole of inaction. Right now, despite the attacker, he was at peace, and so he would enjoy the feeling. If he knew how, he would've paddled. Yet even without him, Tipal had the canoe moving swiftly, and in the hush of dawn, the shore dropped away. They travelled towards the horizon, the green-red now a ribbon of orange and purple and gold. The sea was absolutely still, not even a gentle swell. Yet unable to dispel all of his doubts, Jonan kept a watchful eye on the water. He had the weird idea that at any moment his assailant would burst out of its depths.

Something else happened, however, and Jonan's spine

began to tingle. It was a very faint sensation that made him sit upright and feel more alive. The tingle was an excitement, a danger that he imagined as a flight across an abyss on flimsy wings. Part of him wanted to draw back, yet another part, more powerful, drew him deeper. He knew instantly what it was. It was the siren song of an Obelisk. He saw Tipal watching him.

"What?" Jonan said.

"You feel it?" Tipal asked. He looked surprised.

"Don't you?"

"Not yet. Remarkable, zamir, truly remarkable."

Remarkable, indeed. This was Tipal's territory; he should've felt it first, not Jonan. What did it mean? What could it mean? Had he been sensitised by the attacker or was his imagination working overtime? Hopefully, it wasn't just imagination. With no answers, the canoe joined the others at a tiny island. Jonan now felt like a tuning fork, his whole body resonating to the Obelisk. The group walked across gravel, and there, embedded in the rock, was a curious pillar. Or maybe it grew through the rock? As with the object on Varli, its existence was ambiguous. Solid or black hole? Jonan couldn't say, but obviously, this was an Obelisk.

One by one, the men and women went forward. In silent grace, each touched as close as they could to the pillar then put their hand to their forehead. Moving on, their faces were transformed. Tipal reached for the Obelisk, and his face lit up. Jonan also almost-touched it. A shock, pleasant but electric, ran through his arm. *Just* pleasant, however, was a disappointment. Then Jonan put his hand to his forehead. The charge ran through his head and mushroomed out through the top of his skull. In a delirious daze, he followed Tipal back to the boat. There, he took the paddle, and with an unaccountable skill and energy, he paddled like a demon.

Tipal watched him. Eventually, as the sky turned to a light green, he said, "A curious thing, zamir, that you should feel the energy so soon. In truth, your struggle was good for you."

Jonan stared at the other man. The Obelisk had driven out any thought of the attack, yet now, Tipal had given voice to an idea that Jonan found difficult to accept: in attacking him, his enemy become his ally.

# Chapter 13

Mirena tapped lightly on the door.

"Come in," Evana called. "Door's open."

The postgrad entered the office. "I wonder if you could spare me a few moments?"

The Psychaeologist stared blankly at her, then recognition dawned. "You had a problem and... Jonan, I believe, helped you with it." Her face tightened. Was this pretty young woman here to compete for Jonan? Or to put in a complaint about him?

"I thought you were... friends." The postgrad carefully kept her voice neutral. "So I was wondering if you could help with my research."

Evana relaxed, her tension turning into puzzlement. "I don't see how. It's been quite a long time since I did any research."

"Can I?" Mirena pointed at a chair.

"Yes, sure." The Psychaeologist looked at her clock. "But I've got a client in twenty minutes."

The postgrad sat down and scrolled through her minScreen. "My research is to do with off-planet tourism, looking at why people go where they do." She used her minScreen to project a series of 3-D photos. "There's an increasing minority of nutters who want to hoverboard in live volcanoes, or go deep sea diving in turbulent waters, or free fall through the highest atmosphere." She smiled gingerly. "Actually, I don't know if they say the highest atmosphere or the deepest."

Evana returned the smile. "Highest or deepest, you won't find me doing it."

Mirena shuddered. "Nor me."

The Psychaeologist again looked at the time. "And? Beside these activities neither of us would ever do, what is it you would like me to do?"

"Ah, well, Jonan told me he was going on extended leave to visit some really off-the-track planets. D'you know if he's come across anything that can be viewed as extreme tourism?"

"Extreme tourism?" Evana burst out laughing. Mirena blushed. Evana waved a hand. "Sorry, I'm not laughing at you. Look, it's quite a story, and we don't have time now. Can we meet in a couple of hours?"

With the blush fading, Mirena checked her schedule. "I'm free at five. At the Astrobar?"

"Excellent! Now, however, I have to hurry you out."

Mirena left, and Evana prepared for her next client, continuing work until her minScreen chimed for her to leave for the Astrobar. By coincidence or reflecting Jonan's habits, she sat at the place where he had often met with Yerudit. Mirena entered soon after, and Evana waved her over, launching into a discussion she'd wanted to have with someone, anyone, connected to Jonan.

"At the beginning of the academic year, Jonan met a young woman." She smiled wryly. "Not unusual for him, but this one had a profound effect on his thinking. Not that it stopped him from… playing around. But she then left in a huff, leaving Jonan surprisingly disturbed." The Psychaeologist grimaced. "I used to think he and I would eventually get together, but…"

Mirena thought of her last evening with Jonan and felt a twinge of guilt. "I'm sorry about that."

"Again, not you." Evana took a sip of coffee, wishing she had ordered something a little stronger. "Jonan is a real dreamer." She waved a hand. "More than that, a true searcher. He looked into all sorts of myths, magics, and mysticisms, but when nothing came out of them, all the discipline of those practices turned into a very refined self-indulgence."

The postgrad reflected. "I remember Jonan used to say something like mysticism is the highest form of hedonism. I never really knew what he meant."

"He probably didn't know himself till he met Yerudit. She brought it all to the surface again. Now, he's on a search for her, and from what he's Screened me, it's also turning out to be a search for Obelisks."

Mirena frowned. "Obelisks?"

Evana gazed up to the ceiling's panorama of stars. "They're these strange pillars, or things, found on a few planets. Scientists were really excited when they first found them. But when they couldn't find out what they were, even what they were made of, they kind of faded out from the news. More accurately, blocked out of the news."

"But you know about them?"

"Only because of Jonan and he only knew about them, or was reminded of them, by Yerudit." Evana's gaze shifted down again.

"Does he know what they are now?"

"I don't really know. I only know he's become fascinated by them."

Mirena queried her minScreen. "Obelisks... alien artefacts... government conspiracy... mythology in the making..." She cupped the minScreen in her hands. "It reminds me of a Jonan history lecture. He said ages ago, there were stories about UFOs, but the government ridiculed the rumours, then we found out the Zirenians were observing us and the government knew about them all the time."

"We still don't know much about the Zirenians, either."

"True." The postgrad slid her cup around on the table. "The Obelisks could be what I want. The nutters who want extreme experiences might find those things exactly what they're looking for."

"But not if the government denies they exist. Or refuses to say where they are."

"Even better, Jonan knows how to find them. He could be

their guide."

Evana waggled her head. "Maybe? He likes to think of himself as a kind of maverick, so it might suit him to go against the government." She stood up. "I'd better go. I need to do some shopping if I want to eat tonight."

Mirena walked with her. "I guess you won't give me Jonan's new Screen address. But would you contact him and ask if he'd be interested in being an, oh, an extreme guide?"

"Who funds your work?"

"The government."

Evana grinned. "Even for anti-government research?"

Mirena transferred her e-business card. "WorldGov is flexible, and nowadays, they'll look at anything that'll reduce Terra's population."

"Well, Jonan might be interested." Evana looked at the e-card. "He just might." Curious as to Jonan's response, she Screened her message as soon as she arrived home.

# Chapter 14

After two days, Tipal said, "You next go to Probos, zamir?"

"Yes, zamir." They both smiled at Jonan's use of the word.

"But you like it here?"

"Yes."

"Then why go on?"

Jonan released a heavy breath. "Yerudit." But this time, on hearing the word, it seemed just that, a word.

"Do you expect her to be there?"

"No." Jonan could imagine her. Her reality, however, was ephemeral.

Tipal poked him with a bony finger. "Then you pain yourself."

"I know. But I must go."

Tipal closed his eyes and rested his chin on the bridge of his fingers. When he opened them, he said, "Go to another place first, zamir. Then after that...?" He shrugged.

Jonan showed him the minScreen. "This says Probos. It tells me the optimal route."

Tipal smiled, the sort of smile a jaguar might give a turkey. "But what does your machine mean by optimal, zamir?" he purred.

"It's a parallel, quantum neural net. It adjusts weightings," Jonan replied hesitantly. "Gives the maximal probability."

"Ah, probability. Like the Probability Drive." Jonan shivered slightly. Here were echoes of phobia. "You trust the machine use of optimal. But what of the human sense?"

Jonan looked at him, not realising an answer was actually expected, but as the silence extended, he reached for an understanding. "You mean," he said slowly, "optimal as in the *right* thing to do?"

Tipal nodded. "That. And?"

"The rightness of things? The right intuition?" Jonan paused. "You mean there's a more appropriate place to go to?"

"Yes." Tipal motioned skywards, "There's a barren place up there. Terra has no interest in it."

"What's its name?"

"We call it Yawa. Ariyeh the Tsadkah found it of much interest, and that was his name for it."

"Yawa?" Jonan mused. "Wasn't that the name of an old tribal god? A god of fire and thunder?"

"Indeed, there was such a god, so in naming it, the Tsadkah named it well." Tipal looked thoughtful. "Or contradictorily. Come, zamir, let us peer into our crystal ball."

Jonan gaped. "You are an Occultish?"

"Worse." Tipal grinned. Waggling a finger, he led the way back to the office where, with a flourish, he revealed a Screen. "See? Magic!"

"Some crystal ball," Jonan said sourly. "I wondered how you knew the starship schedule."

Tipal's long face broke into a wide grin. "When the runes fail, we fall back on this." His long bony fingers flew over the buttons, suggesting the runes often failed. "Ah, you are in luck," he cried, "The Shriva leaves shortly."

"The Shriva?" Jonan cried. "This place? The whole village?"

"No, no, zamir! A starship, Shriva its name and Shrivites its occupants. Are you free to go on that?" Tipal looked up, his face shining. "Yawa is of no interest to Terra, but to us, it is of great interest."

"Why?"

"Can you not guess?"

Could he not guess? Of course, Jonan could guess. He gazed at Tipal. The man was human and yet almost alien. The strangeness of it reminded Jonan that he sat here in a crude, hard-backed seat ready to go onto a barren rock of a planet when he could be at home and sitting comfortably in a soft flexi-chair. Strange? Yes, yet he had to go on. The Obelisks now drew him as much as Yerudit did.

"So, what makes this one special?"

Tipal paused. "Ariyeh, the one you react to, was the first human to find it."

"Curious and curiouser."

Tipal lifted a finger. "I know that, Alicia in Fractal Land."

Jonan shifted on the hard seat. "Terra didn't find it but he did? How could he, especially as someone who spurns hi-tech?"

"Exactly, zamir."

Jonan was baffled, but Tipal wouldn't say such a thing unless he believed it. The idea was so amazing that, for once, Jonan thought perhaps he *should* meet this Ariyeh. Perhaps he really did have important understandings? Strange thoughts. The Psychaeologist's head hurt. Strange reality.

"What you're saying is very hard to believe," Jonan said. "Let me think about it."

"Think," Tipal agreed. "Meanwhile we have work." And he made a face like a melancholy donkey.

"Just one moment, zamir. Can I use the Screen to see if there are messages my minScreen can't receive?"

"Of course." Tipal turned the machine. "Shall I show you how to use it?" He smiled slyly.

With a sound somewhere between a snort and a laugh, Jonan shook his head and keyed in his private Screen address. There was one message, and he read it with growing perplexity. "Interesting." He rested his chin on his fists. "Evana, a close friend, is wondering if the Obelisks would be an attraction for extreme off-planet tourists." He snorted again. "Extreme off-planet tourists!"

"Perhaps, zamir, the Obelisk would be of interest to these people," Tipal said. "It is sometimes the extreme that brings answers."

Jonan pushed the Screen away. "Another thing to think about. Let's do this work you mentioned. I'll do my thinking afterwards."

Leading the way to a pool, Tipal rolled up his baggy trousers and waded in. Selecting a length of seaweed, he said, "If the centre is translucent then it is good to eat."

Jonan waded in and began to collect plants. "A good one," he said. "A good one… a bad one…"

Tipal checked them. "Correct, zamir. You learn quickly for a Terran button pusher."

"Something within me seems to have shifted."

Tipal nodded. Jonan had, indeed, made changes. It wasn't long, however, before the Psychoaelogist began to blink.

"The sun is too bright, zamir?" Tipal fetched two wide-brimmed hats from a nearby shed. "The hat is also good to cook." He put one on. "You must boil it with a rock. When the rock starts to crumble, throw away the hat and eat the rock."

Jonan laughed even though he'd previously heard many versions of that joke. But Tipal was such a clown. *Maybe one day,* he thought, *I, too, could become a clown.* Aloud, he said, "Okay, if you reckon I should go to Yawa, then Yawa it is."

Tipal grinned. "You will not be sorry." With that decided, they spent the next two days collecting seaweed.

On the third day, the day for Jonan to leave, Tipal held up a hand mirror. "Do you know yourself?" he asked.

"Metaphysically?"

Tipal shook his head. "Look and see."

Used to a holo, Jonan took the mirror and swivelled his head. His reflection disappeared. Making a long face, Tipal held the mirror while Jonan gazed into it. The Psychaeologist gasped. A stranger looked back. His skin had become brown and leathery, his eyes piercing, and his cheekbones stuck out.

"I had a beard once." He rubbed his jaw. "Just here under the chin, I thought I looked like a buccaneer. What a spacewalker!

But now, this?" He shrugged and they both laughed.

Tipal held out a packet. "This, zamir, is for you."

"A present?" Jonan reached for it. "From you?"

"From here."

Jonan opened the packet, finding loose trousers and a jerkin inside. When he stroked them, they were soft and fleecy. They reminded him of Yerudit. With this present, Tipal was sending Jonan in her direction.

"Thank you, zamir," Jonan mumbled. "It will be an honour to wear them."

"They will become you. And you will need them on Yawa."

The two men were silent for a moment then, fingering his onepiece, Jonan said, "Why d'you say that I'll need them, Tipal? And what about my onepiece? Would you like it? It lasts forever."

Tipal shook his head. "All things must pass. Why not our clothes? People are afraid of death and surround themselves with the permanent, but that is an illusion. The living flesh turns to dust while the armour still shines, then that, too, must rust and pass."

"The shells die, Tipal. But the spirit…?"

The tall man smiled. "Who knows?"

*Tipal knows or has some pretty good ideas,* Jonan thought, *but he won't say*. As for himself? The Psychaeologist sensed a new sense of lightness, a deep down lightness that he hadn't known since he'd been a student.

They went to the terminus and waited for the old solabus. This time, the driver grinned cheerily and even helped stow the Psychaeologist's pack. When the vehicle chugged into the air, Tipal bowed, then continued to wave until the bus was just a dot on the horizon.

# Chapter 15

When he arrived at the terminal, Jonan was amazed at the number of people already there, then he did a rough head count and was amazed at just how few they actually were. He hadn't been with so many people for a century? A week? A month? Impossible to believe this was the proverbial drop in the ocean compared to Terra's billions.

After a late minute rush of travellers, there was a whoosh, and a great starship appeared in the sky. Gentle as an autumn leaf, it floated down, its incredible silence hushing the awe struck watchers. With strange symbols cut into its slender side, it could pass as humanity's imitation and homage to the Obelisks.

The doors opened and a moving stairway slid down. A steward with long hair and moving tattoos did the security checks. No one disembarked although many filed in. On board, Jonan felt bewildered, partly because of the size of the ship, which was massive after his time in a hut, and partly because of the people with their different costumes and skin colour. In addition, he felt like a complete outsider when those already on board greeted the other newcomers with exuberant hugs and kisses or slaps on the shoulder.

Jonan, left alone, felt alone – a lone rock around which streams of people flowed, the feeling heightened after working so closely with Tipal the clown. Wanting communication, communication of any kind, he scrolled through his minScreen and closed himself off from the outside. A hand on his shoulder, however, made him jump, but just as quickly he relaxed when a deep chuckle filled the air. It was Vulcan the warrior, the muscular flesh and blood gate of Varli.

"Jonan," he boomed, "I was asked to look out for you."

“Zamir,” Jonan exclaimed, “it’s good to see someone I know.” He put out his hand, but Vulcan ignored it and placed his palms together. “But how did you spot me in this crowd?”

Vulcan held his nose. “Your clothes.”

Puzzled, Jonan echoed, “My clothes?”

He gazed down at his onepiece; non-tear, non-fade, non-toxic, it was a wonder of modern technology. Able to maintain a constant temperature, Jonan could even adjust its coat of many colours. He had always been proud of it. Now though, beside Vulcan in his olive-hued, homespun rough wear, Jonan saw it in a new light. It wasn’t exactly a sterilised robot’s skin, but it wasn’t too far off. On the other hand, he wasn’t yet ready to wear Tipal’s gift.

“It is a bit dead, I guess,” Jonan admitted. “Perhaps I should attach drying seaweed to it?”

“Perhaps, but then we might cook your suit and eat it.”

“No doubt with a rock.”

Vulcan laughed. “Ha, I see that Tipal has instructed you.” He clapped Jonan on the shoulder. “Come, meet some people.”

Seeming to know everyone, the big man led Jonan from group to group. At first, the Psychaeologist was self-conscious about his hi-tech clothing, but as no one else made comment, he quickly forgot about it. He soon became aware, however, that Vulcan was not only a forger of metal but also a forger of networks.

With meeting so many new people, the two Standard days to Yawa passed quickly. Then, with their final entry into norm space, the passengers crowded around the windows. Vulcan clapped Jonan enthusiastically on the back, causing him to see a haze that he temporarily mistook for a return to Probability Space. When he recovered, Yawa lay below them, a bleak planet of black rock and hard shadows.

They landed at the base of a cliff so bleak that Jonan doubted there was any air outside. But his was the only doubt, and the other travellers cheerfully skipped onto the planet's surface as he still hesitated. Only when Vulcan nudged him did he reluctantly venture onto the rocky ground. Yawa was not at all what he'd expected. Varli and Haja had been tropical paradises. This place was equally hot, but bone dry, and it was impossible to believe that anyone could ever have lived on it.

"Is the whole planet like this?" Jonan asked.

Vulcan shook his head. "Oh no, not nearly as hospitable." Masking a smile, he slung Jonan's bag over his shoulder then casually strolled towards a battered airbus. But before they reached it, it rose and headed towards the hills.

"That was the last one," Jonan said, his face creasing with worry.

"Never mind." Vulcan jolted him with another of his giant slaps. "They will be back. Meanwhile, let us find a suitable watering hole."

Taking him literally, Jonan looked around in bewilderment. But Vulcan gripped his arm and led him towards a shiny black rock face. The Psychaeologist's feet slapped against the hard surface, the echoes swallowed by the surrounding bleakness. But on rounding a rocky outcrop, he stopped in surprise. Laughter and singing burst from the depths of a vast cave. Vulcan entered, and as Jonan's eyes adjusted, he saw he was inside a very busy tavern.

"Food comes from above," Vulcan said, waving vaguely.

"From above?" Jonan echoed. "You mean by starship?"

"No, no." Vulcan chuckled. "This is hard place but crops do grow here."

When they went further in, Jonan's imaginings were thrown back a thousand years. He was in a mediaeval painting of illuminated darkness and exuberance. Going further back and he was living in the body of a myth, the laughing revellers being goblins, elves, and dwarves. Jonan laughed out loud.

"How fitting," He gestured with a sweep of his arms, "to eat here with Vulcan, ancient god of volcanos."

"Hah!" the big man roared. "The volcano rumbles." He slapped his stomach, and it answered with a drum roll. Vulcan cocked his head. "Fugue in G minor." He chuckled, pushed into a space on a long bench then held up a mighty arm to show he wanted feeding. A man strolled along the table, laying down broad leaves that served as plates. Another man served out a type of potato mush from a bucket. A woman served cubes of what Jonan guessed must be vegetable protein.

Temporarily ignoring his food, Vulcan wrapped an arm around the woman.

"Careful!" the other men shouted.

"A kiss," Vulcan said.

"Be off with you!" the woman snapped, and undaunted by his muscles, rapped the big man on his pate with her ladle. But when Vulcan made a face, she kissed his shaved dome, and the men laughed.

This was undoubtedly the strangest place in which Jonan had ever eaten. Although the kitchen was well lit, the long wooden tables only had candles and oil lamps. As a result, the boisterous activity projected mysterious shadows while the huge cave echoed resonantly.

With Vulcan siphoning up information, they were the last to leave. Outside, a partly-filled airbus waited. When they entered, it rose and followed a stony track towards the hills, creaking and groaning with every step. On the shiny black track, it took twenty minutes to cover as many kilometres. In mock exasperation, Vulcan clapped his hands.

"Shriva take me!" he boomed, "We could walk this fast."

"Walk?" another man cried. "We could carry it faster."

The joking continued as the airbus struggled upwards. Jonan, however, wasn't quite so happy. The vehicle strained along a sheer path. To one side, shiny black rock rose steeply. To the other side was a sheer drop. The sun cast a bright light that was reflected from the depth of the canyon as if from black diamonds. The sky, leached of all colour, was as white as bleached bones, the contrast causing Jonan to shudder.

For another hour, they climbed this harrowing landscape until, rounding a bend, they came to a clearing. Several airbuses were already parked there, but Vulcan used his weight to nudge a way through and led Jonan towards a black rock face.

"The Boot Shop," he said, pausing at the entrance to a small cave. Jonan looked and then gaped: rows and rows of shelves were cut into the rock, each shelf containing a bewildering array of boots. With a chuckle, Vulcan pointed at the Psychaeologist's shoes. "Show me," he said. Obediently, Jonan handed him his right shoe. Vulcan felt at the sole. "Huh, too soft. Good for princesses and Terrans but not for Yawa. For Yawa, you need a pair of these."

"Those?" Jonan took hold of a boot. "These are too hard. I can't walk in those."

"Oh, yes you can." Vulcan pointed to the milling mob. Old men in robes, excited boys in shorts, and women in short tunics were all stomping around in heavy boots. "You'll bruise your feet otherwise."

"Dreck!" Jonan muttered. He selected a pair of boots, but couldn't get his feet inside. Too small. The second pair were too big, so that when he tried to walk, his feet slid out. Vulcan just laughed. With the next pair, Jonan lifted his knees and tried to flick the boots off. When they stayed on, he exaggerated the movement. Just right. And the clowning, a zindance for bleak rocks, felt good. Space, he hadn't played about since he'd been a child; Terra didn't encourage her Psychaeologists to act as clowns. "I'll be a Tipal yet," he muttered.

With their boots on, Vulcan set off on an upward slope. Jonan tried to keep pace but kept tripping on the ebonite surface. Vulcan chuckled and grasped his hand. "Copy me," he said and took shorter steps.

Feeling childlike, Jonan imitated him. Other people streamed past. When they grinned, Jonan flushed with embarrassment. Defensively, he again wondered, *was Vulcan the mysterious attacker?* He certainly had the strength, but one glance at his open face and Jonan was pretty sure it couldn't be him. Accepting that, Jonan saw the humour of his situation. By then, of course, they were at the tail end of a rapidly disappearing line. He stopped trying to catch up and settled for a slow but steady pace, more like skating than walking.

Even without the weight of the boots, the slope would've been hard going. The flinty road circled a mound that became a hill that became a mountain. To one side, the view was blocked by shiny black. To the other, jagged peaks receded into the white glare of the sky. Sweat streamed into Jonan's eyes and his breath became ragged.

"Hard work," he gasped.

"The height," Vulcan said. He curled his tongue into u-shape. "The air is thin. Breathe like this."

"Yeah," Jonan wheezed. "I would if there were anything to breathe."

Vulcan motioned to a rock, and Jonan sat for a few minutes. When they continued, he tried to sip the air but it never really worked. He mostly sucked dust.

A century of effort later, a final bend revealed a long, wide single-storey building.

"The community hall," Vulcan said, his chest heaving.

Jonan planted himself in front of the big man. "You're panting, too??"

Vulcan grinned. "Just breathing."

The interior of the building turned out to be a manmade version of the cavern down below, but built of rough-hewn timber. At first, it seemed to be full of rough-hewn people, but that was just an impression created by their noise. They behaved with a gusto that not long ago, Jonan that would've considered quite unseemly. And, as on the starship, Vulcan dived right into the middle of it.

Eventually, Vulcan led Jonan to another long single-storey building, but unlike the hall, this one was narrow and divided into small rooms. The big man selected one empty bedroom and Jonan chose the next. Before entering, however, Jonan touched one ebony wall.

"Is this hard to build with?" he asked.

Vulcan shook his head. "It is somewhere between carbon and diamond. Find the right face and it cuts very easily." He laughed. "And that, zamir, is a very good meditation."

Jonan grunted. "I'm not yet ready to meditate on a rock."

"Meditate on rock?" Vulcan echoed. "Very easy to fall off." He laughed again. "Rest now, I will be back at dusk."

A rest was never more welcome. After the long trek, Jonan was exhausted. Lying down, he immediately fell asleep, not waking until Vulcan shook his shoulder. As he revived, he tried to stretch, but still stiff, he stumbled out into the fading light.

"Can you go a little further?" the big man asked.

Jonan managed more of a stretch. "If I have to. Why?"

"Come."

A stone wall ran around the cluster of buildings. Vulcan sauntered towards it and looked over the top. Jonan followed, and his jaw dropped: beyond the wall was a sheer drop with a vast bowl stretching away below them. In the last of the light, the sides gave off a silver reflection. Tiny blue lights dotted the bowl.

"Incredible!" Jonan exclaimed.

"Incredible, indeed."

Jonan hung over the wall, trying to see as much as possible. "What in space is it?"

Vulcan pulled him back. "It is an old volcano."

"An old volcano? Is that why it's luminescent?"

"Here, yes."

"And the lights?"

"Glozards."

"Glozards?"

"Glowing lizards, lizards that glow. They come out at night. Big things." Vulcan leant against the wall. "It is a tough old planet, but there are several animals here, and like the glozards, they only come out at night."

"And water?"

"Plenty in the mountains, but like the creatures, it goes underground during the day."

Jonan grunted again. "You talk as if the water makes a decision."

"Yes," Vulcan chuckled, "and sometimes I speak as if people do, too."

The sun had now completely disappeared, sucking the heat from the air and leaving a cutting chill. Vulcan tensed his whole body then relaxed. He did it three more times, holding his breath as he did so. He blinked then seemed to have adjusted. Jonan buttoned up his onepiece and pressed a button on its sleeve. He was beginning to feel comfortable when Vulcan raised a broad arm and pointed beyond the bowl.

"Over there," he said, "is the Obelisk."

The Obelisk! Jonan felt another type of chill run through him. Even so, he again leant over the wall. "How do we get there?"

"Boot power."

Jonan stared, yet no matter how hard he looked, he couldn't see any trace of a path. There was just the swallowing darkness and the sparks of the glozards. The effect was disorientating: looking down gave the same view as looking up. The Obelisk was well concealed, and it was going to be hard work to get to it.

As if reading his thoughts, Vulcan added, "We leave at dawn.

You'll see the way, then."

He walked along the wall to a gate. Beyond, Jonan saw a few black glittering steps. The rest of the way, however, was swallowed by darkness. Between the vastness of the bowl and the dome of the sky, Jonan felt insignificantly tiny. The whole of humanity was tiny. It seemed totally improbable that humankind should exist, totally improbable it should be able to traverse the infinite voids of space. Above all, it seemed totally impossible that he should be in this place right here and right now.

# Chapter 16

They returned to the dining room. By now, Jonan was used to communal eating, although he still wasn't used to the exuberance. The Shrivites were clearly excited, in fact, when one started to play a squeezebox, he expected to see the others dance on the tables. They didn't – not quite – but they did touch shoulder to shoulder and sway together like trees in a breeze. Perhaps that was how trees danced.

It was well into the night when Jonan and Vulcan went back to their cottage across an open courtyard. It was now so cold Jonan raised his onepiece to its max. His frozen fingers kept fumbling with the controls, but when he did press the right button, the extra heat was blissful.

Vulcan had taken a cloak from the hall and his reaction was to wrap it around him. When Jonan didn't do the same, the big man boomed, "You are not cold?"

"I was," Jonan replied.

Vulcan jutted his head forward with interest. "But then?"

"But then I adjusted my suit."

"Ah!" Vulcan slumped back, clearly disappointed. "I thought perhaps you had mastered the cold."

It was Jonan's turn to be interested. "Can it be done? D'you know anyone who can?"

"I can do it a little," Vulcan admitted. "Ariyeh the Tsadkah can do it a lot. A lot." Vulcan nodded. He suddenly turned to Jonan. "I've stood next to him on a night like this, and he generated so much heat even I felt warm."

"Hmm," Jonan said.

"Amazing!" Vulcan exclaimed.

"Amazing," Jonan echoed, his tone bringing a frown to Vulcan's broad face. But without further explanation, the

Psychaeologist added, "See you in the morning," and he went into his room.

Not long after, Jonan heard a rhythmic rumbling from the adjoining room and knew that Vulcan was asleep. At first, that sound combined with thoughts about Ariyeh kept him awake, but then he told himself he was listening to the ebb and flow of the sea. After that, the rhythm soon had him asleep as well. But not for long. He awoke shivering. His onepiece was designed for Terran days not for Yawa nights. With the temperature dropping and Jonan not moving to recharge it, the suit was losing power. He tried curling into a tight ball, but that didn't help. His jaw clamped with cold and his whole body began to shake.

This was dangerous. Jonan worried he would become seriously ill, and on a strange planet that could be fatal. It was also ridiculous. All this travel only to die of cold? He had to do something. Like a puppet on broken strings, he stumbled out of bed. He had other onepiece suits, but that was no good. Heat from one outer layer couldn't pass through to another.

As he fumbled in the dark, Vulcan stirred. *Wake him,* Jonan thought, but pride wouldn't let him. No, Vulcan would be a last resort. Desperately, he searched through his bag until his groping fingers found something, the rough clothes Tipal had given him. Tremblingly uncontrollably, he stripped and put them on. They itched but brought immediate warmth. His onepiece went over the top. It might not be the latest in fashion, but it worked and his chilled bones began to thaw.

As he returned to his bed, Vulcan stuck his head around the door. "I heard noise," he said.

"I was cold."

"What about your onepiece?"

"Didn't work," Jonan muttered, "not enough power."

"Hah, Tipal warned me you were thick-headed." Vulcan briefly went back to his room, returning to throw a thick rug over Jonan. "Here, enjoy. Sleep well, you still have two hours."

Jonan grunted. *Two hours*? But he was grateful for the rug. If anything, he was now too hot. But that was all right. Hot was just uncomfortable; cold was dangerous. Gratefully, he sank into needed sleep and was just beginning to enjoy it when someone hammered on his head.

"Umph?" he groaned.

The thunder continued until he wondered if the sounds were his bones grinding in his skull. The rat-tat-tat repeated along with a deep voice. "It is now three-thirty Yawa time," Vulcan called, "and all is well. Four o'clock and it may still be reasonably well. Four five and it won't be well at all."

*Clowns,* Jonan thought. He struggled into bleariness. A huge weight was holding him down. His attacker? His eyes flipped open. A hairy beast? Then he remembered: the cold, the double layer of clothes, the woolly rug. Three-thirty, couldn't he stay where he was? He stuck out his nose. Ice cut at his nostrils. He dug down again. But the cold acted like a knife, cutting away slumber and leaving behind a curious elation. He sat up and peered through a window. Patterns of frost clung to the glass, and beyond it, the sky was a sheet of shining black ice.

Briefly, Jonan was taken back in time, to his youth and to holidays in the Kosciusko Mountains. To a time when there was still snow on the peaks and he could toddle on a ski, a time when comforting hands held him when he fell. Yawa, he now saw, was like that. It wasn't just bleak, it was also an adventure. Evana's extreme travellers? Just bring them here!

Meanwhile, Vulcan was exercising inside his blanket. When Jonan rose, he called out, "Are you awake, Jonan? Or frozen? Did you sleep well? Are you warm?"

Jonan shuffled out, still inside the rug, and growled like a bear. "Ta dum!" He dropped the rug and showed his onepiece. "More ta dum." Jonan slid open the top of his onepiece and showed his Tipal-wear beneath.

Vulcan laughed. "You look like a stuffed sausage. No, an unstuffed sausage. A sausage with its stuffing coming out."

"Should I change?" Jonan asked.

"No need," Vulcan boomed. "There are no meat eaters here."

With the blankets wrapped around them, they went to the dining hall. The stars were brilliant, and Jonan paused to admire them. But as the sharp chill cut at his face, he hurried inside where a fire was burning, its flames greener than those of Terra.

"That," Vulcan said, "is why no-one lives here permanently. The trace elements would turn them into toads."

"Really?" Jonan asked, his mind on hold.

"Look at the Zirenians."

"Ha-ha." Jonan gave Vulcan the eye, a rather bleary eye, then turned at a sound. A man was wheeling a trolley towards them. Jonan squinted; the fellow's skin did have a shade of green.

"Eat, drink," he croaked at them. A long tongue flicked out of his mouth.

Jonan goggled, then Vulcan spoilt it by bursting into laughter. At that, the man took a toy from his mouth. Jonan smiled weakly. "Too many clowns," he muttered.

Vulcan put an arm around him. "Lighten up," he said. "That, after all, is the purpose. Life is to enjoy." Vulcan grabbed a hot drink and a misshapen lump that he thrust into Jonan's hands. "Eat," he ordered.

"No, thanks," Jonan muttered. "It's too early for me."

Vulcan dug an elbow into his ribs. "Eat for heat. Otherwise you will need a hot water bottle."

"A what?"

Vulcan pointed to the corner. A few children were dashing around in a play area. One was swinging a stone jug. Another was trying to bounce a rubber bottle.

"Space, I could've used one of those during the night," Jonan said.

"My fault." Vulcan grinned unapologetically. "I have seen those antiques. Would you like a bottle with a mouse face or a duck?"

Jonan half smiled. "I'll eat."

He was still chewing when a bell chimed and people headed for the doors, and so, swallowing a last mouthful, he also filed out. After the warmth inside, the intense cold was again a shock. It gripped him like a vice, and he had to fight to breathe. The hot food, as Vulcan had said, provided a particle of relief, yet despite the cold, Jonan felt touched by magic. With the thin air and the stars so close, it seemed they all moved within a rare black crystal.

The front of the line had already crossed the rim and disappeared along the trail. The only sign of the path were lanterns and the zigzag lights from startled glozards. The volcano wall to one side, they descended into the swallowing darkness, taking step after careful step until they eventually reached level ground. It wasn't, however, as firm as it first appeared: the top layer was ash so that dust rose while their feet sank. It wasn't quite hell – the biting cold was wrong for a start – but it could well have been limbo. Trapped within the walls of this huge black bowl, ash hovered around each one of them, shining with the ghostly light of ectoplasm.

They went on and on, their mouths fighting to suck in air. Even so, excited children hurried past. Jonan saw nothing to get excited about. At least, not till they came to a steep slope, and Vulcan pointed at stone steps.

"Up there," he said, "is an inner volcano, a live volcano within a dead one."

Jonan moved towards the steps, but Vulcan stopped him. No one else was going up. Instead, they sat in a circle. Jonan tingled with anticipation. In this hollow pit, he expected to observe a religious or spiritual ritual. No, not observe; he was going to be part of it, a pre-dawn ritual as ancient as human consciousness. They were going to summon the sun.

The ceremony began with a sub-vocal note. The vibration crept through the night, into Jonan's spine, and his skull buzzed as if with a mild electric shock. For an infinite time, it disappeared, then came a second time but from a different location and hit his body in a different way. Harmonics and sub-harmonics shivered through him until his muscles rippled. A gust of wind blew into his lungs and burst out again. Gigantic forces held him on the end of strings. Jonan couldn't resist. Nor did he want to. Suddenly he knew. It wasn't just the circle, it was also the Obelisk. This was its siren call – calling out to him.

Between a push and a pull, Jonan rose. Vulcan reached to stop him, but either Jonan forced him away or else he let go because Jonan couldn't be stopped. He advanced to the steps and put his right foot on the first stone. A wave of doubt assailed him, but he shook it off. Alone in the dark, and struggling for air, he began to ascend. After ten steps, he had to rest, and again at the second ten. Below him, the Shrivites continued their low hum. Arms linked, they swayed from side to side. Against the shiny black rock, however, their heads seemed to flicker from place to place, a probability of being here, then a probability of being there. Definite bodies with probable or improbable heads.

Jonan climbed more steps. From there, even the bodies had succumbed to the probability effect. Between the shiny black rocks and the grey ash, they were no more than dark smudges. No more than orbitals of electrons around a nucleus. He hesitated. Was it safe to go on? Safe, unsafe? He couldn't resist. One more stop and gasping for breath, Jonan crested the top.

The scene that greeted him was startling. Expecting a plateau, he found himself on a rim that was only two paces wide. Below him was the perfectly smooth cone of the inner volcano. At its base bubbled a phosphorescent substance that gave off a pungent green smoke, rent with purple flame. Jonan felt an impulse to descend, but one look at the walls prevented him. Volcanic heat had made them as smooth as glass.

Instead, he paced along the rim, the Obelisk pulsing within him even though he couldn't see it. On his right, the smooth cone descended into flames and smoke. On his left, jagged lava fell to volcanic ash. Jonan turned and walked in the other direction. Passing the steps, he looked around wildly. He could feel that familiar electric tingle, but he couldn't see what caused it.

What he did see was a ghost.

A figure suddenly materialised from out of the smoke, his eyes burning like the flames below. Amazed, Jonan watched as the man approached. He came so close that Jonan went to step round him, but the dim figure moved with him. Reacting, Jonan returned to the other side, yet so did the other. Suddenly Jonan knew this was his attacker. He put out his arms to ward him off, but it was already too late. The man gripped Jonan and began to twist him. Jonan held him off, but the stranger was too strong. Slowly Jonan was forced toward the edge. One glimpse of the fire below and he redoubled his effort, but an irresistible power continued to turn him toward a hell of smoke and flames. Still not ready to yield, Jonan spread his legs and dug in his feet. He expected to be pushed. Instead he was held steady. When that finally seeped through, he stopped struggling and looked. There, behind the rising maelstrom of smoke and flames, was the Obelisk.

In that same instant, Jonan realised he was free: the other had gone. He whirled and peered around, but the stranger had disappeared. Jonan knelt and panted. How had the man come? How had he gone? Who was this friend who masqueraded as enemy? Who? Vulcan? But no, his attacker was nothing like as big. Another answer floated at the edge of his consciousness, but that idea was too fantastic and he pushed it away. Instead, he faced towards the Obelisk. No wonder he hadn't been able to detect it, with all the smoke and flames curling into the air, it seemed to flicker in and out of existence. He would never have spotted it, if he hadn't been directed.

Jonan gazed down the glassy slope. How the hell could he get to it? It seemed to require an impossible leap through the air. Smoke drifted up, whirls of orange and purple and green. The Obelisk was now transparent, now translucent, now opaque. Bewildered, he moved his head from side to side, his peripheral vision detecting weird misty images. They seemed to be ghosts of stairs. Ghosts of stairs? That didn't make sense. His scalp crawled, then he focussed again and realised that the smoke settled in unnatural patterns. Something was there, something that made a pathway.

Jonan picked up a handful of ash and threw it. It drifted over the rim, briefly settled on an invisible surface then whirled about. He moved his head and caught glimpses of refracted light. Cautiously, ever so cautiously, he put out a foot. On the point of overbalancing, he lowered his weight. Now he truly understood Yerudit's dance! Holding himself stable on one foot, he tentatively extended the other. He was just about to withdraw when he touched something soft and yielding. He hesitated. Go on or go back? The ash formed a glowing invitation, so that with an inner prayer, Jonan lowered his weight. The cushion beneath his foot firmed up, and the invisible surface became rock hard.

Slowly, very slowly, Jonan threw more ash and took another step. His searching foot found another cushion. Again when he put his weight on it, the force field hardened. He dared to turn. A step away was the smooth wall of the volcano. Between him and it were only wisps of coloured smoke. He seemed to be walking on air. Hardly breathing, Jonan made his slow advance, following the inner wall in a wide spiral. With each step, the pull of the Obelisk grew stronger, and Jonan wanted to throw caution to the wind and run forward.

Controlling the impulse, he approached steadily. The prickling feeling along his spine grew stronger, and without burning, the whole of his back was on fire.

Around Jonan was the smooth black cone of the inner volcano. Above him was the velvet sheen of the sky and its alien constellations. Smoke and flames flickered about him, while molten lava bubbled around the Obelisk. This was humanity's picture of hell, yet Jonan experienced it as a heaven. Peace and power emanated from the Pillar, enfolding him in waves of serenity. Here was an object unknown or ignored by Terra, but it was an incredible wonder. Before it, he felt alive as never ever before.

For long minutes, he remained in awe, but then a movement above disturbed him. Vulcan was waving an object. As Jonan watched, the object emitted a mist that spread and outlined the steps. Vulcan came down, using the spray to mark his way. He also prodded the air with a staff before stepping onto hidden surfaces. A line of people followed him.

"Well," Vulcan shouted, "so here you are, I was beginning to worry. Did someone tell you the way?"

Jonan smiled. "I was shown the way."

"Shown?" Vulcan looked around. "But we were all down there."

"All? You, too? No one passed you on the way?"

Vulcan chuckled. "People always pass me on the way."

Jonan studied the other's broad open face. "But you're sure everyone stayed together?"

"Jonan, I am certain. I know the people here. They stayed for the meeting."

Jonan gazed into the Obelisk. "Someone or something is haunting me, Vulcan. Sometimes as enemy, sometimes as friend."

Vulcan also gazed at the pillar. "The Obelisk is a great stimulation for the imagination, my friend," he said eventually.

"Are you sure it is not your own… intuition."

"As an enemy?"

"We all have our shadows."

"You think I'm just projecting my dark side?"

"It happens."

Jonan shook his head. "I don't think so. At least, it doesn't feel like it."

"The alternatives?"

"Are very strange. I can only think that the Obelisk…" Jonan's voice faded out. Standing close to that strange pillar, he again had the feeling of being on the verge of a deep understanding. But Vulcan waved a large hand and interrupted his thinking.

"The sun rises," he said. "It is proper to see it."

The others were already climbing back up the slope. Reluctantly, Jonan followed. They reached the top of the inner cone in time to see a river of light cascade over the rim of the outer volcano. It spread across the distant peaks in a wave, the edges in shimmering pastels. A rainbow broke from the sky and flickered momentarily above the Obelisk. Silver points danced within the inner cone. Jonan put out a hand, but he couldn't tell if the sparkle was real or just an afterimage.

In the dawn brightness, the glozards vanished, and an intense hush settled over the landscape. The sun rose quickly, and in moments became a burning ball in a white-washed sky. In comparison, the smoke and flames were reduced to insignificance. The Obelisk had gone, and no amount of peripheral vision could make it come back.

They all descended from the inner cone and returned to the ash plain. The shadows were stark now and seemed solid enough to collect. The sun was searing, and the only protection was the dust haze caused by the trudging of many feet. Jonan bounced between elation and sorrow. Yerudit and the Obelisk had become completely intertwined so that the loss of the one reminded him of the loss of the other. Without speaking, he returned to his room. Once there, he brought out the shadow puppet.

"D'you know what this is?" he asked.

"Of course." Vulcan looked at it with affection.

"Sometimes," Jonan said, "I think it's alive. I think it's my attacker. Pretty crazy, het?"

"Alive?" Vulcan said. "Of course, it is alive. Physically, no. But metaphysically? Oh, yes, yes very much indeed."

At this, Jonan shivered. But Vulcan grinned, and for the first time, Jonan recognised the intelligence that hid behind the broad bland face. He also detected a knowledge, the knowledge that reflected the most crazy of his own wild ideas.

# Chapter 17

Once upon a time, Jonan had believed in magic. Then he'd become a Psychaeologist; faith had turned to technology and search had turned to habit. In these past weeks of travel, however, he had regressed; his sophisticated mind had started to accept metaphors and myths as hidden truths, and this more pagan way of thinking accepted that the puppet really had become alive. Not in its own right, perhaps, but as a projection of his mind. Through his guilt towards Yerudit, he had started to think of the puppet as his attacker – and that was the sanest of his ideas, his others were a lot wilder.

Wrapped in thought, Jonan went to the communal dining room and lined up for fruit slices and bean paste. Once he would've turned his nose up at such food, now he gulped it down with relish.

It was good that he rushed as the early sun was already a burning ball. To return to the terminal without frying in their boots, the whole group had to hurry. For a fleeting moment, Jonan did think of staying with the Obelisk. A temptation, but there was no question, he had to go on. Yerudit was his destiny.

Fortunately, Jonan was getting used to being boiled, chilled, or just lightly barbequed, and so he managed the trek down with scarcely a pause. In fact, he did so well that he almost kept pace with the children. When he did catch up with them, they'd exchanged their boots for light shoes and were racing around as if they hadn't already had the long trek. Jonan also returned his boots but did so with reluctance. His Terran shoes now seemed too light, as if they had been designed for pixies in low gravity, and when he walked, he was afraid of bumping his chin with his knees. Feeling light-headed, he entered the food cave and sang out – although not too loudly, "Welcome to

Troglodyte Tavern. Trolls, half price."

And what trolls there were. Everyone was high. After the pre-dawn ritual, the Shrivites were as boisterous as ten monkeys with three bananas. They squawked, they gobbled, they jostled. Jonan wouldn't have been at all surprised if they'd pecked each other and shed feathers. He scratched his head. Did he mean monkeys or turkeys? He was already forgetting his animals.

His thoughts were interrupted by a bell; the starship was ready. He followed the Shrivites to the landing area and was awed. Although metal, the slender shape of the ship was so like the Obelisk. Everyone immediately became quiet, the passengers boarding in silence and clustering around the windows. When the doors finally closed, the captain counted down for take-off, and the ship rose on anti-grav. The bone-bleached light of the sky briefly filled the interior, then the ship translated into the flickering blue haze of Probability Space.

Mathematically, the travellers flipped in and out of existence as though spread through the whole of infinity. Existentially, nothing changed. A paradox. What to believe, the senses or the sciences? But why make such a struggle? In fact, as a complacent Psychaeologist, Jonan really had stopped trying to understand. Especially when he'd realised some of his space phobia clients were themselves scientists. Maybe it was best to ignore the paradox. Science reduced existence to calculation but existence wasn't calculation.

The ship skimmed through space like a stone skimmed across a river. When it touched the surface of norm space, computers did lightning calculations and sent them diving again. Before its first re-entry, however, Vulcan sat down beside Jonan, and the big man drew his hand down his broad face. As he did so, his normal cheer turned into a frown.

"This is me being serious." He roared with laughter, and his expression returned to normal. "Oh, being serious is so hard.

But really, I need to ask. This ship is destination, Hebaron. Before there, we touch down at other planets. What would you like to do?"

The Psychaeologist pursed his lips. He had thought of visiting other Obelisks, but Yawa had shifted something deep within him. "What are you doing?"

"I stay on to the destination."

"Destination is like destiny, het?"

Vulcan grinned. "Could be."

"And the other travellers?"

"Some go to Hebaron. Some leave before."

"And Yerudit?"

"Ah." Vulcan drew the word out with a long breath. "What does your heart tell you?"

"She's in Hebaron, at home."

"So, your decision?"

"Hebaron. It has to be Hebaron."

The big man nodded. "My thought, too." He rose. "But consider deeply."

Jonan was left alone with his thoughts. That was fine with him. Everything was fine with him. Everything? Nothing. His decision made him nervous, petrified. For in going to off-route Yawa and the Obelisk, he had forsaken his previous plan with the result he was now headed directly for Hebaron, Hebaron and his destiny. Jonan gulped. He didn't want to arrive too soon. Suppose Yerudit rejected him? In fact, he didn't want to arrive at all.

As Jonan's mood oscillated, the ship made its first stop. As some passenger-pilgrims left, he even thought of dashing out with them to prolong his arrival time. But he forced himself to face his fears, to stay still, and to focus on his breathing. After all, he was a Psychaeologist, an expert on beating down phobias. On the second and third stops, he was much more relaxed.

Yet when the bell tolled for his destination, Jonan felt sick. *Ask not for whom the bell tolls, it tolls for thee.* If he could, he would've stayed on board. *When destiny beckons,* he thought, *run*. But Yerudit was here. Yet so was Ariyeh the Tsadkah. And, perhaps, this was where he'd have to confront his attacker. Plus, once here, he'd have to reply to that Screen message from Evana. But what to say? Were the Obelisks suitable for extreme travellers? On the one hand, it seemed blasphemous. On the second, third, and fourth hands, they had certainly sent his adrenaline sky-high. So, maybe those crazies were the right sort? A sour thought: *Maybe he should ask the Tsadkah?*

Sweating, Jonan went to a window. Norm space showed a mosaic of silver on black. One shining point was brighter than the others, and even as he watched, it grew. Hypnotised, he stayed by the lookout. A blink later, Hebaron was a disk and its colour had changed. From silver, it had turned to ochre.

His heartbeat increased as the starship penetrated the atmosphere. A palette of coppery golds rushed up to meet them. Jonan blinked, and the motion stopped; they had landed in a field of bright orange sand. Reluctantly, Jonan followed the others towards the terminal, noticing even the air had an orange tint. Waiting at security, he spotted people beyond the gates, and he craned his neck to see them. A foolish hope, of course she wasn't there. Among the copper skins, none had Yerudit's inner glow.

Vulcan had stayed with Jonan. "Do you see her?" he asked.

"No." Jonan shook his head. "What now? Find the Ariyeh?"

"Why?" Vulcan replied innocently. "Is he lost?"

"No." Jonan scowled. "But I am." He suddenly rounded on the other man. "Are you supposed to be looking after me?"

Vulcan scratched the stubble on his shaved head. "Maybe."

"You don't know?" Jonan said. "No orders? No commands? No suggestions?"

"Hmm, yes." Vulcan's eyes glazed with thought. "You

remember Thera on Varli?"

"Yes."

"Thera said to make sure you ate properly."

"Is that all?"

"That was hard enough."

"Nothing about riddles? Nothing about time? Nothing about Yerudit?"

Vulcan screwed up his broad face with thought. "About Yerudit?"

"Yes?"

"She said…"

"Yes?"

"To make sure that she also ate properly."

"Space!" Jonan shook his pack with anger. He was tempted to shake Vulcan. The other waited patiently. When the rage had blown over, Jonan said, "Okay, so I'm the clown. What now?"

"What you already said, the Tsadkah."

"Yerudit is there?"

"Hmm." Vulcan made a sound deep in his throat. "You may be shocked. I will take you."

"More shocks?" Jonan gripped Vulcan's arm. "Him? Her?"

Vulcan shook his head. "Not in that way."

"I didn't mean that."

"Then?"

Jonan shrugged. At that, Vulcan smiled, a smirk concealing more than it revealed. He was subtler than his powerful body and bland face suggested. Yet Jonan found it impossible to believe that the big man was his enemy.

"Come," Vulcan said, "it is far from here. We will need to shuttle."

"Shuttle?" Jonan was surprised. "I thought after Yawa, it'd be camels."

Vulcan whacked him on the shoulder. "There will be worse. Do not worry."

Jonan staggered. "I'm not worrying, I'm just trying to stand up."

"Hah!" Vulcan laughed and strode off.

Jonan hurried after him. He had to admit that he was relieved the meeting had been put off. He still wasn't sure Yerudit wanted to see him. Guilt as well as desire had sent him after her, but she had no reason to feel guilt, and she might no longer have any desire. The primitive customs of this place could even have her married by now. Or... or... Negative thoughts chased after each other.

Strung out with tension, Jonan boarded a shuttle that flew high above the orange-tinted land. It shuddered and thundered. But that only took place inside Jonan's heart, and all too soon, they were landing again, near a small town that shimmered in the desert heat.

Guided into a waiting airbus, Jonan said, "The place is bigger than I expected."

"That is not the Shriva," Vulcan replied. "We have to cross sand to get there."

Jonan grunted. Still, it was another reprieve. He was being given time to absorb the fact he was on the same planet as Yerudit and the Ariyeh. The bus lifted and took them towards the town. A busy market on its outskirts reminded him of the tourist *shooks* in Egypt, and he realised why Yerudit had been so drawn to the pyramids.

At the sight of the market, Vulcan tugged at Jonan's sleeve. "We descend here," he said, "to arrange transport."

"An aircar?" Jonan asked. Vulcan, however, shook his head and headed for a ramshackle building with a wooden fence. Animal noises and animal smells came from it. At that, Jonan exclaimed, "We really are going by camel!"

"Sort of." Vulcan chuckled. "A griffin."

"Griffin?" Jonan echoed. "There's no such thing. Wait a minute!" He clicked his fingers. "When we saw the sphinx,

Yerudit said they reminded her of griffins. But I thought she just spoke metaphorically."

"Oh, no, we Shrivites are very serious people. We never speak metaphorically. Although when we see a sphinx, we do say, I sphinx therefore I am." The samurai-clown kept a deadpan face. The oncoming meeting obviously wasn't depressing him.

Vulcan strode into the building. Jonan followed and marvelled: here were creatures straight out of mythology. They were as high as horses, but with bodies made wider by vestigial wings. With long narrow snouts, whiskers, and enormous eyes, their faces reminded Jonan of seals seen in a zoo.

"Gentle creatures," Vulcan called. "They live on night moss."

"They're indigenous?" Jonan asked.

"Oh, no," Vulcan said blandly. "They evolved here."

"But genetically speeded?"

Vulcan nodded.

Jonan patted one of the creatures. "Are all animals here as safe?"

"No, ecology demand there be hunters. They are the lions and the bears. They eat the griffin."

Jonan made a face.

"But do not worry," Vulcan added, "fire will keep the lions away."

"Great. How far away?"

"Enough." Vulcan gave him another of his giant claps on the shoulder. One of those, no doubt, would also keep the lions away.

The owner approached. "Fine animals, eh? For two, I can give you a special price."

"How much?"

The man's eyes flicked from Vulcan to Jonan. "Eight hundred for the two."

"Eight hundred!" Vulcan laughed disdainfully. "Five."

The man stroked his chin. "You go to Gedi? Well, I too am a disciple. Seven twenty."

"Huh. I can go no higher than six."

"Say, six ninety."

"Huh!" Vulcan began to walk away. "We will do business across the way."

Alarmed, the man called, "Friend, friend, last price." Vulcan hesitated. The man bit his lips. "Six fifty." Vulcan continued to walk away. "No profit for me, no profit for me. Six… six twenty."

"Six twenty, you say?" Vulcan rubbed a big hand across his stubble. The rasping sound covered the lowing of the griffins. "Okay," he sighed, "but I will have to do extra work to make up for it." With a sad expression, he reached into the folds of his green robe and withdrew a leather pouch. From it, he counted out a wad of paper money. With an equally sad expression, the owner took it and counted it out. They both touched their hands to their hearts, and the deal was complete. Then they both grinned; they'd both done well. Jonan was taken aback, he'd never haggled in his life. It just wasn't done on Terra. Not on the Terra he knew.

The owner saddled up the griffins, and Vulcan showed Jonan how to mount. He found it easy but unnerving. Despite all his travels, he wasn't used to heights. Shuttles and starships gave no sense of height, nor did a solabub, but sitting astride this rotund swaying creature did. As the ground rocked beneath him, Jonan found he couldn't bear to look down. Fortunately, they stopped after an hour to snack. But on remounting, that brought on another problem: his stomach.

Not wanting to appear weak, Jonan gritted his teeth and waited. When his belly settled, he relaxed, even starting to enjoy this ride. While he was no buccaneer carousing in a ship on the high seas, this was still an adventure. They'd left the town behind and were now travelling through rolling desert with far horizons. In contrast, although home was lush and tropical, it now seemed claustrophobic. In this clean and spacious desert, Jonan spirit's felt free to expand.

Not long after and it again contracted. After all the riding, his bottom and saddle had collided a hundred times too often while his thighs had rubbed up and down a thousand times too much. His legs were on fire. When they stopped in the shadow of a sand dune, he hobbled off his mount, expecting to spontaneously combust. Vulcan, apparently unaffected, leapt off and scraped at the sand with a stick.

"See," he said, "plants. They come up at night. The griffins eat them."

Jonan, keeping his thighs from touching, asked, "Can we?"

Vulcan rubbed his dome. "Some. Some are good for us. Some mean instant death. Leave them until you know the difference."

Jonan nodded, but his griffin nudged him aside and with a long tongue pulled at the orange-tinted greenery. As his mount ate, Vulcan took bundles from its pack. "We'll eat as well. In this desert, it is best to munch frequently." He touched a sequence of buttons on one bundle, and it blossomed into a nanomesh umbrella.

Jonan gaped, "I thought with your philosophy you would've built a shelter."

Vulcan shook his head. "Too much work for too little benefit. We do what is appropriate." He cut hunks of bread and cheese.

Jonan chewed away. "It's good. Does Hebaron breed cattle?"

"No." Vulcan put on his bland face. "Why?"

"The cheese."

"Oh, that." Vulcan looked sideways at Jonan. "Griffin."

Jonan paused, uncertain whether to swallow or to spit. Eventually he decided to keep going. "Better than synthetics." He swallowed. "In fact, it's pretty good."

Jonan ate too much and drank too much. With the next bout of travel, food plus riding caused his stomach to rebel. In vain, he scanned the desert. "Any decent toilets here?"

Vulcan handed him a shovel. "This is where it's appropriate to work."

"I have to dig?"

"On Yawa, it would be into rock."

Muttering, Jonan walked a good distance away. When he couldn't see Vulcan, he thrust the shovel into the dirt. At the sound, both griffins turned to stare. Embarrassed, the Psychaeologist ducked behind a dune, dug a small hole, and squatted. Jonan smiled: many stories dealt with mind downloading, not many with body downloading. Finished, he refilled the hole and washed his hands with dirt.

Returning to Vulcan, he stretched out beneath the umbrella, closed his eyes, and dozed. Jonan woke when Vulcan shook him and pointed back at the dune. Blinking sleep away, he looked, then snapped alert. A fierce creature was glaring at them, a lean and hungry griffin with slitted eyes and sharp teeth.

Jonan felt suddenly unprotected. "What now?" he muttered

In one oiled movement, Vulcan rose. Hair half-shaved, half-knotted, he was now a true samurai. He reached into his bag. Jonan expected him to draw out a sword. Instead, he pulled out a phasion. "We do not eat meat," he said, "but nor do we become meat."

Keeping eye contact, he picked up a stone and threw it. It landed in the sand and scattered dust. The creature drew back its ears, snarled, and looked like it might attack. As Vulcan raised the gun, Jonan threw a larger stone. It bounced, raising more dust, making the creature sneeze. Rubbing a paw over its face, it growled, then slunk away.

"That was a lion," Vulcan said. "A griffin lion. A fearless beast. It may come back, so better for us to go." He collapsed the umbrella while Jonan gathered up the food. When everything was packed, Vulcan eyed Jonan and said, "You were not afraid?"

Jonan paused to consider. "I was."

"But now?"

Jonan held out his hands. "Pretty steady," he said. "Shaken but not stirred."

"I know that phrase," Vulcan said. "James Bond, Space Agent." He stroked his griffin. "You should thank your attacker."

"Why?"

"He has unstirred you." He patted Jonan on the shoulder. "Remember that."

Jonan patted Vulcan on the shoulder. "Why do I think you know more than you're saying?"

Vulcan mounted his griffin. "We all know more than we are saying. Words are merely pointers."

"Very ontological," Jonan murmured.

Calmed by Vulcan, the griffins continued their rolling walk across the desert as the single sun grew hotter and hotter. Although Vulcan didn't seem bothered by the heat, Jonan's head started to burn, and he touched his hair expecting to feel smoke. Remembering the hat in his pack, he reached for it, but his buccaneer fantasy came to the fore instead.

"Ho, ho, ho, me hearties!" Jonan called out, draping a shirt over his head..

Vulcan turned. "…fifty four, fifty five. At one hundred, I was going to warn you."

Jonan grinned, childishly pleased with his buccaneer self.

Although his top burnt less, his bottom burnt more. The saddle hammered it, his trousers scraped against his flesh, and his legs had become raw strips of pain. Fortunately, they stopped at a small village built around a group of micro-solar panels.

"Together with storage batteries, these power the region,"

Vulcan said.

Jonan didn't listen. With utmost care, he lifted first one leg from the griffin, then the other and gingerly stepped down. Walking bow-legged, he croaked, "Can you do anything for this?"

A copper-skinned local admired his walk. "You elephant rider, friend? I always want to ride elephant."

"Elephants!" Jonan snapped. "They don't exist anymore, and as for me, I'm just goddam sore."

"Ah!" the man cried, his face alight with comprehension, "You want griffin balm?"

"Yeah," Jonan replied. "No. Maybe. What?"

"To rub in, to soothe."

Vulcan nodded. "It is good, an anaesthetic."

"It's not a snake oil?"

Vulcan looked puzzled. "There are no snakes here."

"A Terran expression," Jonan said wearily. "Okay, I'm ready to try anything."

The man gave Jonan a paste wrapped in a leaf. The Psychaeologist shuffled into an empty room, and ever so carefully, pulled down his onepiece. His thighs were red and raw. If this stuff didn't help, he wasn't even going to dress again let alone get back on his griffin. Carefully, he squeezed the paste into his palm and gingerly touched his flesh. The reaction was immediate, and his burning flesh cooled down. With a heartfelt prayer, Jonan covered his skin with the paste, redressed, and then oozed straight-legged again.

"Incredible!" he said to the Hebaronite. "How much is that stuff? I want a bucket."

The man was taken aback. "Price?" he said. "No price. You want, you get."

Thinking he couldn't have been understood, Jonan raised his voice. "Price?" he shouted. "How much?"

But the fellow just grinned. Exasperated, Jonan looked to

Vulcan, but he was also grinning. "I told you," the big man said, "what the griffin eats might be instant poison, but what they pass out is instant balm."

*Balm?* Jonan gasped. Had he just covered himself in griffin pooh? Good thing he hadn't tasted it! Still whatever it was, the pain had gone. When Vulcan swung into his saddle so did Jonan – although his swing was more of a crablike scrabble. But it was such heaven to have a numb bum. *To sit and not to burn,* Jonan thought. *Aye there's the rub.*

He wondered if the griffin and its balm was a metaphor. For Jonan, the Tsadkah had been a constant pain in the bum. Would actual contact with him also act as a balm, a psychaeological balm?

# Chapter 18

They were still travelling when the sun dropped close to the horizon. Jonan scanned the terrain in search of lions. Vulcan noticed.

"We continue," he said. "We are very close."

Very close. That could mean anything. Too tired to argue, Jonan jiggled around in the saddle. If they didn't stop soon, he would just fall off. But Vulcan was correct. They rounded yet another orange-brown dune and saw a large lake, ringed by semi-regular lines of cultivation. This, obviously, was Gedi. A wave of relief swept over him, quickly followed by a wave of anxiety.

"How many people live here?" he asked.

"No people," Vulcan replied. "Just a thousand souls."

Souls, a thousand souls. This place was special to Vulcan. Jonan hoped that it would also be special for him. The approach, however, was not auspicious. They were still an hour away, time enough for the paste to wear off, but too close for Jonan to drop his pants and add more. So with a sore bum, he clung wearily to his mount as they continued, but on reaching the outskirts of the town, he forced himself to appear alert. The griffins revived as well, flapping their vestigial wings.

From the fields, men and women waved. To everyone, everywhere, Vulcan was a friend. He waved back and to those close enough, he called, "And this is Jonan from Terra."

Their reaction surprised Jonan. The workers leant on their tools and nodded.

"Vulcan," Jonan whispered, "they know about me?"

"Yes." Vulcan beamed. "You may be only the second Terran to come this way."

"Only the second?" Jonan turned in his saddle. "And who

was the first?"

"The first? Ah, a mystery."

"To whom?"

"To the moment."

Vulcan didn't have a mouth that could clamp, he was too generous by nature. Instead, he just grinned, the sort of grin that told Jonan he should already know the first Terran. Had he been told? He was too tired to remember. Too much had happened, and he suspected the Obelisks had affected his thinking. But none of that mattered now. Vulcan had motioned for the griffins to stop. They were in Gedi.

It was the unexpected that Jonan had expected. A Terran town was composed of wide avenues, plastiment houses, and ornamental parks. This place consisted of narrow streets, house of all types and sizes, plus trees among an explosion of flowers. Yet whereas home was always busy-busy, just-thrown-together Gedi conveyed a deep sense of tranquillity. Also, despite architectural ingenuity, Terran houses always looked the same – including Jonan's, although he spent a small fortune on preservation. Here, and he doubted there were any architects, each house was individual. Jonan had lectured often enough about holistic and organic, he'd just never realised how far away from it he'd been.

He found one house particularly attractive. The roof and doors were made of wood, the walls from pink stone plus another material unfamiliar to him.

"What's this?" he asked.

"Mud brick."

"Which is?"

Vulcan yawned. "You will see, my friend. You will see."

"You sound very certain."

"When you build your own house."

"Me? Build?" Jonan blinked. "Can't I rent this one? Who lives here?"

His face a blank, Vulcan replied, "Ariyeh the Tsadkah, of course."

"Oh." Jonan's mouth made a little circle. "Oh!" he repeated.

Vulcan's face split like a melon. "Your vocabulary has become very small, my friend. I thought Terrans were more articulate."

"Yuh." Jonan gulped. "Especially Psychaeologists."

Vulcan waved a hand. "Relax, my friend, they will not be here now."

"You're sure?"

Vulcan nodded.

"But they are here, on-planet?"

The big man nodded again.

Jonan rubbed his neck, gone stiff with tension. As it eased, he realised that every time he thought he had to make a giant leap, it had been broken down for him. This last step, to meet his maybe-friends/maybe-enemies in their own home, was also being softened. Relief followed upon relief, they were deliberately making it easy. Jonan was grateful. Yerudit was thinking of him.

Vulcan dismounted, tied his griffin to a post, and knocked on a wooden door.

"It's open," a soft voice called.

They entered, and Jonan was stunned. A woman was inside. Yerudit's mother? He'd never once thought about a mother. Yet the similarity was striking: same height, same slimness, same beauty. Space! He'd thought of neither mother nor father. As Jonan struggled to absorb this, he was given another moment's reprieve as the woman skipped forward and threw her arms around Vulcan. But then a terrible thought hit Jonan. This house belonged to Ariyeh the Tsadkah. So if this was her mother then the Tsadkah must be her father! His whole body shook, quivered, and turned to jelly. Why this should seem so terrible, he couldn't say, but it overwhelmed him. Once more, he sensed the play of powerful forces around him. But his moment of reprieve was over, the woman had turned.

"I am Hulva," she said, "Yerudit's mother."

"Yes. Yes, I guessed."

"You are Jonan."

"Yes."

She looked at the Psychaeologist expectantly, but he didn't know what else to say. Vulcan came to his rescue, clapping Jonan on the back so that he couldn't speak anyway. "He is looking for Yerudit," he boomed. "Or perhaps," Vulcan raised his eyebrows, "he hunts for her?"

Hulva smiled. "Who the hunter?" she murmured, "Who the hunted?"

"Indeed," Vulcan agreed. "And who the hungry?"

Giving a hearty and totally unapologetic laugh, Hulva bustled around, plates of food appearing as if by magic. Jonan used the time to look around. The lower floor, of timber and brick, conveyed exactly that air of antiquity he'd tried so hard to create in his house. The absence of plas-coatings made a big difference. It meant extra work, of course, but the Ariyeh with his teachings wouldn't worry about that.

A spiral staircase led to the upper floor, and Jonan eyed it with envy. His house only had one floor, but he would've given away the roof to have a spiral staircase. In the upper storey, the sloping ceiling must turn the rooms above into triangular cubby holes. For the first time in his button-pushing life, Jonan's fingers itched. His whole body did. He also wanted to live in a house like this. His fingers wanted to make a house like this.

"Who built it?" he asked, already sure of the answer.

Hulva's eyes glinted. "We did."

"We?"

"Ariyeh and I."

"With your own hands?"

Hulva turned up her palms. "With our own hands." She smiled. "I did use lots of cream, though. There is a cabin for you. It is nice, but not like this."

"He will make one," Vulcan said.

Jonan stared at him. "I'm not here for long. Not that long."

Vulcan shrugged. "What is time? Huh, is that not what Thera said? Time and probability and Yerudit. There is your riddle."

"Tush, Vulcan, do not tease." Hulva took Jonan's arm. "Let us show Jonan where he's staying."

They left the house and walked through an orange-tinted rain forest. Not sure if there was a pattern or not, Jonan asked, "Is this wild or cultivated?"

Hulva gave a musical laugh. "Very very carefully uncultivated."

Vulcan eyeballed him. "Zennish," he whispered.

A little further on, they stopped at a cabin with a thatched roof. Vulcan touched the round walls. "Mud brick," he remarked. "Easy to make. Even Ariyeh would not need help."

"Even Ariyeh?" Hulva questioned. She pointed at a grassy area. "Do you want to build your own hut, Vulcan?" she said sweetly.

Vulcan spread his arms. "Okay, okay, he can build mudbrick. He just sometimes forgets the mud."

Jonan looked from one to the other. For the first time, he saw hope that the Ariyeh was not all perfect. A little further on, they came to a little building with square walls and round turrets at each corner. Vulcan, delighted, strutted into it.

"This new one for me," he crowed, "a warrior's castle,"

He wanted to stop there, but Hulva urged them on. "Just one more house," she said. Jonan thought the interest was its curious structure: a honeycomb built of tiny solar panels. He had a different understanding when she added, "This is where Yerudit lives."

Jonan's breath rushed out, and he found it difficult to breathe in again. He was relieved when Vulcan took the attention away from him.

"Jonan will not be building houses," The big man chuckled. "He will be digging tunnels."

Hulva smiled, but having shown Jonan the house, she didn't stop but led them to the river. "The waterwheel on this side is used for grinding, the other side is more blowy and that's where we have our windmills." She pointed at a range of low hills. "You can't see them from here but that's where we have combined solar-wind turbines."

"You know a lot about power generation," the Psychaeologist said.

"It's always interested me." Hulva's face lit up with enthusiasm. "Although we don't use it much, there's also geo-thermal power. The idea here is for people to generate their own power, but we also have plenty of public power for hospitals and schools."

"And those that don't want to generate their own power?"

"No one is forced to do anything, Jonan, and obviously the sick or frail must be helped." She looked thoughtful. "But the people here want to, they like to construct."

"The philosophy of using your hands?"

"Yes." Hulva patted Jonan on the arm. "But that is only a metaphor."

The Psychaeologist grunted, "For?"

"You will know. In time, I am sure you will know."

Jonan sighed. "Why do I get the feeling I'm being led by the nose?"

Vulcan laughed. "Because you are lucky, my friend. You have the required nose."

Jonan pursed his lips. "To help build a utopia?"

Hulva patted his arm. "Or an anarchy. Here, people move in and out of work, in and out of study, in and out of play. It works – it just means we are less regular in paying our taxes."

The Psychaeologist scratched his head, aware that the reply had just sidestepped his question.

They returned to Hulva's house as people were returning from their work. Most travelled by peddle power, but Jonan also saw a powered balloon, a primitive solabub, and even a flying broomstick.

"People build what they like," Hulva said. "The only restriction is on the use of fossil fuels."

"The black rock I've seen here," Jonan asked, "that's a form of coal?"

"A form of carbon, yes, easy to burn." Hulva pointed up to the clear sky. "We'd lose that, of course."

"So what is your economy based on?"

Hulva smiled. "Sustainability. In the early days of Israelistine, there were communal farms called a kibbutz. Hebaron is like that, particularly here, people with other drives go elsewhere."

A passing woman waved at them, and Jonan thought, she seemed to take more than a passing interest in him. So did other people, stopping to chat and to create brief stops that he appreciated as they took his mind off the coming meeting. But when they were back in Hulva's house and time passed, his unease returned. The sun set and turned the surrounding hills to an orange-gold. A warm breeze brought unfamiliar but pleasant odours. Yet despite the beauty, Jonan couldn't really relax.

"When d'you expect them back?" he finally asked.

She placed her hand to her heart. "I did think tonight. But now, tomorrow."

"They've been away long?"

"Today."

Jonan looked into the orange-gold sunset. "Did you know we would arrive today?"

"Yes."

At Hulva's direct reply, Jonan felt terribly empty, but when she smiled encouragingly, he asked, "Why did they go? Why did *she* go?"

"One reason they went," Hulva replied, "is because there are useful herbs that can only be found at night." Jonan tried to pull at his non-existent beard. "Plus, I think she was nervous."

"Nervous? Her?" He stared into Hulva's tawny eyes, nearly laughing when she nodded.. "You know," he confessed, "when the starship landed, I was so scared I almost didn't get off."

"Thera said that would happen," Vulcan murmured.

Jonan rounded on him. "So you *were* there to look after me."

"Oh, no. Who, me? No, never."

Jonan wanted to turn his unease into anger, but again Hulva patted him on the arm. "You and Yerudit both have fears," she said. "Perhaps too much is expected of you."

"Too much?"

"Or perhaps you expect too much of each other."

Jonan gazed at an orange fern, at its wide lacy fronds, and weighed Hulva's words. He compared *too much is expected of you* to *you expect too much of each other*. Whatever they might expect of each other, it seemed others had even greater expectations of them. "These expectations seem very heavy," Jonan murmured.

"Be grateful," Vulcan cut in. "What is a life lived without expectation?"

"Happy?" Jonan muttered.

Vulcan lifted his hand to give Jonan one of his thunderous thumps, but Jonan shook his head – he just couldn't take one right now – and Vulcan's hand floated away.

"You are right, my friend," the big man said. "You have travelled far, very far. Perhaps you should rest."

Jonan nodded. His head throbbed with new ideas, and he knew he had to be alone. He rose, and his companions both touched their hands to their hearts, a gesture that warmed him. Giving a half bow, he took the grassy path that led to his round hut, and once inside, he started to unpack. On finding the shadow puppet, he carried it to the window sill, and contemplated the shadow created by the bright moonlight. His oil lantern added further projections and they rippled in a shadow dance. Jonan sat on the bed. He was tired and he was wired, depressed and elated, discombobulated and... He was so confused, he didn't know what he felt.

He rose again and moved the puppet out of the light and onto the table. Then he lay down on a hard and lumpy mattress, made no doubt from griffin. He fidgeted, closed his eyes and stared at thoughts that came and went as abruptly as starships popping in and out of Probability Space. Sleep seemed a universe away. That was it, no more sleep. Ever. He'd just think. He'd just... He'd... Sleep came and took him, after all, a universe away. But only for a blink, or an eternity. The universe clanged, and he jerked into wakefulness.

The past months had not only hardened him, they had also sharpened him. Eyes still closed, his mind flipped on. Without moving, he strained to hear. Nothing. He held his breath; so did the night. There was complete silence. But someone or something had woken him.

Heart pounding, Jonan opened his eyes a fraction and caught a flicker of movement. Feigning sleep, he looked again. And froze. The oil lantern was still on, and the shadow puppet projected on the wall. It had moved. Jonan gulped. Every thought turned to ice.

He wanted to shrivel. He wanted to give up, to surrender, but this was one attack too many. Someone must be holding the puppet against the moonlight. With a growl, he threw off the cover and leapt up. In response, the dark shape of the puppet pressed on his chest. Brushing it away, he hit out. His punches blocked, he reached out and grabbed. Grunting, panting, and cursing, he wrestled.

The noises must've carried. A voice called out, "Jonan, Jonan, what are you doing?"

With relief, Jonan saw Vulcan's bulk burst through the doorway. Yet instead of helping, he ran behind Jonan and held him in his muscular arms. Trapped! In desperation, Jonan kicked and wriggled, but he was helpless. Panting, he paused then realised the other man had stopped fighting. Chest heaving, he tried to relax, and when it was clear he'd given up, Vulcan released him. Bewildered, Jonan turned. To his alarm, Vulcan was grinning.

"Jonan," he said, "meet Ariyeh the Tsadkah."

# Chapter 19

Jonan reeled. "You're the Tsadkah?"

In the lantern's light, the dark figure nodded.

"You live here?" Jonan didn't know what he was saying. "Have you been on Hebaron all the time?"

"All which time?"

"Since I've been travelling!"

"As you mean it, yes." The man laughed. The wrestling seemed to have invigorated him.

Jonan didn't understand. Had the Tsadkah been on Hebaron or not? The Psychaeologist was certain this was his attacker. But then how could he have been here all the time? Did he have a double? A twin? Yet this man and his attacker felt identical, and not just in physical appearance. The energy was identical. The stance was identical. Even twins couldn't be so perfectly matched. Jonan's mind whirled. But when the Tsadkha suddenly moved, Jonan flinched and clenched his fists.

The Tsadkah only smiled. "Good," he said, "you are back." Jonan faced him warily, but the man merely put the shadow puppet back on the table. "Dress," he added. "Yerudit is waiting."

"Why did you move the shadow puppet?" Jonan asked.

"I gave it to Yerudit, but she gave it to you. I was a little put out by that." He made a face. "When I heard you were here, I wanted to see it." He put a hand to his heart. "Yes, I should have waited, I am sorry to have disturbed you." He didn't sound at all sorry.

Not knowing what to believe him, Jonan just grunted, and too agitated to feel shy, he started to dress. But although the room was warm, he kept shivering, his mind skipping from planet to planet. At each of them, he endeavoured to recall his attacker. Surely, this was the man? The idea was overwhelming. Vulcan, however, put a hand on his shoulder.

"Finish dressing," he said. "Your journey is over."

But was it? Jonan stared at the Ariyeh and wondered. The man looked quite different to the other Hebaronites, being short and stocky, olive-skinned and red-haired. He didn't have the musculature of Vulcan either, yet strength simply oozed out of him. He had an aura that emanated power. It was almost brutal: frightening yet fascinating. *He's a dinosaur,* Jonan thought, *a primeval being*. He wanted to resist this stranger, yet at the same time, he felt drawn to him.

Jonan kept his eyes fixed on the Tsadkah even as Vulcan handed across his onepiece. He fumbled it on and then followed the Ariyeh out. In the bright moonlight, more orange than Terra's, Jonan could see him more clearly. Or tried to. The other's appearance was still somehow elusive, as elusive as an Obelisk so that from one angle, he looked Indu; from another, Anglo. There was something ancient and deeply mysterious in the man. Jonan shook himself. He was projecting.

When they reached the Tsadkah's house, the door was open and lamps were lit. Hulva was sitting at the table, another person standing at her side. One hand held Hulva's, the other gripped the back of a chair. Yerudit, and she was nervous, as nervous as Jonan. Flanked by his escort, he halted. Jonan and Yerudit were like two ships in a storm, their bodies braced yet leaning towards each other.

Finally, Yerudit sighed. "I'm glad you came."

As softly, Jonan replied, "I couldn't stay away."

"You've changed."

"I've been changed."

Suddenly, the others didn't matter. Yerudit hurled herself towards Jonan, and he opened his arms to receive her. They kissed, pulled apart, kissed again. When they finally separated, he was surprised to find that the others were still there. Jonan looked at each in turn, so many thoughts tumbling through his mind. The centrepiece, however, was the Tsadkah.

Hesitantly, Jonan said, "You never told me the Ariyeh was your father."

Yerudit studied his expression. "You were so sceptical. But I wanted you to know I followed the ideas because I believed in them, not because he was my father."

"Oh?" Jonan reached for his non-beard. "Was I that sceptical?" Yerudit nodded. Jonan found that hard to believe. Had he changed that much or was it just that the sheer presence of the Tsadkah had made a believer out of him? Like a magnet drawn to a pole, Jonan turned towards the mysterious man. Out of the many questions, he asked again, "Why did you wake me like that?"

The other looked at him with a gaze so piercing Jonan had to look away. Like the volcano on Yawa, this man's dark eyes bubbled with layers upon layers of depth.

"I didn't wake you," he said. "I held myself so that I was barely there, but you were waiting to be awoken."

"You mean I woke myself?"

"Yes." The Tsadkah chuckled.

Jonan dug deep into his memory. In his earlier days of searching, he'd come across a philosopher-mystic called Gurdjieff who used to say, *Man thinks he is awake but he is still asleep*. "I think I understand."

"Good."

The Tsadkah's voice was deep, not as loud as Vulcan's but more penetrating, and Jonan thought, potent with portent, a man both warm and threatening, a human version of a tropical storm. Stroking Yerudit's fingers, Jonan considered the Tsadkah's explanation: *Awake* meaning more alert, a heightening of awareness. But why? For what? For Yerudit? For this society? Did he have to protect her from attackers?

Attackers? But there was only one attacker. His thoughts went back to the crucial question.

"Why have you been following me? And how?"

"I?" The Tsadkah seemed amused. "Why do you say that?"

"I was attacked on every planet." Jonan paused. What he had to say next was so crazy.

"Yes?"

"I never really saw who it was but…" He had to steel myself. "I'm sure it was you."

There, it was out. In response, the Ariyeh seemed to flicker. Jonan looked at the others, but they didn't seem to notice. He rubbed his eyes and shook his head.

"Hoi," the Tsadkah exclaimed, "and you call yourself a Psychaeologist?"

He was clearly teasing. Although uncomfortable, Jonan asked, "What have I missed?"

Although he scarcely moved, the Tsadkah seemed to prowl around Jonan like a Hebaron lion around its prey. Even his words were hunters. "Take your own question," he said. "The why."

"The why," Jonan echoed. Without thinking, he released Yerudit's hand and considered the images that went through his mind. If the impossible was possible and it had been the Tsadkah, then what had been achieved? What changes? Jonan spread his arms wide. "I can only think to make me sharper? To harden me?"

"Not harden," Yerudit put in. "You're much less hard now."

"Not harden, then." Jonan sought for words. "To shock me. To flip me one way or the other."

"Which way?"

Had the Tsadkah flickered again? Were Jonan's eyes playing tricks? Surely not. So many questions. He had to focus on one thing at a time. In answer to the question, he murmured, "To make me stronger?"

"Yes, that would be a reason." The Tsadkah smiled warmly. "And you have done well."

Maybe the Tsadkah thought Jonan had done well, but Jonan still knew he had been given no answers. He threw up his arms. "But why? Why make me stronger?"

The Tsadhak focussed on Jonan, and Jonan found it truly awe-ful, sinking into the other's eyes, falling through layer after layer until he span in a vast emptiness, an insignificant as a particle in a vast spinning galaxy. Yet that scrutiny also declared that he *was* significant. Dizzy, he fought to wrench himself out of that vastness until normality – whatever that was – returned. From an enormous distance, he heard the Ariyeh.

"For the Obelisk."

"The Obelisks?"

"*The* Obelisk."

Vulcan laughed. "Heavy, no?"

Jonan shook his head, then raised a hand to touch it. It was a relief to know it was still there. Yerudit gently grasped his other hand. Vulcan stood with his arms crossed and his eyes slitted, and Hulva smiled compassionately. They formed a still life. But if there was an answer in this still life, only the Ariyeh knew, and he was unfathomable. Like the Obelisks.

Though still not expecting an answer, Jonan asked, "How, then, did you follow me?"

"Follow?" The Tsadkah grinned. "Hulva, have I been away?"

She shook her head, but again, Jonan detected layers of subtle understanding between the two.

"What?" he said, leaning towards her.

Hulva blinked slowly, considering what to say, but before she could reply, the Ariyeh said, "You still have the shadow puppet." Puzzled, Jonan nodded. "Hoi, and you a Psychaeologist," the Tsadkah said yet again. "What do you think?"

He'd turned the question on Jonan. What did he think? What *did* he think? He thought crazy ideas. Hulva was lying? No, he didn't think that. Instantaneous matter transmission? He couldn't believe that either. Then what? What could a Psychaeologist believe?

"That… that it's psychaeological, that the shadow puppet brings out associations?" Jonan sensed he was working towards a solution. "That any anger that I have towards Yerudit, projects as aggression towards you." The words came out jerkily, but the ideas fitted, fitted all too well; pure displacement behaviour. Jonan had been fighting with his own images.

But the Ariyeh checked him. "But what of this last time?"

"This last time?" Jonan thought back. "You said you were scarcely there. Was that me? Was that you?" Completely bewildered, he had no idea what he was saying.

Jonan's confusion increased when the Ariyeh said, "What do you really understand by Probability Space?"

At that, he again seemed to flicker, and this time it hurt: Jonan felt as if *his mind* was trying to move out of normal space and into Probability Space. Was this an attack, or was the pain actually a result of his resistance? Holding his head, Jonan muttered, "I know just what most people know."

"Which is?"

"That Probability Space is to do with the probability of where one exists."

"D'you believe that such a space itself has existence?"

Ah. This was how Jonan challenged his phobic clients. But he didn't have a phobia. Or did he? "I don't understand. If it didn't exist, how could one travel in it?"

"One travels, yes. But *in* it? Suppose 'it' is just a name?"

Jonan's mind struggled. Words and meanings. He knew what the Tsadkah's words meant, but he resisted their meaning. "I don't understand," he protested. "If it were just a name, how could physicists use it? Starships do travel from place to place. People don't get out at the same place but give it a different name."

"Huh," Vulcan boomed. "A good joke, my friend, a good joke."

"But what, Jonan, if the name and the thing-in-itself were different?" The Tsadkah looked around. His gaze fell on the wooden table and he rapped its surface. "Solid, het? Yet science says that it's mostly empty space with a sprinkling of atoms and molecules. So, it is both solid and empty. But in reality, a table is a table all the way through."

The Tsadkah grinned, transforming his air of wisdom into one of pure mischief. "Yet physics goes further. Break the smallest particle and it becomes a wave, so what is tiny is also infinite. Then add the idea that once two tinies interact, they are forever entangled." He smiled. "As with you and Yerudit, myself and that shadow puppet. So there are different perceptions of reality and one, perhaps, is the more real. Perhaps there is a reality where we might achieve things that baffle both our common sense and our science."

*A more real reality?* Jonan had had a philosophy once; he'd been a holist ranting against reductionism. But that had just been theory. Now he was being told that there was an application. His head pounded. The Ariyeh flickered. There was the answer, but it still eluded Jonan's grasp. He couldn't understand but sensed that he balanced on the edge of an abyss. If he stepped back, he would be safe. If he stepped forward, he would fall. To fall… perhaps to fly?

Hoarsely, Jonan whispered, "You mean Probability Space and the probability of existing somewhere are different? That one can change one's probability of existing somewhere without actually going through the Space?"

"Without going through the computations. The idea that space is three dimensional is drilled into us when we are young. Take away that cognitive conditioning and space is no longer three dee. It just is." The Tsadkah sat on the table. "Sitting in three dee or just sitting?"

They were talking madness, dwelling on the far side of sanity. Yet if the other man was mad, he was also magic. The Tsadkah glowed. He seemed dangerous, radioactive. "You accept," he said, "that a transmitter on Hebaron can communicate with a receiver on Terra."

"If they are attuned."

"Suppose, then, that I or the Obelisk were a transmitter."

"And the receiver," Jonan said, "was the shadow puppet?"

"No, the Obelisk."

"Obelisks?"

"The Obelisk and those attuned to it."

The abyss opened again. Jonan was on the edge, teetering, then sinking not flying. There were resonances here: physical, psychical and psychaeological. *The* Obelisk, not Obelisks. And those attuned to it, such as the Ariyeh. Jonan had the shadowy impression of something vast. He could almost feel he was more than three dimensions; he could almost sense that dimensions no longer existed.

The very notion of dimensions was wrong? That hurt. That really hurt.

Jonan shivered. Tunnels opened before him, ghosts travelled within them and then ghosts within ghosts. An infinite regress. Probability Space. He'd never really understood it, yet he'd always assumed it existed. Now he was being told that it was an illusion, a convenience, useful for physicists to do their calculations but with no actual reality. Though reality itself was no longer real, that too was only a name. And why? Because the Ariyeh flickered. First you see him, now you don't. In mind or in reality, here was the mystery.

Grasping at ghosts, Jonan tried again. "And the Obelisks? What are they? Who made them? Where do they come from?"

"They?"

Resisting what he was starting to accept, Jonan cried, "But I saw them on different planets!"

"Big fingers from the one hand," Vulcan said.

"Multi-dimensional fountains from a multi-dimensional pool," the Tsadkah added. He was like an underground fountain himself, life bubbling to the surface from depths Jonan couldn't sense. "Even though dimensions are just an illusion, a construction."

Jonan sighed, "How can this be?"

"How can anything be?"

"Who built them... it?"

"It may not have been built."

Jonan's mind whirled. "Not built? You mean it's... alive?"

"No."

"Then it's dead?"

"No. We just do not understand it to say what it is."

Jonan was sinking, his mind in a whirl. Nothing was what it should be. He went to a window and gazed at the unfamiliar stars. He was so far away from his certainties. So far. Yerudit stood beside him and also looked out. He could see her reflection in the glass, and his heart ached. He was empty, and yet her presence still moved him. Beyond mind, they were still linked. Strange to think that not long ago, he'd thought he had all the answers, handed them out as readily as pills. Now, he had no answers, only questions. Questions piled upon questions, building up in pressure. He had to try once more.

"If Probability Space is just a word, why do people have phobias?"

"A Screen shows a starship flicker out of existence," the Ariyeh said. "That sows the seeds of doubt. Who can be sure existence will flicker back again?"

"Or how?" Vulcan put in. "The most probable probability is with your foot in your mouth, your eyes on the end of your fingers, and as for your pipi…" He roared with laughter. But at Jonan's confusion, he added, "Do not be so grave, my friend, the cosmos has always been mysterious."

True, but Jonan had always been cosy in his infinitesimal corner of it. Now its vastness was being spread before him, and that was not cosy, not in the least. He tried yet again. "What about the Zirenians? Perhaps they built the Obelisks… Obelisk?"

"Ah, the little green men!" The Ariyeh's face sparkled. "Technologically they are a thousand years ahead of us. Morally, hundreds. But as to the mysteries just an hour away, at most a day."

"So they didn't build them?"

"No, although they take more interest in them than we do."

At a sudden thought, Jonan said, "We met a Zirenian on Luna. Is an Obelisk there?"

"It is in many places, perhaps everywhere. Only its concentration varies."

This was too much. The sleep that had been stolen from Jonan returned with a vengeance, and his eyes closed as if smeared with glue. Immediately, Vulcan's broad arm closed around him.

"Sleep." The Ariyeh intoned. "You need to rest… sleep."

Exhaustion, new concepts, and the mesmeric force of the Tsadkah's words shuttered Jonan's eyes. He made the thousand mile journey back to his room with just enough awareness to notice the pre-dawn light and to feel Yerudit's kiss. And somehow, they felt they were the same.

When he awoke again, a rust coloured moon was high in the sky. Too heavy to move, he gazed at it through the window. He had no idea where he was, and memory only provided fantasies. Deciding he was still dreaming, he told himself to sleep within the dream, and so he did, until a terrible idea hit him.

He dreamt he was back home, sleek and plump as before, his little buccaneer's beard still attached to his chin. He was pressing a button to create a fragrant shower, pressing another to prepare his well-chosen breakfast, then a third to orientate his lustrous solabub. Time compressed, and he was forever pressing. Pressing, pressing, pressing. His hand became a blur. Press... press... press... Press... press... press... His hand flickered. It was there. It wasn't there. It flicked. Flickered. Flick. Flickered.

Movement awoke Jonan. His fingers were still flicking. He looked at them, and his stomach churned. That dream! He gazed at the ceiling, hoping beyond hope that the dream wasn't true, that his travels were not just an illusion, the hardships only imaginary, that a kiss was not just the breeze.

Gradually he worked out where he was and which dream was the most compelling. He was on Hebaron, with Yerudit. The bristle on his chin was real, the leanness of his body was real, and the sharpness of his senses was real. A tremendous relief swept over him. Yet at the same time he was amazed how such a simple dream had filled him with such an awful horror.

# Chapter 20

Jonan slept again and when he resurfaced it was still dark but with Yerudit sitting beside him, her hand resting lightly on his chest. Seeing him move, she asked, "Are you rested?" He nodded but she still scrutinised his face. "I mean really rested?"

Jonan checked his body. "I'm okay." He put his hand on top of hers.

"Good." She used their joined hands to pull him into a sitting position. "I want you to come to a meeting." With a new shyness, she added, "I'll wait outside."

Jonan hurrying to dress, recalled fragments of his dream so that when he was outside, he said, "I don't think I can go back to my old life again."

Yerudit put her head to one side, the rust-tinted moon giving her a golden halo. "Why not?"

"I had a dream," he grinned wryly, "about pressing buttons."

Yerudit nodded. "That's not the way for a man to live." She smiled and began to walk. Jonan took her hand and hoped for a long walk in that peaceful night. In a few minutes, however, they turned off the main street and entered a courtyard rimmed with bushes. Forty to fifty people were already inside. "Our Ico centre," Yerudit said.

"Ico?"

"Icon." She smiled. "Sometimes iconoclast."

Jonan peered through the entry. "So few? Vulcan said there were a thousand souls here."

"There are many Shrivites but only a few are here at any one time." Yerudit put her lips to his ear. "Plus, we prefer to meet in small groups." Her hot breath swirled around his face. "Except for special occasions."

"What counts as special?"

"A Terran who stays." She giggled then indicated that they should enter.

As Jonan sat, his heart sang. In this peaceful courtyard, with Yerudit at his side, he felt at home. He closed his eyes and let the silence enfold him. In a few minutes, electric tingles ran along his spine. He shivered and opened his eyes: feeling, rather than hearing, the subsonic hum he'd experienced on Yawa.

When the sound was almost audible, the Tsadkah rose. To the unheard sound, he added unseen movement, so subtle he seemed to shimmer. He flickered and became like a river current, tangible yet having no reality of its own. Moving in and out of existence, existence moved in and out of him. He was the constant shift from the improbable to the impossible.

Time moved. Time stood still. A moment was an eternity; eternity, a moment. Profundity. Depth. Deeper than anything he'd experienced before. Jonan closed his eyes and sank down, a leaf gently, gently floating. The incredible stillness held for long moments. Only gradually did it give way. Eventually, though, thought returned and he opened his eyes. People were already leaving. Yerudit stood, motioned to him and took his hand. Staying close together, they went back to his room, lay down on his bed, and after their long long absence, their pain began to heal.

When the sun was a copper ball in an orange sky, Yerudit rose and looked out the window. "Time to eat," she said.

Standing beside her, Jonan said, "You can tell from the sun's angle?"

"From that, yes." She laughed, adding, "But didn't Tipal tell you about the cosmic lines of hunger?" Still laughing, she led him to a courtyard where branches intertwined to provide a cool shade. A man in flared trousers and a loose shirt placed a handwritten menu on the table. "This is the Glen." She indicated the greenery above them. "Our version of the

Astrobar."

Jonan smiled. The relaxed atmosphere couldn't have been further from the high tension Astrobar, and he looked forward to sharing a leisurely breakfast there with Yerudit. But not long after they'd eaten, she rose.

"I've got to go now," she said. "I have to work."

"Must you?"

"Yes, really, I've got to cover the plants."

Jonan held onto her hand. "I'll help."

Yerudit looked puzzled. "It's physical. There're no buttons."

"All the better." Jonan also rose.

But just then Vulcan entered the courtyard. "Huh," he boomed, "work."

"But," Jonan protested, "I was just going with Yerudit."

Vulcan chuckled. "You call that work?"

"Covering trenches," Yerudit said dryly.

"Huh." Vulcan wrinkled his nose. "Pooh work. But Ariyeh wants Jonan to come with me."

"Oh, hot-metal work." Yerudit fanned her face as if too hot. But then she grinned. "You'd better go. It's probably more symbolic."

Vulcan chuckled and slapped Jonan on the back. This time, Jonan showed enough presence of mind to ride it. "Come," the big man said, "and I will melt you."

"How?"

"Making irrigation pipes, my friend." He flexed his great muscles. "Melt and smelt. You will enjoy it – fire is in your nature."

Jonan made a face. If fire was in his nature, he might want to smelt, but he was pretty sure he didn't want to melt. But not wanting to seem reluctant, he followed Vulcan to a building made of connecting domes and cylinders. On seeing it, Jonan laughed out loud, this was the perfect place for the trolls on Yawa to beat out their swords and shields. Entering, he was struck by the variety of machines, recognising only two: an old-fashioned anvil and a modern phision cutter. Anything in between was a mystery.

Vulcan, however, strode confidently among the machines. "Not too hot," he muttered. "Not too easy... not too dangerous. Huh, I have it! This one." He pulled at a trolley with cylinders on it. Putting on a mask, he twiddled the knobs on one cylinder. "Stand back," he called, then laughed as a great tongue of flame roared out. Jonan jumped but Vulcan just laughed again. "Come, I will show you how to werld."

Not sure if his companion had said *weld* or *world,* Jonan waited for further instruction. But without saying any more, Vulcan abutted two metal pipes with a clamp then peered through his protective helmet. With that and his green robe, he looked like a space-age version of the god of fire, his namesake. It only needed a few robots trolls to complete the image, but lacking those, Jonan alone watched as Vulcan focussed a fierce flame over the join. The metal grew hot, glowing cherry-red and with the clamp turning the pipe, Vulcan melted a grey rod onto it.

"This is the flux," he said, "to make the werld easier."

"Weld or world?"

"Yes, werld."

Finished with the flame, Vulan used an air machine to cool the join and then rubbed it with a block. "See," He held out the work, "you can hardly see the seam."

Jonan gingerly put out his hand, but feeling no heat after the blown air, took the pipe and inspected it. He was amazed. The seam was invisible; Vulcan had made a perfect connection. With an unexpected surge of emotion, Jonan gripped the pipe to his chest.

"Show me," he said fiercely. "Teach me to how to weld... world. Oh, I get it, werld."

Vulcan looked at how Jonan clutched the work. "You have

been deprived," he said. "Come, I will show you." He pointed at the pipe. "Werlding." He grinned cheekily. "It joins one world to another. We will start with the phision."

"No," Jonan said, "show me with the flame."

Vulcan rubbed his pate. "Okay, but I will have to watch you carefully."

For one, two, three hours, Jonan practised playing heat over metal, his new strength finding its use. But he smiled wryly at the idea of fire as a symbol of purification; he was now filthy with sweat and flux. Well, maybe that was a purification. Or maybe, he really was melting. Who cared? He loved it.

When they stopped, Vulcan beamed. "Good, het?" Jonan nodded. "Fire is in your nature. I see it in your eyes."

"And is fire also in Vulcan's nature?"

"Fire and earth. Fire and earth. I, my friend, have a large component of earth which means that often my pipes carry sludge instead of water." He laughed. "Come, we have finished."

He led Jonan to a sparkling river, so clean Jonan could see ochre coloured rocks as clearly if they were on the surface. Small fish darted in and out of their shadows.

"We wash here!" Jonan exclaimed.

"Here? Pollute?" Vulcan shook his head. "Wash here and we have your guts for garters!"

"Oh?" Jonan scratched his head. "What are garters?"

Vulcan rubbed his dome. "It is an expression, Jonan. Are garters not the strings on a guitar?"

"No, the strings are strings." Jonan waved a hand. "But never mind garters, I really am smelting and melting. So what is it about washing and the river?"

"For washing, my friend, we take a bucket. Then, when we are clean, the river is for swimming." Vulcan went to a large rock that matched the landscape and rapped on its surface. "Open, sesame" he said in a commanding tone.

Not expecting magic, Jonan was still surprised, then

amused when the big man opened a door in the rock face. "Rock is better looking than shed, het?"

With a chuckle, Vulcan went into the fake rock and came out with two buckets. Jonan dipped one in the river, and although the water was heavy, he managed to carry it – requiring only one change of hands when his companion wasn't watching. In his tiny bathroom, he observed as Vulcan poured water into the tank at the top of the shower.

"Pour in here," Vulcan said, "and, hey presto, gravity gives you a shower. Dirty water then runs out through the drain. Come." He led the way to the rear of the cottage. "The waterbox collects the run-off and it catches the rain."

"And then?"

"The waterbox purifies the water, of course."

"Of course," Jonan repeated. He paced around the water purifier, an octopus of a device with transparent pipes but with no visible motor. "But how does it work? What powers it?"

Vulcan pointed at the sky. "The sun. This special glass causes evaporation. The vapour runs inside the glass and is collected in channels. An old Terran invention, only the materials are modern." He slapped the construction. "Now, a Hebaron export to other planets."

Jonan peered at the swirling vapour. "We might have these on Terra but they're big and centralised."

Vulcan grunted. "To make it easier to tax you." He tapped the waterbox. "This also takes sea water so even in the driest times, we can drink."

"Very clever." The Psychaeologist rubbed his arms, moving flux and sweat around on his skin. "I'll take a shower," he said, "but I'll pass on drinking my recycled water."

"Another way in which the cosmos links us," Vulcan picked up his bucket and began to walk away, "we drink each other's recycled water."

Jonan, snorting, returned to his washroom, tipped his

bucket into the tank, and on the turn of a tap, watched as gravity created a gentle spray. As he soaped off the grime, he had to smile; this was a world away from his perfumed auto-shower. Several worlds, he reminded himself, no wonder Yerudit had been amused at him. Yet with all his home gadgets, he had never felt so alive, so happy. In a croaky voice, he began to sing a modern version of the old folk song, *Waltzing Matilda*.

"Once a jolly spaceman jumped into a big wormhole
Under the belt of the Trousers of Time
And he sang as he travelled and turned into topology
Who'll come space waltzing, space waltzing with me?"

Jonan sang, remembering bits of verses. He felt great. He looked down: his belly was flat and he could see his toes. He grinned, it was a long time since he could last seen his tootsies. Dressing, he adjusted his onepiece down a size then he set off for the Glen. On seeing him, Yerudit pretended to sniff.

"So you didn't melt into flux and sweat?"

"I did."

"But you're so clean."

"Burnt off," Vulcan said, sitting beside her. "Jonan did well, het. Soon we will have Terra completely out of him."

"Not all, I hope," Ariyeh murmured, and his eyes glinted. If eyes could werld, Jonan thought, it would be those eyes.

Vulcan looked at Jonan as if taking his size. "No," he laughed, "leave a little of Terra in him."

"What is this all about?" Jonan asked.

But Ariyeh shook his head. "In time, you will know."

Jonan looked at the Tsadkah and shivered. He didn't like not knowing, but he suspected, knowing might be even worse.

It was strange to eat with the Ariyeh. Even at his most relaxed, power oozed out of him as if he focussed it from the air around him. In contrast, it was pure pleasure to eat beside Yerudit. Her essence was compassion, plus she was beautiful, even more than he'd remembered. In the filtered light, her skin and eyes shone like molten gold.

When they left the table, Jonan walked with Yerudit along the river, stopping at a little bay with deep, clear water. The copper sun beat down, and a yellow-gold mist rose from the river's surface.

"This is my favourite place," Yerudit said dreamily. "We can swim here."

"Now?"

"No, later. I need to sleep now, but I wanted to show you."

"It's lovely."

"Yes."

Jonan gazed at the view, but his mouth opened in a giant and undignified yawn. When he managed to regain control, he asked, "How long've we got for sleep? D'we have to work again in the afternoon?"

"No," Yerudit replied, "we only do a few hours a day. Usually, before it gets too hot." She nestled into him. "The rest of the day is for study or practise or..." She laughed wickedly. "Pleasure. You know," she added and looked directly into his eyes, "I missed you very much. I didn't think I would but I did."

"I didn't intend to come after you. But I did."

"Yes, some things are bigger than both of us." Yerudit put a hand to her mouth and giggled. "D'you hear what I just said?" Laughing, she dragged Jonan back to his cabin and locked the door. "Good," she said, "no one will interrupt us now."

"Very good." Jonan said.

"Very, very good."

Slowly Yerudit undid the buttons of her blouse. Whatever inhibitions she had shown before completely disappeared. She swam into Jonan's arms, and they joyfully kissed their clothes away. Finally, however, they dozed. After a time, Yerudit separated her long legs from around Jonan and brushed her dark gold hair from her face. "There's one more thing for you to learn," she said.

"You have my full attention," Jonan said.

Yerudit laughed. "Not that. Something different. The Tsadkah is teaching now. You don't have to go…"

"But…?"

"But you do. I'm making you."

Jonan nodded, accepting that to want Yerudit was to want to know her world. They showered and returned to the Ico Centre. A dozen people were there, moving in a staccato manner to a complex rhythm. The Tsadkah moved among them, demonstrating and correcting. When he saw them, he came over. With his burly frame and wild hair, he seemed enormous. Or perhaps it was his aura. Not only was he father, he was also teacher.

Yerudit touched her hand to her heart. "May we enter?"

He looked at them with those awe-full eyes, but touching hand to heart merely replied, "I am your servant." Some servant. It was, Jonan thought, like a king being at their service. If he didn't want them to enter, they hadn't a hope. But it was a formality. With his permission they stepped forward. With a little bow the Tsadkah asked, "What do you know of the dance, Jonan?"

"What I taught him," Yerudit replied.

"And you have practised?"

"Daily."

Ariyeh smiled. "Good," he said, "you don't look like a sleek smug self-satisfied seal."

"Dad!" At the change in him, Yerudit gently slapped his arm. "I never said such a thing!"

He twinkled. "Someone did." Then he changed again. "Come, show me what you know."

The limelight made Jonan awkward. Not only the Tsadkah, but the others also stopped to watch. Yerudit looked worried; after all, she'd taught him. Yet once he started, Jonan felt fine, concentrating so hard, he almost forgot he was being watched.

Then the Tsadkah assisted. With small adjustments to Jonan's posture, he showed how the Psychaeologist could use less muscular effort but generate more breath power.

His closeness was strangely familiar, bringing shadows of memories that Jonan couldn't then explore. Later, though, when he was resting, he had time to think back. There was no doubt in Jonan's mind that the Tsadkah was his attacker. His aura, the feel of him, was unique. It had to be him. There couldn't be two people with such an aura. But how? Against all Jonan's previous beliefs, he began to seriously consider that the Tsadkah had appeared to him because of a psychic link with Yerudit and the shadow puppet. Or more accurately, the Tsadkah had appeared to appear to him. But how did this relate to Probability Space? What did the words mean and what was the reality that underlay them?

Space. It all seemed to revolve around the notion of space. *What then is space?* Jonan asked himself. He thought back to his student days. A lecturer had compared the universe to the lungs, said that through a process of folding, the maximal volume was packed into the minimal space. So that what seemed distant along the surface of the lung, could actually be quite close by going across it. So what was infinite in two dimensions could be infinitesimal in three. Probability and fractals extended the number of dimensions, but the principle remained the same. Could the Tsadkah, through the Obelisk, actually turn this principle into a practise?

Jonan's mind ached with these thought as he watched the Tsadkah respond to questions. To each one he replied with his body. The body existed in space. The negative space of the body was... space. With exquisite control, the Tsadkah showed how minute differences created different sensations. Jonan watched until his head hurt, until he was a headache away from an understanding.

The others asked questions, and Jonan drank in the

answers. There was so much he wanted to know: more about Probability Space and reality; more about psychic links and the Obelisk; more about the flicker. Especially the flicker, for even as the Tsadkah spoke, it happened. He was there, not there; there, not there. Jonan wasn't sure if everyone saw it or only he did, but he *was* sure it had to do with the Tsadkah's notion of space. Eventually, there was one statement he couldn't let pass.

"Mind," the Tsadkah said, "is space,"

"But if mind is space," Jonan couldn't stop himself from calling out, "then what are the objects contained within it?"

The Tsadkah turned to him, the brown eyes like a flame. He was man turned demon. This was the Devil and he was asking for an account: *Who are you and what have you done with your life?* Before that fire, Jonan had to turn aside. Yet when the Tsadkah spoke, his tone was surprisingly mild. It was as if he couldn't contain the life force that burnt through his eyes, but he could modulate that which flowed through his mouth.

"When you were practising," he murmured, "what did you feel?"

"Peace?" Jonan ventured. "Stillness?"

"And stillness is?"

"No thought? The absence of thought?"

"And space is?"

He tried for a parallel. "No object? The absence of objects?"

The Tsadkah smiled, and Jonan felt warmed in the way that a distant sun can warm. "Space," the Tsadkah said, "is a cognitive creation which separates object from object. Mind is the divider. D'you understand?" Jonan shook his head. The Tsadkah nodded. Life left his eyes, and for a moment, Jonan was staring at a human husk. When he came back he smiled again but this time it was like basking in the radiance of the noonday sun. "Have you ever," he asked, "practised a sport? Really practised?"

"Yes," Jonan replied slowly, smiling as he recalled his

student days as buccaneer. "Sword and archery."

"Sword and archery," the Tsadkah echoed. For a moment, Jonan thought he would laugh but the humour that came into his face was not mocking. "Excellent! Excellent!" he cried. "Tomorrow, then, we shall all become archers."

And the next day, he showed them what he wasn't able to convey in words.

# Chapter 21

Vulcan raised an imperial finger.

"More werlding?" Jonan asked.

"Net, weapons." That explained Vulcan's staff and yellow robe. The latter left his right shoulder bare, and the sun reflected off his rippling muscles. As before, the back of his hair was tied into a topknot. They were once again in samurai territory. "Come," he rumbled.

"Where to?" Jonan leapt to his feet.

"To make bows."

Jonan fired a pretend arrow. "Bows as in bows and arrows." Vulcan nodded. "Ah ha!" Jonan cried. "Ariyeh is serious?"

"Ariyeh? No. The Tsadkah? Yes."

He chuckled, a volcano in preparation, then searched in the folds of his robe and held out what seemed to be another wooden staff. But when Jonan took it, the weight told him immediately that this was no staff. This was a wooden scabbard, a sort of bamboo sheath, and inside was a metal sword. He turned the scabbard in his hands. He'd told the Tsadkah he'd used the sword and bow. Well, here was the sword. Tentatively, he slid out the blade and cautiously cut the air with it. The years rolled back. The grip felt great. Impulsively, Jonan began to twirl the weapon.

"Hold still!" he cried.

Not knowing if Vulcan would obey, Jonan danced around him. The blade slashed through the air, its shining arc coming to within inches of the other's body, but Vulcan hardly reacted. If anything his face showed amusement plus a sort of paternal pride. Irritated by that, Jonan began to jab closer and closer. Vulcan shifted his weight but otherwise still appeared unconcerned.

Jonan wanted to bring the blade closer still, but didn't dare risk it. Yet even as he thought it, the idea was taken out of his hands. At lightning speed, Vulcan shot out his staff and twisted it under Jonan's right armpit. It locked his arm, and the sword dangled uselessly. Jonan pressed against it, but Vulcan just grinned. At that, Jonan pulled away and hit at the staff with his left hand. Pulling free, he again attacked. This time, Vulcan deflected. Jonan went the other way, but with the same result. By now, they were both grinning. Jonan raised the blade once more, but Vulcan was faster. The end of his staff made a blurred arc and hit Jonan behind his knees. He yelled, went straight down, and the staff pressed into his throat.

"Enjoy," Vulcan growled, "but concentrate. Do not let your emotion take over." Then he laughed. "But good for a Terran, truly well done." He put out a big hand and pulled Jonan to his feet. "Come, we must saddle up the griffin." He turned then waddled forward, holding onto his bottom. "Though do not forget the balm."

Jonan laughed, rubbing his backside in rueful memory. "Could you teach me the staff?"

"Huh!" Vulcan rubbed at his stubble. "It is one of the dances."

"Can you teach it?"

"If the Tsadkah wills." His hand rested thoughtfully on his pate. "But I do not think it will be necessary."

"Why?" Jonan sheathed the sword.

"Because it is already in you."

"What? How?"

Vulcan scowled in thought. "What we do is speed and timing. What the Tsadkah does is outside of these. It is... different. You will learn that, I think."

"This is about space again, isn't it, Probability Space? Do you really understand all that business?"

"What business?"

"You know, that somehow someone can shift to somewhere."

"Huh, that is a lot of somes."

"Do you?"

"Ah, Jonan, you do ask questions."

"Do you?"

"Let me ask you a question. Suppose someone, the same someone, can exist everywhere. Could that someone then change to another somewhere?"

"Exist everywhere?" Jonan unsheathed the sword until reflected light dazzled him. "I don't understand."

"Nor do I. But somewhere, some place, some time! Ask the Tsadkah."

"Oh, yes, he knows everything!" Jonan snapped.

"It is not what he knows, it is what he can do." They walked on in silence. Vulcan sighed. "You know physics?"

"A little."

"Electrons move around atoms in orbits that are not orbits but are orbitals. Orbitals are probabilities of electrons being somewhere, and they jump from shell level to shell level. Add relativistic effects, stir in a billion particles in a great dollop of a starship, and you have the improbable science of Probability Space."

"And?"

Vulcan shrugged. "Who knows? I only know elementary physics. Ask the Tsadkah."

Jonan put the scabbard into his belt. "You know." He hesitated. "When I look at him he seems, well, to sort of flicker."

Vulcan grunted, then scratched his chin. "You think he flickers. What is flicker to you?"

"To me? Well," Jonan said slowly, "I have this weird idea he actually moves. Either that or he affects my perception, which is equally weird."

"Two weirds! Which would you like?

"Like?"

"What do you think he is doing? Better still." Vulcan turned and poked a thick finger into Jonan's chest. "If it were you, what would be your doing?"

"Me?" They walked on, Jonan wondering about his *doing*. When he noticed houses built into the slopes, he absentmindedly asked. "Why there?"

"We build into the cliffs for coolness," Vulcan replied.

"Good. And that?" Jonan pointed to a huge pot on legs.

"A solar battery."

"Good." Jonan hardly noted the answers, he was too preoccupied with *his doing* and the questions were just a way of buying time. But when time didn't supply any answers he added, "I can't think what my doing might be. Except..." He paused. "I guess in this context, it's the very act of watching my own mind."

"Exactly!" Vulcan exclaimed. He touched the scabbard. "Discrimination. The sword."

"The sword," Jonan echoed. "The sword of discrimination. I read about that when I was... searching." The excitement returned. He was reliving his student days, buccaneer and sword, samurai and bow, weapons meant for fighting but often presented as symbols for the sharpening of the mind. Was his earlier interest a premonition? Jonan chuckled. In hindsight, could he say that he'd had foresight? Like the winner of a gravity-free footie game, Jonan raised his arms high.

He lowered them again when Vulcan brought the griffins. With their large eyes and seal faces begging to be petted, Jonan just had to stroke them. In return, they thrust their noses into his armpits.

"Good," Vulcan grunted, "somebody someplace somewhen likes you."

Grinning, Jonan saddled up and threw his leg over the saddle. His backside twinged, but it was merely a memory, quickly overcome by the mild euphoria that bubbled inside. He was centuries back, back in 2100, back in ye Olde Wilde Weste.

As they rode Vulcan pointed out landmarks. "Windmills for grain and energy," he said. "A waterwheel for turbine power. Over there are parabolas for solar energy."

"Vulcan," Jonan said cheerily. "why're you telling me this? Yerudit and I may soon be returning to Terra."

"Perhaps, my friend." Vulcan still pointed. "In these fields, everything is together: vegetables, fruits, and flowers. Not a monoculture, not like Terra. Terra likes to isolate the dominant strain, genetically modify. That gives them control which in turn gives the semblance of understanding."

"You're being unusually philosophical, Vulcan."

"Huh!" He grunted and rubbed his pate. "You ask so many questions, it has set my head in motion."

They rode on in silence. Then Vulcan pointed towards the sun. Shielded by thin cloud, its light was soft so the hills were bathed in copper and the lake was a palette of pastel pinks. Birds flew over the water or dived into the rippling surface. On the ground, plants unfolded and interwove their petals into a carpet of many colours.

Jonan felt at peace, but when they entered the forest the griffins began to sniff the air, and he felt charged instead. The mounts lifted their pointed noses and whinnied, obviously wanting to stop, but Vulcan urged them on. Then from the side came a muted roar, and Jonan's hair stood on end.

Vulcan immediately slid off his mount, leading it with one hand. The other gripped his staff. Jonan put his hand on the sword, and they advanced with caution. There was another menacing roar and suddenly a great shape reared forward. The griffins mewed with fear.

"Shout!" Vulcan bellowed. "Shout as loud as you can!" With resounding blows, he drummed his staff against a tree. The griffin lion roared again, pushing the bushes aside and creeping forward. "Run!" Vulcan shouted, pointing away from the creature. "Run!"

Jonan started to back off, but Vulcan didn't. Unable to leave him, Jonan returned. Vulcan tried to push him away, but Jonan, refusing to budge, held up his sword as the huge beast advanced. The copper sun glinted on the blade, momentarily dazzling Jonan for a second time. Inspired, he directed the rays into the creature's eyes. Blinded, it shook its head then charged, but the two men had already moved. As it roared past, Vulcan whacked it on the back then again drummed on a tree. Jonan shouted and again reflected bright light into the creature's eyes. Slowly, the griffin lion backed away. Vulcan made short bellowing dashes forward and back. The creature gave one mournful wail then turned and crashed into the forest until they could no longer hear it.

"Good," Vulcan said. "Excellent." He made to pat Jonan. But shock had set in, Jonan trembled and gulped for air. "Sit," Vulcan said. "Let it happen, let it happen. That particular creature is rare here. Next time, we will carry a stunner."

"Next time," Jonan stuttered, "I'll wear a suit of armour. Space, why am I talking about *next time*? There won't be a next time. I'll be back on Terra." He pushed himself up. "Okay, I'm okay. I'll be okay."

Vulcan eyed him for a few moments, decided *okay* was okay, and then gave a nod for them to remount. They continued on, coming to trees with a deep red hue and trunks that split into several parts. Some did so midway and looked like giant harps. Some twisted from the ground like giant corkscrews. Others spiralled into giant shells. Jonan didn't know much about plants, but he knew these were quite different from any on Terra, although they might be similar to underwater plants. But this forest was not their destination, and they pushed on towards a grove of slender trees. Vulcan rode among them and tested the branches. At a particularly springy one, he grunted with satisfaction and nodded at Jonan.

"Do your thing," he said.

Jonan unsheathed the sword. As he drew it back, however, Vulcan seemed to be looking at him critically. "What?" Jonan said.

Vulcan shrugged his wide shoulders.

"It's something, I know." Jonan looked at the branch in his hand. Silver-brown buds were ready to blossom. "Killing?" he said. "Creating pain? Needless destroying?"

Vulcan nodded.

"Okay, then let's use a fallen branch instead."

Vulcan picked one up. He bent it and it snapped. "Dry."

"So? We're stuck. We can't kill a live one while a dead one is no good."

Vulcan shook his large head. "So, what else?"

"What else? You want me to play guessing games."

"Think."

"Okay. All right, I've thunk. You tell me. What else?"

"You think you have thunk." Vulcan rolled his eyes. "We apologise."

"We apologise? To a tree? You must be joking!"

Vulcan solemnly faced the tree. "Oh, tree, forgive us for our transgressions."

He looked sideways at Jonan. Jonan pulled down his mouth. "You want me to say that to the tree?"

"You would not?" Vulcan looked shocked. Then he chuckled. "No, my friend, just a little thought will do."

But it turned out to be more than a little thought. Jonan thought about the lion griffin that had attacked them. He thought about how everything preyed on everything else. How everything was food for something else. What difference if one were sorry?

At his hesitation, however, Vulcan acted. "Do not question!" he roared. "Do it!"

His shout led to action. With one smooth slash, Jonan cut through the branch. Sap flowed out. Orange as blood, it trickled over Jonan. Rust coloured and sticky, he apologised in his heart.

They took several branches back to Gedi and soaked the wood overnight in minerals. In the morning they put the branches out to dry. Every so often Vulcan tested them. While still flexible he bent them and added string. To finish, the two men rubbed wax into the wood, creating a line of gleaming long bows with taut strings.

In the afternoon, they took them to the Tsadkah. He tested them, finally saying, "Good, very good. Now, practise."

Vulcan rubbed a hand over the smooth dome of his head. "Jonan also wants to shake hands with the staff," he said.

"Yes?" The Tsadkah looked from one man to the other. "Are you teaching Yerudit now?"

Vulcan nodded.

"Then teach Jonan as well."

The Psychaeologist grinned with delight. Not only was he doubling up on his learning, he'd also be spending more time with Yerudit.

Following the suggestion, Vulcan led the way to the Ico Centre where Yerudit was waiting for her lesson. Vulcan began with a demonstration. "This is an attack." He bought up his staff and made it whistle down. "This, a defence." He twirled the stick in a sideways arc. "Now, do it as I call it."

The two advanced across the hall as Vulcan called, "Hit, defend. Hit, hit, defend. Defend, hit, defend."

Jonan's staff flew out of his hand. "Sorry," he panted. "Sweaty."

Vulcan waggled a finger. "You must ask your opponent not to make you sweaty."

Next, he placed Jonan and Yerudit so that they faced but their staff's couldn't touch. Vulcan called who was to attack, but at first, Jonan was hesitant. Yet when Yerudit lightly whacked him on the head, he realised he had to be more focussed.

"Now, in touching distance." Vulcan ostensibly crossed his fingers. "Yerudit to strike only. Jonan to defend only. Go!"

When Vulcan swept his hand down, Yerudit immediately swung her staff. Jonan moved to the side and deflected. But her blow was so strong, it still pushed into his side. She grinned.

"Extend, Jonan," Vulcan called. "Extend through the staff."

The Psychaeologist held up a hand, and the others waited. Next, he straightened his arms, but no, being stiff wasn't the answer. Then, in a flash, he understood the zen sayings he liked to quote in his lectures: extending his mind through his arms was the answer. Ready once more, he nodded, and Yerudit again attacked, but this time, Jonan visualised the staff as an extension of his arms. He was amazed and greatly satisfied when, with hardly any physical effort, he saw Yerudit's staff fly out of her hands. From then on he was magic.

Later they went on to the bows, aiming at targets made of thatching. At first, their shots went wide, but slowly the arrows crept closer and closer to the bullseye, eventually touching its edge. Naturally when the Tsadkah arrived, Jonan immediately shot wide. But as he made no comment, Jonan's arrows again approached the bullseye.

"Good," Ariyeh smiled. "Do you see now that mind is space?"

"Um." Jonan let down his bow. "I hadn't really thought about it." He twanged the bowstring. "I can see," he said carefully, "that one has to see across the distance. I'm not sure, though, that that supports a whole philosophy."

"Philosophy, hoi!" Ariyeh grinned. "Let's go."

He began to walk away from the Ico Centre. Though Jonan was taller, he found it an effort to keep up. Soon others also joined in, clearly knowing something was about to happen.

They laughed and jostled like children following the Pied Piper, marching away from the lake and towards the surrounding hills. The Tsadkah stopped at a rocky outcrop, measured thirty paces from it, and there he placed the target.

"Jonan," he said, "now try."

"Where from?"

The Tsadkah's manner had changed, his voice had become more commanding, and when he pointed, he sparkled with energy. "Midway between target and edge."

Jonan sighed with relief. He had half thought he'd be expected to stand on a slippery rock while balanced on one foot on the edge of a precipice. Casually he took his place then, with dozens of eyes on him, he took a deep breath. He let it out. He took another breath, aimed, and fired. Squealing, the crowd ran back. The arrow hit dirt. Vulcan slapped his head with his staff. Since he could hardly do worse, Jonan relaxed. The second arrow hit the edge of the bullseye. The third was dead centre.

"Excellent," the Tsadkah said. "Further back." Jonan uneasily walked towards the edge. "Stop!" He was two paces from the sheer drop. "Good, now try."

Jonan lifted the bow. Although on solid ground, he was all too aware of the precipice behind him. Cautiously, he fitted an arrow and released it. There was a small but definite recoil. Jonan turned and gulped. He was that fraction closer to the edge.

"Another step back," the Tsadkah called.

Jonan now stood half a step in front of the edge, a steep drop right behind him. When the Tsadkah threw a stone over, Jonan listened out for it, but it was a long time before he heard it crash. He turned back to the target and slowly lifted the bow. His heart thudded and sweat dripped into his eyes. He tried to put everything aside and focus. It felt as if his eyes stretched straight across the space and glued themselves to the bullseye.

He almost understood that mind was space. Yet even as he thought it, his concentration broke. He shivered and let down the bow. One part had understood, but another part had seen the recoil hurl him over the edge.

Gently, the Tsadkah took the bow and placing Jonan to one side, stepped back until one heel rested just over the edge. Calmly, he lifted the bow and took aim, a lone figure against the orange-tinted sky. His arm drew back, held taut and then... everything changed: Jonan saw along the same sight line as the Tsadkah did. Yet it was not a sight, it was the actual identification of arrow and target. One didn't have to hit the other, they were already conjoined. Except for the thwack. The arrow hit dead centre, and the sharp sound broke the spell.

The Tsadkah looked at Jonan. One nodded. The other understood. Vulcan shook his large head. "We learn and learn," he grumbled, "yet still he stands alone."

The Tsadkah laughed, lifted the bow and shot another arrow. Yet no one watched it, their horrified gaze was on him. In slow slow motion his rigid body toppled backwards, and he disappeared. Everyone surged to the edge, stopped then cautiously looked over. A roar of laughter greeted them. Ariyeh the Tsadkah was reclining comfortably in a safety net!

# Chapter 22

Did the net matter? No, Jonan thought. If it hadn't been there then the Tsadkah would've just hovered. Well, that was what he now believed. Yet even with the net, one had to be brave to just fall like that. Jonan couldn't do it, nor could Vulcan, to judge by the look on his face. The Tsadkah might laugh, but their main feeling was simply one of awe.

Bedazzled, they began the descent. Yerudit slipped her hand into Jonan's, and he held on tightly. Between her and the Tsadkah, his previous life with its ease and casual affairs had faded into superficiality. He felt part of this hardy group, and that gave him a warm glow of pride. They made him feel special, chosen, but also humble. They were so far ahead of Jonan that he panted to catch up.

But certainty revolved on the wheel of doubt, and uncertainty returned the next afternoon. After their work, Yerudit and Jonan paddled out to an island, stripped, and dived into the water. Yerudit swam like a golden fish, constantly slipping from Jonan's grasp and glittering just out of reach. Yet once on land, she came to Jonan, and they merged joyously in the shade of the bushes.

The air swirled around them, and they half dozed in their private heaven. The pleasure, however, became tinged with memory. Jonan began to think of his house on Terra, his work at the university, and his frequent affairs. At first these were distant images, half-formed memories of a different person. But as he dwelt on them, they grew stronger. He opened his eyes, but the images hung like paintings against the orange-blue backdrop of the sky.

Yerudit noticed. Turning, she murmured, "What, Jonan?"

He sighed. "I have to decide soon. I'm supposed to go back."

She paled. "Do what you must."

"I still haven't replied to Evana. Would the Obelisks be of interest to extreme travellers?"

"What d'you think?"

"It feels like a sort of sacrilege."

Yerudit nodded. "That's how I feel about it too."

There was a long silence as Jonan summoned up his courage. "If I did go back," he muttered, "would you come with me?"

Yerudit's tawny eyes misted. "I'd hate to leave but… yes, I suppose."

She gripped his hand, and Jonan's thoughts became chaotic. He didn't want to leave, yet all he owned was on Terra and he hadn't left his home with the idea of leaving it for good, he'd only left it in order to find Yerudit. Also, he had to admit, he'd hoped to unmask the Tsadkah. Now he found he didn't want to tear Yerudit away from this place. Nor did he want to leave. But different values and different ways tore his mind in two.

Jonan sighed. "I don't want to go, but how to decide? All these things in my head – how do I choose?"

Yerudit stroked his hair. "Of course," she said, "your poor old head. All these changes to your body, but your funny little mind is trying to catch up."

"Yes? Body here, mind in Probability Space?"

"More like Improbability Space." Yerudit's face lit up. "You know, Jonan, we could ask the Tsadkah."

"Hardly unbiased," Jonan protested.

"Of course, he is. Ariyeh might not be. But the Tsadkah is."

"A fine difference."

"A big difference. Come on, let's go."

Yerudit didn't leave room for argument but hurriedly dressed. Jonan followed suit, and they paddled quickly back to shore where she dragged him through the tree-covered walkway to her parent's cottage.

Seeing Hulva, she called, "Mum, is Dad in?"

Hulva laughed. "Yes, dear, but who is it exactly that you want? Dad, Ariyeh or the Tsadkah?"

"All three, all three! Jonan has lost his mind!"

Hulva peered over a glass retort. "Losing can be finding."

"Yes, Mum. And losing can be losing."

Considering the importance of his decision, Jonan was surprised at Yerudit's enthusiasm, but he guessed any decision would be better than no decision. As Jonan thought about it, Ariyeh came in. As usual his broad frame emanated strength, yet he moved with a lightness a panther would've envied. In contrast, Yerudit was a kitten that bounced around with happiness.

"Jonan is perplexed," she explained. "To go or not to go?"

Ariyeh, listening, gazed out the window into the sky. His face became withdrawn and unreadable. In a moment, though, it cleared and Jonan expected a pronouncement. *The wise one speaks.* Instead Ariyeh simply said, "Tomorrow, we go to the Obelisk."

The Obelisk. So much was happening Jonan had temporarily forgotten about it. Yet now, at its mention, he shivered. An *it* rather than a *he* or *she* would make his decision. Yerudit was delighted, shining with an energy that reduced Jonan's worries, and she informed everyone they met of their intended visit. As a result, the Ico Centre was packed for its evening session.

"Why have they come?" Jonan whispered. "Bread and Circuses or to wish us luck?"

Yerudit brushed his cheek with her ember hair. "To share."

Uplifted by her vivacity, Jonan did not expect much more from this meeting. But the congregation created a hum that was markedly different from before. One moment, it stretched Jonan into an infinite line, the next he was compressed into an infinitesimal point. He waxed and waned until vibration reached the level of sound, then realised why the effect was different; the men and women were alternating. Jonan was surfing on sound waves, on the sinusoidal harmonics of melodies.

Ariyeh the Tsadkah was also a part of it. Usually he was slow, controlled and flickering. Now, however, he was also fast. No, fast didn't describe it, he was instantaneous. It was not just an aura that flickered. Space was eliminated, and Jonan swore that while staying absolutely motionless, the Tsadkah actually translated from place to place.

The meeting closed in a silence as deep as the ocean and as vast as the sky. Everyone stayed until the last stars had vanished and dawn was just a fading palette. One by one, people rose and dispersed.

"Dawn," Yerudit yawned at the rising sun, "and time for breakfast. I'm famished."

"I'm starving too." Jonan bounced on his toes, feeling curiously energised. "I could eat a griffin."

"It is a day's journey," Ariyeh said, "with you *on* the griffin. We will leave after breakfast, stay overnight, and return tomorrow or the day after."

Jonan scratched at stubble. "A lot of work for one or two nights," he said.

"But then you'll know," Yerudit declared. And she was right… almost.

After eating, Jonan took his bag towards the stable. On the way, Vulcan stopped him. "Here," he said and handed across a stunner.

"I need this?" Jonan was surprised. "Can't the Tsadkah control animals?"

Vulcan shook his head. "Minds have to be in tune. Wild animals are difficult."

They entered the stable and the griffins mewled with delight. Jonan's recognised him, flapping its vestigial wings and rubbing against his hip. He threw the saddle over the long body, made sure everything was secure, then climbed on. The group set off, away from the lake and into the sharply outlined hills. It was already hot, but they went on for an hour then stopped to drink. On the second hour, they paused again. On the third, they stopped to eat in the shade. Yerudit sat with Jonan, Vulcan with Hulva and Ariyeh. The food was plain, local nuts and rice, but Jonan ate with gusto, sharing with his griffin when the animal nuzzled him.

After the break, they pushed on for another two hours. The sun was high now and their shadows were just short stumps between their feet.

"Put up the shade," Ariyeh said. "Time for a rest."

They dozed. Except for the Tsadkah; he kept watch.

When they continued, Jonan's legs were stiff but not burning. They were well into the foothills now and still climbing. The track was flinty and slippery, the sun a white-orange globe. The way was hard, but Jonan didn't feel uncomfortable. On the contrary, he felt the peace of feeling tightly linked. The Obelisk was affecting them.

When the sun was just a low orange ball, the Tsadkah brought them together. "This is a dangerous time of day," he said. "Keep the stunners ready."

Jonan thought of the lion griffin that had attacked them the day before and gratefully felt for his weapon. He was pleased to know he wouldn't have to kill, yet if anything came he'd be ready for it. Or so he thought. Yet with the heat and the travel, he was saddle weary and his eyes kept closing. When a pebble bounced down the slope, he startled and looked up in search of the cause.

"A bad sign," Vulcan rumbled. "Scavengers."

Damn! Jonan gripped the stunner and forced his sleepy eyes to stay open. He scanned the way ahead, but saw no other creatures. After a few more swaying steps, his eyes again drooped. A big mistake. The group rounded a corner, and a pack of muscle, teeth, and claws surged towards them. Dog-sized creatures poured out of the hillside crevices.

The griffins howled. Ariyeh jumped down. "Put the griffins in the centre!" he shouted.

They all dismounted, held the griffins with one hand, and fired the stunners with the other. The dogs took the blasts full on. Most shook their heads dazedly and staggered off. Some, hit in mid-flight, didn't stop until they crashed against a griffin. One huge creature just shook its shaggy head and staggered backwards.

It looked like the creatures were retreating when the big one suddenly broke through their ranks. Like a coiled spring, it leapt directly at Hulva. Jonan shouted, but as its gaping jaws hurtled towards her, she froze. Without thinking, Jonan threw himself forward. The creature knocked Hulva down, turned towards him, and locked its teeth onto his arm. With a ferocious roar, Ariyeh sprang forward, dug his thumbs into the animal's jaws, and forced its mouth open. Then, as Jonan pulled free, he flung the beast down the slope. Seeing no other threat, Ariyeh carefully lifted Hulva who clung to him, shocked but otherwise unhurt. Jonan, however, was bleeding, and the slopes were covered with unconscious animals.

The mewling and growling had stopped. The dogs still on their feet retreated, while the ones on the ground were stunned or panting. Vulcan moved among the griffins, stroking and murmuring. Ariyeh inspected Jonan's arm. Jonan, despite the pain, felt fantastic. He was a true hero, a true buccaneer.

And then he fainted.

When he came to, Yerudit was holding his hand. She smiled, and Jonan twitched his lips in response. He tried to use the other hand to push up, but his arm felt odd. Looking down, he saw it was bandaged, and although he expected it to hurt like hell, it merely throbbed. Vulcan held up the paste.

"From your bum to your arm," he said.

Wondering how long he'd been out, Jonan gazed into a sky, now silvery with stars; he'd been out for hours. He tried to sit up, but still weak, Yerudit had to help him. At the movement, however, Hulva came over and also supported him. Ariyeh opened a bottle and dripped a blue liquid onto Jonan's lips.

"Not more griffin balm," Jonan mumbled. "Just need to close my eyes for a moment." He lay back and fell into a deep sleep.

It was light when he awoke again, and Vulcan was inspecting the injured arm. "It looks well," he said, rubbing on more paste. "Rest more."

But Jonan struggled up. "I'm okay," he said, "Let's go on."

Vulcan waggled his head. "Typical Terran." To the Tsadkah, he said, "Perhaps we should have come by vehicle?"

The Tsadkah shook his head. "He must first learn about the land. That is also why we did not bring tents or the secure sleeping bags." He approached Jonan and looked into his eyes. The Psychaeologist felt, or imagined, a gentle mental probing, then the Tsadkah nodded. "Let's go."

Vulcan helped Jonan onto his mount, and although he swayed from side to side, he managed to stay on. They travelled slowly, however, and stopped frequently. After two more hours, the land changed, the texture of the rocks becoming smooth and glassy as if it had once been fired. The ochre darkened into claret, and they could have been moving within a crystal goblet. Vulcan tilted his head to one side as Jonan had seen him do on Varli so many ages ago.

With a nod at him, Ariyeh said, "Listen."

Jonan half-closed his eyes. At first, all he could sense was the throb in his arm, but he pushed beneath that and found the unstruck sound, the unsounded hum. As before, electric tingles ran along his spine, increasing his concentration. Jonan heard the chime of bells and an electronic clink… clink… clink… He looked around, but the source was not outside, it was inside.

His body was charged, and the hairs on his arm prickled with electricity.

The Obelisk! As they got closer the effect increased. Drawn to this siren song, Jonan forgot the burning heat, his dry throat, and the pain of his arm. The living presence of the others, however, was enhanced; they lived together in this song. And though profound, it was not heavy. It was the bubbly champagne of life. It was angels' faces with clown noses and absurd limericks. When they finally saw the Obelisk, Jonan laughed aloud. In the distance a black crystal sparkled. Morning rays sparkled from it, lit them all, and turned the Tsadkah into a cloudy fire.

Yet on coming closer, the effect diminished. Perhaps the Tsadkah had countered it, for when they stopped, he virtually ignored the Obelisk. Instead, he took nanomesh from his pack and constructed a shelter. While he did that, Vulcan uncovered Jonan's arm, showing it was still raw but not infected. The big man was about to add more paste, but Jonan took it and gingerly rubbed it on by himself.

Eager to go closer to the Obelisk, he said, "What now?"

Ariyeh eyed him with amusement. "Now?" he replied, "There is no now."

The Tsadkah took a round fruit from his pack, crushed it, and added dried herbs. Grinning manically and with mysterious passes, he mixed in spices. Meanwhile Vulcan started a small fire, and on placing a log from his pack onto it, the flames then emitted an unfamiliar but pleasant odour. The Tsadkah put his mixture into a bowl and heated it over the smoke. Jonan breathed in and his synapses started going crazy.

"In the no-now," the Tsadkah said, "the warrior's dance."

He started to move, and as fumes from the fire drifted over them, the group began to copy him. The fire and the fumes transformed the Tsadkah. He was a giant spark, a fallen star, a splintered spark off the Obelisk. As the hills around them gleamed smooth and glassy, Jonan felt a great expansion, both outward and inward. He focussed, and the song of the Obelisk returned, a strange sweet sound that filled him so that he became the sound. He/it/sound moved to the Tsadkah's dance, moved him to the familiar steps that Yerudit had taught him, moved him through the arduous sequence of balance and movement. With effortless effort, Jonan reached a pitch of physical and mental agility.

When they stopped, Jonan's whole body quivered. They sat, and the Tsadkah, a pillar of fire, poured the juice into a small china cup. He took a small sip and passed it to Hulva. She sipped and it then came to Jonan, a golden liquid with a taste of spiced wine. When they had all partaken, they held hands and rose. Then the Tsadkah pushed them into a second series of movements, followed by a second round of the drink. In all they did that seven times. Or seven times seven. Or seven times seven times seven.

When they finally stopped, the Tsadkah, sometimes a living flame and sometimes a pillar of frozen light, said, "Listen."

In listening, Jonan struggled to pull in the tangled webs of his mind, his whole body abuzz. The sensation intensified and white flame seared along his spine. Without burning, it coursed upwards, burst into flower, and spread into the brachiating network of his nervous system. Where it touched, it cleansed.

In the distant reality, the Tsadkah spoke.

"Look."

He threw a stone against the Obelisk. It didn't make contact but slid down an invisible slope.

"Touch."

They tried but as always an invisible field kept them away.

"Listen."

They listened and the hum filled them. Then, as they focussed, the impossible happened. The Tsadkah walked into the Obelisk. The air became a black ripple and he was its centre, a black ripple within a black ripple. Then he was out again, yet he still rippled. If the surface of a lake could be turned to fire, or to waves of light, that was how he rippled.

"Listen with your hands," the fire said.

"Listen with your hands," the ripples echoed.

"Listen with your hands," the light repeated. "Listen."

Jonan reached out. Listened. Was drawn in. The light intensified. He chimed black. He reached out and touched light. He fell. He floated. He was intensely alert. He was in a misty dream. Reality was a wondrous illusion. He was in the Obelisk, and all the worlds existed in him. He breathed out and was with Thera in Varli. Another breath and he walked with Tipal on Haja. Another breath and he was two figures that fought on the edge of a volcano.

But this immensity was too much. Whatever strange juices had bolstered Jonan's mind, their power faded. Space became reality. Touch became solid and light burnt. In a red, glass-smooth landscape that reflected the copper sun, Jonan watched as a fierce ember of a man reached out and gently, ever so gently, unwound his bandage. Jonan then gazed at his arm in wonder. His wound was healed, completely healed.

# Chapter 23

Under the spell of the Obelisk, the rest of the day passed in a haze. It was almost too much for Jonan. That night, stretched alongside Yerudit in their mesh shelter, he kept asking, "Was it real? I mean really real?"

"Your arm is healed," Yerudit said.

"Yes, but the wine, the herbs, the atmosphere?"

"Your arm."

"But did I really go into it, become part of it? Did he?"

Yerudit cradled Jonan. "Did *we*? We were all part of a oneness. And as for you, you might," she admitted, "have been a smallish pillar of frozen light. That was one reality." She snuggled closer. "But who wants to go to bed with a *smallish* pillar?"

Jonan laughed, and then frozen light kissed her and hugged her and entered her. They then lay together until they both slipped into a deep deep sleep. In the night, however, a curious noise awoke Jonan. It was laughter, his own laughter. He was intoxicated on life, a feeling that followed him back into sleep. As did an image of the Tsadkah. The impossible image of the Tsadkah within the Pillar of Frozen Light.

In the morning Jonan awoke brimming with exhilaration. What did it matter what was dream or what was reality? Only this divine Obelisk intoxication mattered. Leaving the nanomesh shelter, he was surprised to find Ariyeh was packing.

"We're not staying tonight?" he asked.

"I allowed for two nights." Ariyeh shook his head. "But for now, we are done here, and enough is enough."

"Enough can be too much," Vulcan added.

"But..." Jonan began.

Ariyeh shook his head, silencing Jonan. But the Psychaeologist set his jaw, mentally promising to return. The Tsadkah saw this and laughed.

Vulcan also saw, and laughed. "Only a Terran," he said. "Trust a Terran." He draped his arm around the Psychaeologist. "Absorb the experience until *to be* also means *to give*. Come," he added, "we must feed the griffins. Feed them from your heart."

Jonan grinned. "Bliss balls and joy sandwiches coming up." And in his heart, that was what he provided.

Just as he finished the feeding, Ariyeh came over. "Jonan," he said, "may I change your name?"

"My name?" Jonan was taken aback.

"It will help get push-button Terra out of you." Ariyeh glanced over his shoulder. "And help keep the Obelisk in."

"To make me more what I am?"

"And more what you are not yet." Ariyeh laughed.

Jonan scraped at his chin. A rough sound, he liked it. He wondered how he could ever have been satisfied using cream. Now, he had a new ritual. Nearly every day, with a sharp knife and hot water, he carefully, very carefully, separated stubble from flesh. Yes, it was true, push-button Terra was gradually being taken out of him, although no one would yet take him for an off-worlder.

"What would you like to call me?" he asked.

"Yonan," Ariyeh replied.

"Yonan." Jonan rolled the sound around on his tongue. "It's not very different."

"We could try Xanochleraniphangen for something different. But you would not pass as a Zirenian."

"Is that what they call themselves?"

"Xanochleraniphangen will answer to X."

Jonan laughed. "Why Yonan? Is it significant?"

Ariyeh chuckled. "It means he-who-dances-with-Obelisks."

"Dad!" Yerudit protested.

"Okay, it doesn't. In one of the ancient languages, it means a gift."

"A gift? Of what? To whom?"

"And when?" Ariyeh shook his head. "Questions. Questions."

"Yonan it is, then." Jonan laughed again. He'd entered a new era. His mind state had changed, or else he was euphoric from the closeness of the Obelisk. Only Obelisk from the outside, he thought, but condensed light from the inside.

They loaded up and mounted the griffins for the journey back. As they travelled, the sun rose until, when it was too hot, they retreated within their temporary shelter, Jonan choosing to keep watch. Pressing on, when the sun was low, they kept a watch for carnivores. But none attacked, and although uneventful, for Jonan the journey back was also a journey forward.

Ariyeh led them directly to the Ico Centre, and Jonan was surprised to see that everyone entering carried a plate of cakes or fruits or sweets. A Shrivite he hardly knew pulled him to a table.

"Eat, Yonan," he cried. "Drink, Yonan. This celebration is all for you."

Jonan turned to Yerudit. "How did they know about my name?" he marvelled. "Did you tell them before we left? Did you use a minScreen?"

"Perhaps the Obelisk told them," she replied, her tawny eyes glowing with amusement. "Or the Tsadkah passed it on the wind."

Jonan caressed her neck. "Passing on the wind or just passing wind?"

Yerudit burst into raucous laughter, spitting out food. Squeezing his fingers, she stepped away from the table and began to dance, slowly at first then faster and faster. Hulva joined her, then Vulcan, and then the Tsadkah. Jonan joined in as well; the others clapped and chanted, their voices setting him afire. He was changing. But to what? The Tsadkah knew, but he, Jonan/Yonan, didn't. One day, he would – he hoped.

Perplexed, exhausted but happy, Jonan finally crawled into bed. So much had happened, he couldn't even dream. Nor did he make it for the morning meeting at the Ico, clicking awake just in time for breakfast. But he found that deep below the level of awareness, and deep below the level of dreams, changes were taking place. Had taken place. There was no decision to be made after all, no weighing of pros and cons. He asked for handmade paper and a manual writing instrument, then wrote:

> *Evana, I won't be coming back to Terra. Please sell my house, my solabub, everything. Will Screen you later.*
> *Love,*
> *Jonan.*
> *P.S. Keep my bub if you want it.*

The letter would go by shuttle, and he could imagine how Evana would receive it. She'd probably try to find a slot for it in her Screen, and its contents would undoubtedly shock her. He was giving up everything: his house, his position, even his much-prized solabub, and the gesture to leave the bub behind bothered him more than leaving his position. But as for the money from the house, he'd use that in Hebaron's unusual economy.

Expecting Evana to receive the letter within a week, Jonan looked forward to her startled reply. Most probably she'd say he should wait and not succumb to a romantic gesture. Jonan grinned: what better than a romantic gesture?

Thinking of Evana, Jonan recalled his lectures about downloading minds to computers. For years Artificial Intelligence had progressed to a certain point then hit a brick wall because, many believed, the excitement of space travel had taken scientists in other directions. Jonan thought differently.

AI started with independent units of data that had to be related. Mind, on the other hand, started with wholeness. Data were particles; mind was a force field. Data could be isolated from mind, but data couldn't be put together to produce mind. He was a Gestalt. He was a holism, perhaps even a holo-ism. Jonan smiled.

Data was a particle, mind was a force field? That reminded Jonan of the famous equation, $E=mc^2$, usually explained as the enormous amount of energy that could be released from a small mass. But turned around, and he could say that an enormous amount of energy was condensed into a tiny mass. So, could he also say that an enormous amount of intelligence was condensed into a tiny bit of body? Or, put another way, Obelisk/particle from outside but frozen light/wave from inside?

Phew! Jonan fanned himself with his letter. So if mind wasn't just the end product of information processing, then what was it? He could find only one alternative: the brain didn't make mind, it was merely the receiver of it. The real reality was consciousness, and his brain only made manifest a tiny aspect of it. As with an ancient radio, the device didn't produce the symphony, it was only the conduit for it. Jonan almost staggered. What an idea! Too big an idea to think about now. He'd have to work on it later.

For now, though, there was another matter to work out, one of the primary reasons he'd come to Hebaron, a reason that had even travelled with him, the shadow puppet. It still sat on the edge of the table, and with its oddly sinister profile, Jonan had become reluctant to touch it. But as the days passed, he knew it was an issue he had to face. In fact he was surprised no one had mentioned it in all the time he'd been in Gedi.

So early the next morning, alone in his cabin, Jonan arranged the shadow puppet on a chair as if for a heart-to-heart. But face to face with it and he felt too silly to speak, plus his thoughts were too unclear. He looked out the window: good, the sun was rising, time to go to the Ico Centre. Suspecting the shadow puppets were a jump too far, he threw himself into the Ico practise then into work. The morning passed, and Jonan was happy to forget, or repress, thoughts about the puppets. Yet when he met up with Yerudit for lunch, he could hear Thera's voice saying, *Puppets, now there's a riddle and a half.*

"You seem abstracted," Yerudit said.

"There is one thing," he replied, "in my cabin."

"Yes?"

"The shadow puppet…"

"Ah." Yerudit drizzled sauce over a salad. "That's a big topic. Show me later"

Less mindful of his food than he intended, Jonan ate, and when their plates were empty, he simply looked enquiringly at his companion. She nodded and they rose, Jonan feeling an unexpected urgency that turned to puzzlement on opening his door. He paused: that space-damned puppet had changed position again.

"What?" Yerudit said, seeing his expression.

Jonan blinked. This puppet was even more of a joker than the tall bony Tipal; best to ignore its antics. "When we met, I interrogated the Screen about Hebaron. Mostly it told me about the shadow puppets, yet since I've been here, the only one I've seen is mine."

Yerudit laughed. "They're a legacy from the old days. Many of the first off-worlders came from the Indus. They brought their ancient traditions and that included the puppets." She made her voice deep and echoing. "But come Yonan-formerly-Jonan and I will instruct you."

They went past the Ico Centre, then following a winding path through dense forest, they came to a building new to Jonan. Like so many in Gedi, it was odd-shaped and highly individualistic. Made of red timber, it looked as if many pyramids had been casually stacked together. Some stuck out at odd angles while some bent over like the horns of a jester's cap.

"Behold," Yerudit said, "The puppet shop."

They stood in the doorway, and Jonan's first perception was of a host of little people sitting or standing on top of rough-hewn benches. As his vision adjusted, he recognised the figures as the shadow puppets. Whole ones were on the benches, while disjointed arms, legs, and even heads hung from the walls. He found the setting extremely creepy, especially as they weren't neatly stacked, but were arranged in small groups, giving the impression he had interrupted a group of gossiping neighbours. No doubt, as soon as they left the room, they would once more start muttering to each other.

"Tiny people," Jonan whispered.

"They are," Yerudit whispered back, "to the degree that we make them."

Not daring to raise their voices, they went into another room. Jonan thought he heard the susurration of voices behind them and spun around, but of course, nothing had changed. The second room contained the innards of the puppets: leathers and dyes, wood and rags, wires and clays. Some puppets were worked by string, others by sticks. Yerudit showed Jonan how to move the sticks on one, then she went behind a screen, turned on a lamp, and held the puppet to the light. Its shadow projected onto the screen, its nose long but its chin receding. When Yerudit moved the puppet, Jonan found the projected movements oddly disquieting.

"Witchy," he muttered.

"What?" Yerudit poked her head out from behind the screen.

"Strange, it reminded me of me."

"It's the dances we do."

"And?" Jonan asked.

"I understand movement. I know how to make it move like you."

Jonan shuddered. "You can't use it to control me, I hope."

"Not me."

"Can anyone?" Jonan paused. "Oh, the Tsadkah." Intrigued by the puppet's movements, he asked, "Can I use one?"

Yerudit looked thoughtful. "I don't know. The important ones are only for special occasions."

"Such as?"

"Nothing regular, but for what we call: moments of insight."

"So does that mean I can use one?"

Yerudit bit her lips. "They're pretty powerful, Yonan. Are you sure?"

"I'm not sure," he admitted. "They unsettle me, but I still feel some sort of affinity with them."

"Well, I'd feel better if we..."

"Asked the Tsadkah. So would I." Jonan threw a salute. "Standard Solution One. Let's go."

They found Ariyeh in the the Ico Centre courtyard. He was teaching, and so they waited until he was ready for them. Putting his hand to his heart, he came over. His mane of wild hair reminded Jonan of a lion, but he suspected, the energy was more that of a fire-breathing dragon.

"The shadow puppets," the Tsadkah said.

Jonan gasped. "How did you know?"

"Your expression. What else is there?"

"My expression?"

Jonan did an inventory of his face. It only told *him* that he was grinning; obviously it told more to the Tsadkah. He looked again at the other man. A natural thing to do, but a mistake. His eyes had become bottomless pits, and Jonan could feel himself falling into them. Involuntarily he thought of the Obelisk, but resisted. To the man or to the pillar, he couldn't tell. In that moment he had to decide to lose himself or to resist. Almost at once, he thought, *To hell with resist, just let go.*

There was a flip, a mental switch, and suddenly the world reversed; Jonan was seeing himself through the Tsadkah's eyes. He saw someone tall and lean, a longbow waiting to be released. He saw Yerudit beside him, copper and strong, an arrow waiting to let fly. A second flip, and he saw a king and queen on an ancient copper coin. But it was the third flip that really mattered. Jonan saw Yerudit at the end of a long tunnel. An impossible perception, but he saw the totality of her, even though she was standing by his side. It was how he had seen her on their very first meeting. Now he knew the cause: the Tsadkah.

He was right, but he was also wrong.

"Yes," the Tsadkah said, "we will teach."

Jonan's eyes, which were open, opened. Released, he backed away. The Tsadkah turned away from him, and his gaze swept over the town and settled on the blue lake. From there, his gaze rose along the slopes of the orange hills until it finally rested on the fierce ball of the sun. On the Tsadkah's face was the most curious and exquisite expression Jonan had ever seen: the closest that he would ever see to sadness, the closest he would ever see to glory.

# Chapter 24

Evana pushed the sheet across the table. Initially, Mirena didn't read the words on the paper but just felt the texture with her fingers and smelt its earthy odour with her nose.

"Nice," she said, "handmade and probably very rare."

Evana shook her head. "Read it. It's from Jonan."

"Jonan?" Mirena stopped feeling the paper and scanned the message. She frowned, read it again then laughed. "He wants to stay on Hebaron? Impossible! It's just not him!"

"Nor has he replied to my question about extreme tourism." Evana's eyes flashed. "I'm really worried about him."

"But what can you do? He's so far away."

Evana gulped the last of her coffee and made a face – it hadn't been made with Jonan's finesse. "I know exactly what I'm going to do, but I might need your help. I don't yet know how, but I'll keep in touch."

# Chapter 25

Vulcan beckoned. "Come," he said, "I will teach you the way of the puppets."

"But I thought the Tsadkah..."

Vulcan waved a large hand. "It does not matter who teaches. All that matters is how the learner learns."

"Oh." Although disappointed, Jonan tried not to show it. "Okay."

But it didn't feel okay, especially when they went to the Ico Centre and Vulcan merely twirled his staff.

"Show Vulcan," he said.

"Show Vulcan?" Jonan echoed.

Vulcan hit air. So Jonan hit air. Vulcan parried air. Jonan parried air. Vulcan twirled the staff. Jonan twirled the staff. He was doing well, he thought, when Vulcan stopped.

"Space," he boomed, "I see Yonan. Now show me Vulcan." Puzzled, Jonan pointed his staff at the other man. "A literalist!" Vulcan said. He bent and shuffled around the court. "Now," he repeated, "show me Vulcan." This time Jonan understood and shuffled around like a mangy ape. Vulcan slapped his pate. "Space take me! Do I look like that?"

Vulcan again hit air. "Now, Yonan," he exhorted, "show me Vulcan." Jonan imitated as best he could. Vulcan danced around him. "More Vulcan, Yonan. More Vulcan."

They went through the basic movements a third, fourth, and fifth time. Each time Jonan thought he had captured the other's stance, yet each time Vulcan shook his head. They went at it for thirty minutes, fifty, over an hour.

Jonan wiped his forehead. "I'm stuffed," he muttered.

"Stuffed with Yonan and stuffed with Jonan," Vulcan said agreeably. He eyed the Psychaeologist. "Okay, we stop today, more tomorrow."

They went at it again the next day and the next and the next. Then Vulcan asked Yerudit to attend.

"Watch," he said to her. To Jonan, he added, "Copy." He moved and Jonan copied him. Vulcan stopped. "Which was Vulcan?"

"You," Yerudit immediately replied.

"Huh!" Vulcan poked Jonan in the chest. "You do well, but she can still see who is who. You have the outside but not the inside. This time, copy with your guts."

Jonan immediately stuck out his belly and did a fair copy of Vulcan hitting air. Vulcan laughed then scratched his bald crown, looking like a man in severe pain. It was a relief when his face suddenly light up. "Huh, Yonan, I have it. Listen! Listen to my movements, listen to my body."

That did it. Shifting from his eyes to his ears, Jonan touched the heart of the movements, and in three more days, Vulcan again invited Yerudit.

"Now," he cried, "who is Vulcan."

"Ah!" she exclaimed. "Now he's got you."

"Space, *now* he is beginning to learn quickly. Trust a Terran." Vulcan secured the staff by pressing it into wall clips. "Tomorrow, we move on."

Tomorrow turned out to be what Jonan had expected a week ago: mask making with Vulcan showing how to cut and stitch leather. To add realism, they made ovals for the eyes and slits for the nose and lips.

Vulcan put one on. "This," he said, "is my original face. Now put on your mask and show me Vulcan."

The mask acted like magic, Jonan's movements having to expand into the vacuum caused by no longer being able to use his facial expressions. In this overdramatized way, he mimed the earth/fire essence that was Vulcan. The air quivered with the would-be samurai's hopes and failures: to want be a

Tsadkah yet only to be a networker. When he stopped, Jonan was surprised to see pain in Vulcan's eyes.

"Ah, Yonan," he said quietly, "you show too much, far too much."

Jonan removed the mask. "I was a Psychaeologist." He rubbed his forehead. The leather mask dangling, he asked, "Does it go deeper with the puppets?"

Vulcan's reply was evasive. "Yes," he said, "you are ready for them now."

The next day, they went to the puppet shop. The puppets still sat in frozen gossip so that even Vulcan trod lightly. After a brief search, he handed Jonan a puppet moved by sticks. The body was segmented. Movement of different sticks moved the arms, or the legs, or the head. Vulcan switched on a small lamp to light the back of the screen. Jonan, standing to one side, held the puppet to the light so that he could see its shadow. While he stayed behind the screen, Vulcan went to the front, so that he could also see the projected shadow.

"Now," Vulcan called, "show me Vulcan."

He was stocky and square-faced. The puppet was narrow and long-nosed. Jonan laughed. "With this? How can I? It doesn't look anything like you. "

"Do you?"

"No."

"Then?"

"But at least I'm human."

"So are the Zirenians."

Jonan made a face. "Broadly speaking. Okay, here goes." Tentatively, he moved the sticks. The puppet twitched randomly. Vulcan grunted, waiting for Jonan to get more control.

After a while, Vulcan murmured, "Do not move them, Yonan. Listen for them to move."

Jonan froze. The long-nosed shadow froze with him,

waiting for life as he waited for inspiration. Jonan tried to listen. His mind reached out, searching for the hum of the Obelisk and through that to the essence of Vulcan. His arms began to relax, his hands to move, and the shadow jerked. Startled, Jonan froze and waited again. Space, now the shadow wanted to move, but he was blocking it. Sweating to dampen down his own intentions, Jonan found the self of the puppet. It came to life, first hesitantly, but then with greater momentum, and the shadow began to tell a story.

When Jonan's concentration flagged, the sticks slid down and the puppet died. Vulcan came from the other side of the screen, gently released the Psychaeologist's grip on them, and led Jonan out into the fading heat of the day. His face was wistful. "You know, Yonan," he sighed, "you know much more than you know."

Uncertain what to say, Jonan studied his hands. In his student days, he'd learnt about embodied cognition, the idea that parts of the body had their own intelligence. The young-him had thought it all too fanciful, the now-him thought it all too believable: Jonan could express Vulcan because his body had absorbed the big man's mannerisms. He thoughtfully stroked his chin; he'd have to think more about embodied cognition. Not now, though. For now, puppets dominated, and Vulcan was asking for something new.

"Choose a person," he said.

Jonan made the puppet dance.

"Huh, Yerudit, of course."

He turned the puppet into a powerful fist.

"Very good, the Tsadkah. Try more difficult."

Jonan opened himself, focussed, and let the puppet move.

"An animal?" Vulcan slowly said. "But upright and intelligent? Space, a non-human. I know, a Zirenian. You convey well, my friend, very well indeed."

Two days later, Ariyeh said, "You are now ready to show."

"Yes?" Jonan asked, "To whom?"

"To the whole village."

"To the whole of Gedi! A few, surely."

Ariyeh grinned wolfishly. "We will be outside."

Then the Tsadkah replaced the Ariyeh, looking beyond Jonan and into the burning sun. Jonan tried doing the same, but even the sky was too bright, and his vision flecked with dots, he stared instead at the ground. When the Tsadkah looked at him again, his intense eyes blazed a question, leading Jonan to drop inside himself. What, what was it? But he knew immediately. He'd mentioned embodied cognition, and with that idea, he'd taken the puppets as just another exercise, playing the Psychaeologist. Now he was reminded that they were much more. Their purpose went deeper. He had to go beyond Psychaeology.

And all of Gedi was to be his audience. To see how competent he was? No, that didn't seem likely. To scoff at him, the inner Jonan, the outsider? Probably not that either. Even so, a whole snake pit of emotions arose. There was fear, of course, that hardly needed explanation, but there was excitement, too. With an audience he could really show himself, show the buccaneer that he was. His primary feeling, though, was self-doubt. He was afraid that in revealing himself, he would show himself to be inconsequential.

The expected, as expected, turned out to be unexpected. Vulcan reconstructed the puppetry in the Ico Centre. Dozens of Shrivites sat and watched him as dozens more piled in and searched for spaces. A sea of faces waited in a profound silence, watching Vulcan adjust the projector. At Jonan's insistence his own shadow puppet sat beside it. Ariyeh rose, raising his arms, the setting sun and the rising moon pale flowers at the ends of his fingertips. The silence thickened. Gradually, his arms fell.

"We see a brave man tonight," he declared. "For anyone who is willing to show his inner self must be brave. Open your hearts to him. Open your hearts as he will to you. Do not sit and judge, less you yourself be judged."

With that short speech, he sat and Jonan was alone. In typical greeting, he placed his hand to his heart then, trying to appear calm, moved behind the screen. In the shadows, his pulse raced, but Vulcan had trained him well. Instead of thinking about nerves, he put his mind to listening. Within that focus, he structured what he wanted to say and how he wanted to say it. He was going to speak of his recent past: the romance of his meeting with Yerudit and the uncanny tunnel perceptions that had brought them together. He would woo them with his intellectual questioning about the real and the unreal; his confusion between reality and illusion; and his not knowing where the Obelisk ended and where the Tsadkah began.

But how to begin, how to turn Jonan off and let the story unfold? The silence extended, Jonan listening to it. Gradually, his hands began to move and the shadow puppet flickered. A story began, but there were too many threads, and they became entangled. Jonan sought for clarity but became repetitive. He froze, the shadow puppet motionless.

"Tell us about your family," the Tsadkah said. "How you became a Psychaeologist? What did you hope to achieve? Show us your face before you were born. The fire that ignited your soul."

Jonan was taken aback. He had come prepared to reveal only what he had prepared. Now the Tsadkah was asking for more. He was really asking to see Jonan's shadow side. Jonan shivered. He'd been such a fool. He'd thought all along that the shadow puppet was called that because it projected its shadow on a screen. Now, at the very last moment, he realized the shadow it projected was his own shadow self.

He cast back over the thirty years of his life. As an only son in the post-Climate Change chaos, his parents had lavished all their love on him, but there had been a strange vacuity in his adult life. On the one hand, he'd learnt to indulge. On the other hand, through Psychaeology, he'd sought for meaning. Yet that too had become an indulgence. Meaning had become manipulation, search had become seduction. The buccaneer had become a bore.

As Jonan's little story unfolded, he felt so small as to be beyond notice. He'd been given the magnificence of a life and done so little beyond what was comfortable. He felt naked and beneath contempt; he wanted to crawl away, to disappear. The shadow puppet with its long nose and receding chin became his nemesis, all his self-hate projected onto it.

The Tsadkah, however, wouldn't let Jonan crawl away. Instead he began to probe and guide. Everything the Psychaeologist wanted to glide over, he forced Jonan to explore. They went into strange byways. Every momentary impulse that had flashed across the strata of his mind was excavated, his deepest depths and sickest images revealed. He stole from a blind man and left him bleeding. He ripped atmosphere from the Zirenian and watched him bloat. He abused women and enjoyed their moaning.

Nothing was hidden. To a rapt audience, he showed himself to be not a man but a worm. Less than a worm, a maggot, a parasite. The Tsadkah's voice went on, quietly insistent and as inexorable as the sea. Jonan, totally drained, lost all sense of what he was doing. No, he didn't lose sense, but he became detached. He no longer judged himself. The Tsadkah commanded and Jonan obeyed; the images, through his hands, worked the puppet. There was no Jonan any more. No shame, no pride, no nothing.

"The Obelisk."

Shock! Jonan thought he had gone beyond feeling, but now his mind went into a spin. What was he supposed to be? An object? A life? A multi-dimensional force? His hands quivered.

The puppet's sinister shadow oscillated across the screen. With what little energy remained, Jonan turned inwards. He focussed so intently on listening, it seemed his ears must crawl down his spine. He strove to find the essence of the Obelisk, the source of the pure chimes that entered his head, but probably didn't come in through his ears. He tried to identify with what appeared to be solid but in reality – *reality?* – was a black pillar of frozen light. In a final effort, memory turned him inside out. Fatigue flipped into energy, and a hissing spitting flame surged along his spine, a fire-breathing dragon that mushroomed out through the crown of his head. He became the crystal Obelisk. He became the black pillar of frozen light.

He was no worm. He *was* worm and not-worm! No thing; he was thing and not-thing! He was the universe. His not-nothing was everything. A great roar escaped Jonan's throat. Holding the sticks aloft, he howled across the stage. High above the screen, the puppets wobbled. A mad intoxication gripped him, and without a thought, he dashed towards the screen. Still roaring, the sticks upright, he threw himself at it and plunged forward.

The Tsadkah caught him. Hulva caught him. Vulcan caught him. Jonan roared and Yerudit howled. The Obelisk had been pierced. Jonan was at its essence. He had broken through his barriers.

# Chapter 26

Jonan had burst through the screen at four in the morning, but hours later and he was still being celebrated. He had shown his shadow side and had expected to be ostracised. Instead, he was made even more welcome. Not that it now mattered. The very process had cleared him, right down to his synapses, and he could sense the potential of tremendous powers, an attunement to the Obelisk that begged to be developed.

With this new awareness, Jonan spent two days in which to believe he was king of the cosmos, the master of no surprises. Consequently, he was extremely surprised to be surprised when he saw a quite unexpected sight.

Vulcan, who had the knack of meet and greet, was waiting at the solabus terminal for any new arrivals when a handsome woman alighted, wearing the latest Terran fashion. As Vulcan approached her, she looked around as if in search of someone.

"Het." He touched his palm to his heart. "Are you looking for Yonan?"

She eyed the big man with caution. "I'm looking for Jonan." She raised her voice slightly. "Is Yonan how you pronounce it out here?"

Vulcan grinned. "Owt here we do pronunce kwaintly. We a bit slow on the uptake." He scratched his bum. "But if you follow me, we pro'bly come to the zame person."

Evana tilted her head. "You're having me on, aren't you? I'm sorry; I didn't mean to sound condescending."

The big man whistled. "You are quick, I can see why Yonan respects you." He looked at the sun's position. "He will be at the Ico centre now." He glanced at her shoes. "Can you walk in those?"

Evana pressed a button, and the high stilettos lowered. "Now I can."

Vulcan shook his head. If nothing else, Terrans were ingenious. He led the way through the village, Evana's attention switching from one sight to another. "This is an amazing place. I'd call it quaint, but I don't want to upset you."

"Quaint!" Vulcan snorted. "You mean it is an anachronism, but you think I would not know the word."

Vulcan turned a challenging look on Evana, and she coolly stared back. But when her lips twitched in an incipient smile, he immediately burst into laughter.

Arriving at the Ico centre, they stopped to watch a tall, lean man in the centre of the hall practising with a staff. Evana observed with interest as he turned and span, the stick blurring into invisibility.

"He's very good," she whispered, "almost magical."

Vulcan indicated the man with his chin. "Yonan."

"Yonan," Evana repeated, committing the name to memory. "And Jonan, where is Jonan?"

Vulcan repeated his gesture. Puzzled, the woman followed his gaze and suddenly it struck her: this leathery whirling dervish was the smooth and plump bon vivant she'd known for so many years. "It can't be! Surely, it's not. It is? It is!"

Her last cry was so loud, Jonan stopped and looked to see who had called out. His jaw dropped. "Evana? No!" But belying his words, he ran to hug her. "It's so good to see you." He stepped back to study her face, the staff held behind his back.

"Phew!" Evana forced out her breath. "Is there somewhere I can sit? I'm totally flabbergasted."

Grinning, Jonan pressed the staff into the wall clips. "There's an excellent place where we can sit." He took Evana's hand. "Vulcan, can you ask the others to meet us at the Glen?"

"Of course." With a smile at Evana, the big man touched his hand to his heart, his gaze lingering on her as he turned.

Jonan, still holding her hand, said, "I think you've made a hit there."

"Nice muscles," Evana replied. She then faced the Psychaeologist. "But I can't believe how well you look. You've lost so much weight, but you still look ten times the man you were."

Jonan blushed. "I'm just growing into myself." Holding her hand, he led the way to the Glen, and they sat at a rough-hewn table shaded by intertwining trees. A young woman brought freshly squeezed fruit juice.

Evana ignored it. "I haven't sold your house or your solabub or your anything, Jonan. I thought maybe you'd been hypnotised or perhaps forced?"

"Hypnotised? In a sense, maybe. But forced?" Jonan chuckled. "No, no way. Impressed, yes. Forced, no."

Evana picked up her glass and sniffed at her drink. "Smells okay," she conceded. She took a small sip. "Oh, that's beautiful."

"Handmade. Well, actually, foot made."

Evana laughed so much that bits of pulp flew onto the table. "Really, Jonan!" She used her hand to clean the table. "What's happening? What are you doing here?"

Before he could answer, however, Vulcan burst into the courtyard. "Beware, beware!" he cried. "The Terrans are here."

Ariyeh was immediately behind him. Usually, his energy was contained in everyday life, but Vulcan's excitement had carried across: the Tsadkah sparkled.

"Oh!" Evana gasped. She half rose from her seat then, like a puppet with broken strings, flopped down again. "Oh," she repeated. "Now I see."

"Welcome!" Ariyeh drew her to her feet and engulfed her in a big but gentle hug. Hulva did the same. Yerudit, however, was more circumspect, glancing rapidly between Jonan and the newcomer. Sensing her inner turmoil, he grinned, then rose and put his arm around her.

Vulcan stepped forward. "If we are hugging, I am well known for my huggyness." And he also enfolded Evana, perhaps longer than necessary.

"No doubt," Ariyeh said, "you came because you were worried about your friend."

"Yes. When he asked me to sell all his belongings, I thought a cult might've got hold of Jonan and was forcing him to give them all his money."

Hulva took Evana's hand. "You are a good person to come this distance to protect Yonan."

"Huh!" Ariyeh sparkled. "We do not want his money, but something more precious, his spirit."

Evana considered her friend. "Looking at him now, I think Jonan has just regained it."

There was a short, comfortable silence. Jonan broke it. "You Screened me about extreme tourism, but I haven't replied because I didn't know what to say."

"What is extreme tourism?" Ariyeh asked.

"Some Terrans go off-world in search of extreme activities, dangerous ones," Evana replied.

"Such as dancing on the edge of volcanoes?" Ariyeh asked.

The Tsadkah's smiled, and Jonan knew he was referring to Yawa.

Evana tilted her head for a moment then nodded. "I guess. Anyway, a friend of Jonan wondered if the Obelisks would suit those sorts of tourists."

"Tourists!" Vulcan snorted.

But Ariyeh looked at Evana with interest. "These tourists, I suppose, would be a special type of person?"

"I don't know." Evana slid her glass around on the table. "I guess they're people who aren't satisfied with the usual run of things. Some are towelpackers, some are ultra-successful business people."

"Normally, we would not welcome tourists." Ariyeh laughed. "But considering how well Yonan has turned out, the extreme type might be just what the future needs."

"The future, Dad?" Yerudit looked at her father. "What're you planning?"

The Tsadkah returned her gaze. "You will see, but as for Evana's question, I think she would have a better understanding if she goes with us to the Obelisk."

Evana looked alarmed. "I didn't say I was an extreme tourist."

Hulva touched the newcomer's arm. "Do not worry, there is little physical danger. But your response will probably answer your question."

"Thanks." Evana tried to smile. "But if that was meant to be reassuring, it didn't work too well."

Jonan lent forward. "I think you'll find it exciting. There's only one thing that bothers me and that's Evana having to ride on a griffin."

Vulcan shook his head. "Not necessary. I have taught you how to werld, Yonan. One reason is to make irrigation pipes. Solabubs is another."

"Gedi has solabubs!" Jonan could hardly believe it.

Ariyeh nodded. "We use appropriately. The griffin was best for you. The solabub will be best for your friend." He turned to Evana. "But not yet. Rest for a couple of days, and then we will travel."

"That's good." Evana nodded. "It's not so much the rest, but I'm in such a whirl, I need time to adjust."

"Time is relative and… you're almost a relative." Jonan smiled, a quiet energy rising in him. "So adjust as we show you around Gedi."

Evana gave him a quizzical look. *Time is relative?* This new Jonan bubbled with good humour – and bad puns. So to adjust to him, as well as to this new setting, she spent time walking and swimming with Jonan and Yerudit. Mostly, though, Jonan was sure that she was more interested in him and Yerudit than in the sights.

On her second evening, they were eating in the shaded Glen when Jonan asked, "So, what d'you think?"

"I'm impressed, genuinely impressed," Evana replied. Evading his real question, she added, "There's a deep sense of purpose about Gedi which is really good. But I wonder, how does it get along with people working just a few hours a day?"

"We make puppets," Yerudit replied. "And we sell... some." She grinned. "Hebaron also has engineering skills, such as water purifiers, that sell off-world."

"Does my werlding add to the economy?" Jonan asked. "And...?" He tried to remember. "Vulcan said something about making solabubs...?"

"You'll see."

Evana waved her hand; she didn't care a fig about Hebaron's trade relationships. "But as to what I think about you two? I should be so blessed."

Jonan was stunned. He'd never heard such a word from his old friend.

Yerudit glowed. "Thank you." She smiled. "Well, you might be blessed." Her smile turned into a giggle. "I've known Vulcan, man of fire, for a long time, and something is definitely heating him up."

Evana also smiled. "I like him, as well."

Jonan thought it showed. She seemed happy here, more settled in herself than he could recall. Because of Vulcan? Probably.

Evana glanced around the Glen, then gazed up towards the unfamiliar array of stars. "So vast... so big, and I'm so tiny. The evening sky gives me that do-I-matter feeling?" She rubbed her eyes. "Yet what's the point if I don't." She paused, then added, "And if not now, when?" She laughed. "Now, where in space did that come from? Must be Shakespeare. Everything's Shakespeare." Evana yawned. "Better get to bed before I get too mystical."

"Early is good." Jonan rose. "Up early tomorrow then we all get mystical."

Jonan and Yerudit walked Evana to her cabin. Afterwards, as they went on, Yerudit said, "I like her, and it's good to see her with Vulcan. They twinkle together."

Jonan chuckled. "Two days and they already twinkle together?"

Yerudit elbowed him. "Not that. She's so quick at spotting when he's joking."

They went to bed, and bodies touching, drifted into sleep. Primed to awake early, they rose with the first rays of the sun. Eager to get started, Jonan, not having fully absorbed the idea that Gedi had solabubs, headed for the griffin. So he was surprised - yet once more - when Vulcan motioned for him to wait. Minutes later, the big man returned in a gleaming solabus.

Jonan clicked his fingers. "I forgot," he exclaimed. "Of course, Evana couldn't go by griffin." He walked around the shining vehicle. "No dents?" Jonan marvelled. "Is this from Terra?"

"A thousand probability spaces upon your head!" the big man exclaimed. "I built it!"

"You built it!"

"Both the engine and the bodywork."

"It's absolutely fantastic!" Admiring the vehicle, Jonan asked, "Is this what you meant yesterday, that Hebaron sells solabubs off-world?"

"I thought you'd be surprised."

"I'm astounded." Jonan walked around it. "Can I make one like this?" He turned to Vulcan. "Can you teach me?"

"You learnt to werld quickly enough. I am sure you can learn to make a machine like this."

Ariyeh touched the smooth body. "Even for the Obelisk, it would help if you learnt the skills."

Jonan frowned. "But no machine has had any impact on an Obelisk."

"That is correct, Yonan, no machine."

The Psychaeologist was perplexed, but he knew Ariyeh wouldn't explain further. This was something Jonan would have to discover for himself. Instead, he turned again to the vehicle, comparing its lustre with his own when Vulcan extended his arm.

"Come," Vulcan said to Evana, guiding her to a seat in the solabub.

Jonan was so impressed by Vulcan's ability to switch from warrior to gallant that he completely forgot his thoughts about lustres as he followed the others into the solabub. The big man Vulcan drove in manual mode, and it wasn't long before he pointed out the window.

"See," he said, "we have left the fields behind us. Now, it is nearly all black rock."

"And Jonan walked all this way?" Evana asked. "He could never have managed this before."

"There are many things he can do now he could never do before."

"And werlding?" Evana smiled at Vulcan. "You said he could do that now. What is werlding?"

Vulcan began to answer, but Jonan put out a hand to stop him. "From the outside," he said, "it's about connecting one metal to another. From the inside, it's about connecting one world to another."

Ariyeh patted Jonan on the knee. "See, you already know why learning to make a solabub is relevant to understanding the Obelisk."

"But that," Jonan protested, "is still a sort of unknowing knowing."

Ariyeh smiled. "Your body knows."

As he spoke, the black rock that surrounded them became

smooth and glassy. Jonan tilted his head. Below the level of hearing he could almost hear the song of the Obelisk. The Tsadkah nodded, and almost everyone became more alert, more alive. Only Evana didn't.

She gazed at them. "What's happening? You're all… gleaming."

With a great sense of coming home, Jonan worked to contain his joy. "One day," he said, "one day, you'll know… I hope."

Vulcan stopped the solabub. "We walk from here, an easy walk for twenty minutes." He held out his big hand. "Hold on to me and it will be easier still."

Evana held on, Jonan smiling as the sight evoked the image of a small child holding onto an adult for comfort. They stopped a few steps from the Obelisk.

"It looks," she said, "like a frozen wave."

"To me," the Tsadkah said, "it is frozen light."

"A hologram is frozen light." Evana wasn't sure what was more scary, the strange Obelisk or the wild man beside her. "And you can walk through a holo, but Jonan told me nothing can touch an Obelisk."

"Light is light."

Without any herbs, without any chanting, without any dance, the Tsadkah walked forward. At the pillar of frozen light, he kept walking. When he merged with it, Evana gasped. She might've fallen but Vulcan caught her. Moments later, a living flame emerged: the Tsadkah was aflame, a fire that didn't burn. They waited in silence, in awe, until once more he became a person.

Evana shivered. "That was so scary."

"But is it an answer?" Hulva asked.

"I suppose so." Evana scrunched up her face. "But I can't even tell people about it without sounding completely loony. Which would attract other loonies, I suppose." She brushed back her hair. “I’m surprised Jonan has survived, no, thrived on such… such things.”

“I had a strong motivation.” Jonan took Yerudit’s hand.

“Motivation and strength, plus a deep longing for truth,” Ariyeh said.

Evana studied him, awe in her eyes. “Can you imagine it? Extreme tourists bashing their heads against an Obelisk when told, or even shown, that a man actually walked into one!”

Ariyeh led the way back to the solabub. “The Obelisk has many faces. Some may well suit your extreme tourists better than others.” He smiled. “Perhaps you would like to work with Vulcan on such a venture?”

Evana’s face lit up. “Sounds like a good idea to me.”

“And to me,” Vulcan boomed. “I already have some interaction with Terra.”

“You do?” Jonan exclaimed.

“Huh! Who do you think is the off-worlder who gave your solabub its lustre?”

“You? Of course, you!” Jonan slapped his forehead. “I did think, but then… One look at this and I should’ve known.” His hand moved along the solabub. “And you can teach me this? How to add layer upon layer?”

The Tsadkah laughed. “Yonan, that has already begun.”

# Chapter 27

The return to Gedi was uneventful. The main difference was in Evana. "Space!" She touched her head. "I've gone through an extra dimension... or ten. Is this what people mean by spiritual?"

Vulcan patted her hand. "You feel the enormity of the universe. A universe of which we are all part." Seeing the others listening, he blushed. "Hmm, I do not like to talk about it. I simply ask what can I do."

"And what can you do?"

The big man grunted. "Try to follow the Tsadkah into the Obelisk." He laughed. "But all I do is bang my head against it."

"Then what should I do?" Evana asked.

Ariyeh intervened. "Form your groups of extreme travellers. The more you bring them to the Obelisk, the more its mystery will open up to you." He grinned. "And do not forget, Vulcan will help."

"Indeed." Vulcan's beaming face made him appear to be more a little boy that a muscular samurai. "I will be happy to go with you."

"Excellent." Evana took out her minScreen. "I'll make a note to extend my leave. I can send it from Gedi, can't I?"

"Vulcan has a Screen in his workshop," Hulva said. "We can power it up."

The big man nodded. "It will send a message to the spaceport. From there..." He clapped his hands. "To the universe. No problem."

As soon as they were back in Gedi, Vulcan led the way to a ramshackle wooden hut containing an optical processor with a bunch of wires and tubes hanging off of it. He smiled. "We do not use it much, but just wait, I connect this to this, that to that, and… magic." He flipped a switch, the machine buzzed and lights randomly flashed. When the Screen didn't settle down, he looked quizzically at Hulva. She stepped forward and began to trace out connections.

"I love engineering problems," she said, and making adjustments, soon brought the Screen to life.

Evana sat and after a moment's thought, sent: *Can I beg, steal or borrow extra time?*

Three days later, an eternity for usual Terra communications, she received a reply: *Leave granted*.

For a second time, Vulcan cranked up his home-made Screen. "In a few days," he said, "there will be a starship to Haja. A good place to see the Obelisk, and there you can also meet Jonan's friend, Tipal. You can leave then?"

"That's fine," Evana replied. On the next day, Jonan showed how well he could werld, and on the day after, she brewed herbal concoctions with Hulva. On the day that Vulcan again brought out Gedi's solabub, she sighed. "You said today, but it seems so soon."

The big man patted her arm. "The Obelisk on Haja will help you see that, in truth, you do not leave."

Evana smiled. "If I don't leave, then how can I arrive?"

Vulcan clapped his hands. "See, I knew you would understand!"

Jonan hugged Evana. "Travel well and take care," he said.

Yerudit also hugged Evana. "Travel well and have fun." With a big grin, she glanced sideways at Vulcan.

The big man entered the solabub, and with exaggerated motions, pressed its buttons. "Look, Yonan," he called, "I can press buttons like a Terran."

Then there was a soft sound as the Screen took control, and the vehicle slowly began to move. Vulcan waved, knowing they were just a probability space away, whilst Evana, not as used to space travel, looked back, face pressed against the permaglass.

When the solabub was a distant point, Yerudit said, "They get on so well. They seem very good for each other."

"Agreed." Jonan took her hand. "She saw through that samurai-warrior stuff much quicker than I did. And you know what Vulcan said about leaving, but not leaving? The Obelisk links people. It's like in physics, once particles interact they remain forever entangled." With a smile, he pointed at his chest. "We're particles, and the Obelisk entangles us."

"Entangled?" Yerudit thought for a moment. "And when we die, are we still entangled?"

"Space, I have no idea, but I don't feel that I *can* cease to exist. I can't feel that anyone does." Jonan started to walk. "After we… after we Obelisked, I began to think differently. Terra is terrified of death. They are Terrafied. I was terrafied."

"But not anymore?"

"No… I don't think so."

Yerudit stopped walking. "If I died, would you miss me?"

Jonan couldn't answer straight away, gazing at her, and gazing inside, so that when he spoke, it was as if the words were drawn from a deep deep well. "I would miss you very much, very much. And yet I wouldn't think you had ceased to exist."

"You're very strong, Yonan," Yerudit said. "Your heart is strong."

They kept walking, their feet taking them to the odd collection of pyramids that made up the puppet shop. "It's so counter to all I've been taught." Jonan walked among the shadow puppets, nodding to them as if to friends. "Science teaches that the brain creates consciousness, but now, because of the Obelisk, I think consciousness is more about resonance."

"Resonance?" Yerudit's forehead creased in thought. "That's when you strike one tuning fork and another will vibrate at the same frequency."

"That's what I'm thinking. The real reality is universal

consciousness, and our brains just resonate to a narrow bandwidth of it." Jonan paused. "By brain, I don't mean just the grey blob on top of our spinal cords. I mean all the chemical and electrical messages in our bodies, the whole caboodle of embodied cognition. So my body is like an ancient radio that's tuned to pick up one particular station." He waved his hands like the conductor of an orchestra. "Take a radio apart and you'll never find the music. The radio doesn't make the music, it only makes it manifest."

"Is radio different to a Screen?

"A Screen is digital. A radio was… and-a-log… agital… analogital?" Jonan shook his head. "I don't remember. Nowadays everything is quantum digital." He gazed through a window, almost directly at the sun, then he grinned. "I know, let's ask the Tsadkah."

"Hoi," Yerudit laughed, "that's my line."

Still laughing, she grabbed his hand and ran out of the puppet centre. "My intuition, or my resonance, or my whatever points me to the lake."

Jonan wasn't surprised when they found the Tsadkah sitting by the water, carving a small log. Against the rippling surface, he seemed to shimmer.

Without any preamble, Yerudit said, "Yonan suggests that brain doesn't make mind, but rather it's like a tuning fork that resonates to a tiny fraction of an underlying universal consciousness."

"It's how I respond to the Obelisk," Jonan explained.

"Yonan," the Tsadkah held up the log, showing a puppet head in the making, "your life of button pressing has been your undoing." He smiled, reminding Jonan of the mischievous Puck in an ancient Shakespearean play. "In your travels here, you have been undoing that undoing."

Jonan turned his hands to show his newly gained callouses. "It's been tremendous fun learning to make things, especially learning to werld, and I'm really looking forward to making a solabub."

"But now, Yonan, I want you to view that doing as a metaphor."

Yerudit frowned. "Hands as a metaphor?"

Jonan wriggled his fingers. "I don't understand." He touched his forehead. "Or maybe I do. It's something to do with making things, and being a Psychaeologist, and of course, the Obelisk."

Ariyeh moved away from the water. "I am a doer, not a thinker. What I can do, I have struggled to put into words for you. Yet, to go further, Yonan, we need both thinking and doing." He sat on a rock and motioned for the other two to join him. "When I was young, I had an awe-ful experience. I come from a hot country bordered by a warm sea in which I often dived. Naturally, I sometimes dared myself to stay down as long as possible. But being young meant being foolish and so, one time, it was much too late by the time that I headed for the surface. With my lungs bursting, I decided, so, if I was going to die, I might as well relax and enjoy it."

The Tsadkah resurfaced, emitting a fierce but contained energy. "I did die. And I did enjoy it. Yet amazingly, in this death or near-death, I moved out of my body. I saw myself in the water below and also in the sky above. But I was not sorrowful, instead I had the most intense feeling of bliss, the most complete and utter state of bliss."

There was a profound silence. Even the birds were quiet. "A tour guide," Ariyeh was back and he smiled, "although not an extreme tour guide, found me and thought I was dead. Yet up to date on first aid, he put himself to work. Amazingly, and reluctantly, I returned to my body."

"You've never told me this before," Yerudit murmured.

"Before you were born, I told it to the puppets."

"But what's told to the puppets stays with the puppets."

"Precisely. But now is the time for you to know." Ariyeh

took his daughter's hand and held it between both of his. "I was then a gardener's assistant. It was heavy work, but it suited me as I had no taste for books. But after that experience, I began to search. Finding yoga, I used my savings to go to India. With different gurus, I meditated in steamy jungles, on icy mountain tops, and in deep deep caves. I learnt body control, but that was not what I sought.

"From India, I turned to magic. In the Indus, I learnt to use blood and puppets. That gave me control over other people – but nor was that what I wanted. In South America, I learnt astral travel with shamans." Ariyeh smiled sadly. "Despairingly not right. Almost crazy, I was ready to try anything to realise that state again. In frustration, I even turned to drugs."

"You!" Yerudit was shocked.

Ariyeh shrugged. "I was desperate. Stimulants, tranquillisers, psychoactives, I tried them all. I did not eat properly. I did not work regularly. I did not come by my money honestly. I hit rock bottom, supposedly where you cannot go any lower. But I did. I loaded my pockets with stones, my stomach with drugs, and walked into the ocean. That was where it began, and that was where I would end it."

This time Yerudit reached out and took her father's hand.

He smiled at her. "But it did not end. I stretched out in the water and sank down, and as my breath ran out, I did not fight it. As I prepared to die, acceptance acted like a thrown switch, and gave me what those other efforts could not. I moved out of my body, and once more, everything had meaning, everything had bliss. Unwittingly I reached out, or more likely the Obelisk reached out for me, for in that state I heard one word: Yawa, Yawa repeated over and over again."

Ariyeh chuckled. "I was lucky. All this happened in the shallows so I simply rose, removed the stones from my pockets and walked to the shore. Then I searched on a Screen for Yawa. The only connection..." He turned to look at Jonan. "Perhaps

I should say, my only resonance was a minor reference to an obscure planet, but I threw myself into work and saved enough money to go there, although I had no idea as to why.

"Few people lived there, but the air was breathable and so, with a small backpack, I began to explore. The Obelisk directed me to a live volcano within a dormant one, and there, without questioning what I was doing, I immediately descended the invisible steps. To my amazement, I found an Obelisk and entered a frozen pillar of light. From then on, everything has changed, everything has been completely different."

Ariyeh stopped speaking, and it was only after a long silence that Jonan said, "And the pilgrimage to the other Obelisks?"

"That came later, but Yawa always remained special for me."

The Tsadkah gazed at Jonan with a look so intense that Jonan had to look away. He turned instead to the lake and the distant ochre hills, as starkly defined as cardboard cut-outs. The whole setting was beautiful, almost unreal, only the people within it were real. Although, Jonan reminded himself, the Tsadkah also had more than a touch of the unreal.

Jonan sighed. "And hands as a metaphor?"

The Tsadkah smiled. "Not only hands; for Vulcan, it was a concept. As a physics teacher…"

"Physics!" Jonan exclaimed.

"He was obsessed: how could an infinitesimally small particle also be a wave that went on for infinity? It was a theoretical idea, but one that led him to demolish a physics lab. Then it led him to search."

"Vulcan was violent?"

"He was always physical. But Yonan, we also have Shrivites who physically lack hands, and although they may use artificial aids, infirmity has turned them into seekers. But I am not an analytical thinker, Yonan. When I look for words, I only find a headache. But you *are* analytical, and just as you will learn to use the intelligence of your hands to make a solabub, so you can learn to use the intelligence of your mind to understand the Obelisk. You will, I am sure, go much further than I."

Jonan unexpectedly shivered. Going further? What an idea! Yes, it was true that like the Tsadkah, he once had experimented but failed. How incredible that now, he was being given the opportunity to try again, but this time with guidance.

# CHAPTER 28

The next day Jonan exploded into wakefulness. Beside him, Yerudit opened her eyes and smiled. "A new day, a new skill."

"Ah!" Jonan was balanced on toes and finger tips. "But with Vulcan away, how will I learn to make a solabub?"

Yerudit gave a smile as mysterious as any of the Tsadkah's. "When the student is ready, the teacher will appear."

Carrying a bucket, Jonan headed for the shower. "Breakfast here or at the Glen?"

Yerudit laughed. "The Glen with, perhaps, the teacher."

Showered and dressed, they walked hand in hand to the shaded eating area. Ariyeh and Hulva were already there.

"And the solabub maker?" Jonan asked.

"Here." Ariyeh pointed at his wife.

"Hulva!" Jonan's voice rose to a squeal, part genuine surprise, part act. "As I keep saying, just when I think nothing else can surprise me, something comes along and knocks my socks off." He lifted his feet, shoes but no socks.

"My father taught me," Hulva said. "I taught Vulcan."

"Wasn't that physicist already a metal worker?" Jonan asked.

"He was a theoretical physicist who became a very good werlder." Hulva smiled. "But I use phasor-werlding not the hot werld that Vulcan likes."

"And you also know the mechanics?" Jonan asked.

"I made the tracking system for our solar panels." Hulva blushed lightly. "I also improved them."

"Excellent!" Jonan clapped his hands together. "I'm really looking forward to this. When can we begin?"

"After we've eaten!" Yerudit laughed. "You're such a different person to the one I first met."

Jonan also laughed, and although he was happy to eat, he

was quick to follow Hulva when she rose. She led him to a building made of giant metal cranks and cogs.

"My father was a literal man," she said. "This, he believed, was how a place of werlding should look."

Jonan viewed the odd shaped building. "I thought we'd go where Vulcan taught me."

"That is for agricultural machinery." They passed through a doorway shaped like half a cog and into the workshop. "The inside walls are boringly flat," Hulva said, "for safety." She went directly for two similar machines, adding. "Safety gear on, Yonan, then copy me."

To Jonan's amusement, Hulva pressed a button to start a box-on-wheels welding machine. A narrow tube hissed, and she ran the open end along the meeting of two metals. She pulled at the join, showing that the metals had fused together.

"And it cools instantly," Hulva said, "so as long as your hands are not in the line of fire, you are not in danger."

"Excellent! Can I start?" And scarcely waiting for an answer, Jonan pressed his machine's button, grinning when a phrase came to mind: *on the press of a button*.

Pressing buttons was so familiar, that the Psychaeologist quickly adapted to this new form of werlding, although it amused them not to reveal how well they were doing. But the work progressed so smoothly that just six weeks after they'd started, Hulva decided to unveil the new gleaming, multi-layered vehicle.

Yerudit walked around it. "It's amazing!" she exclaimed. ""The best I've ever seen. From one angle it's as copper-coloured as Hebaron, from another it's as blue-green as Terra."

Jonan touched his nose. "Trade secret."

"And our first journey?"

"Not a secret." Jonan circled his hand. "Just around the block."

"But? I'm sure I heard a but."

He pointed east. "After that, to the Obelisk, but we'll go by my friend, the griffin. I want to try my first experiment."

"Which is?"

"Second trade secret."

Yerudit took his hand. "Yonan, you're becoming as mysterious as the Tsadkah. So when do we leave?"

"In a few days." Jonan scratched his chin, having not shaved for a week. "I'm making a brain wave analysis machine, a simplified version of an Image Enhancer. I'd like to test it out on the Tsadkah."

"Is that your experiment?"

He shook his head. "Not the main one."

With the brain wave machine completed, they left Gedi on the griffins. As always, the big creatures were eager to travel and nuzzled against Jonan as he saddled them up. With Ariyeh and Hulva, they set off through the harshly beautiful country, making only short stops and pressing on even when the sun was high. At dusk, Ariyeh kept to the front, stunner ready in case of carnivores. But the way was clear, and just when the moon lifted above the surrounding hills, they reached the Obelisk. And although it glistened in the moonlight, even before Jonan saw it, he heard it: an inner chime that lifted him as if he were surfing on the waves of the mind.

As on their first visit, Ariyeh lit a fire and made mead, adding careful measures of herbs and spices. They ate and rested, a cool wind refreshing them. When the stars came out, Ariyeh at last seated them around the Obelisk.

"Listen," he said.

Jonan could already hear.

"Sound," the Tsadkah said.

Ah, this was different. Jonan waited. When no explanation came, he listened more intently. Each vertebra chimed, each was resonating, he thought. He put his mind into bringing the resonances into one whole. His mind twanged. He tried again and a purer note sounded. His personal consciousness became a standing wave of a single frequency, and he mentally laughed at the sheer absurdity of the idea.

"Listen," the Tsadkah repeated, "sound. Listen... sound. Listen... sound."

In his uplifted state, Jonan fumbled to attach electrodes from his modified Image Enhancer to his own head. Yet as soon as they touched, the dials went crazy. He laughed again; if he attached the electrodes to the Tsadkah, the machine would probably explode. Let it go, let everything go, and he became the silver chimes of a melodic bell.

He was silence... black... unfrozen... harmony... vibrations. He was the colour of harmonious chimes. He was energy and goodness. Within the reach of the Pillar, the Tsadkah was a projected shadow. They had all become the play of light of shadow puppets.

Night progressed. Question became answer. Death became understanding. Jonan was the Obelisk and the Obelisk was him. Not-I was the Obelisk and not-I was also him. He was Yerudit and the Obelisk was him and Hulva was the Tsadkah the Obelisk was him. Ripples and vibrations and waves. Sound and colour and spectrum. I and not-I, all contained in the Pillar of Frozen Light.

Sounding the source, listening for the source. Freedom. No cell, no body. No death, no not-death. All place, all time. No place, no time. Mind was the creator. Death was the mystery. Life to be lived, but not to be grasped...

Day came and the sun shone directly into Jonan's eyes. He blinked. Black chimed and faded, slivers of silvery sound splintered. He looked into the sun. The sun and he, directly. Opposite him was the Tsadkah, face ablaze. Yerudit and Hulva were curled in sleep. Their pulse, however, beat within him.

Listening for inner sounds, he once more linked himself to the Obelisk, but this time he held onto a part of himself. He was searching for a memory... a feeling... an otherness... To guide him he focused on the blue-green image of Terra and then on the crazy commercialism of Luna. Eventually, in time taken out of time, he found a connection, a resonance of a different flavour. He held it for a little while but soon, too soon, his mind began to weaken, the link began to fade and Jonan returned.

Ariyeh smiled at him. "I see you are already experimenting. What did you do?"

Jonan also smiled. "Is it okay if I don't tell you?"

"You mean I must wait?"

"If that's okay? I don't think it'll be long."

They both grinned. Jonan was creating his first mystery. Yerudit awoke, saw the light in his face and took his hand. Without speaking, Hulva stirred, looked from her husband to Jonan and simply nodded to herself as if this was what she had expected. Ariyeh rose and hugged Jonan, then he reached for Hulva and together they all went to the griffins.

Jonan paused before mounting. "For a while, I thought you'd sent Yerudit to catch me."

Ariyeh frowned. "Not to catch," he replied. "To find out what you were."

"I know now that you'd never do that." Jonan put one foot in the stirrup, and with a cheerful grin, swung his other leg over the griffin. "It was our resonance to the Obelisk that did it."

The sky brightened, and linked by a deep sense of communion, they had no need to speak on the long trek home.

On the first morning back, Jonan dabbed green paint onto his right index finger.

"What's that for?" Yerudit asked.

"It's psychaeological." Jonan smirked mischievously.

He went to werld during the morning, and practiced with the staff in the afternoon. All the time, he searched for the sense of connectedness to the Obelisk. "So this is what Ariyeh the Tsadkah experiences," he thought. "Sometimes my everyday self dominates, sometimes the Obelisk. He flickers not in space but in mind."

On the next morning, Jonan renewed the paint on his finger and Yerudit again asked, "What is it for?"

"While you were asleep at the Obelisk," Jonan waved his finger in the air to dry, "I linked to it with a particular intention. This is to remind me of it." He didn't say what the intention was, but he wasn't surprised when it happened.

A short, green, and warty visitor rode into Gedi.

The Zirenian stopped a Shrivite who was gawking at him and said, "Takes me to your leader." His space suit was flexible enough for him to put his hands on his hips. "I wants to have a words or two with him."

Naturally, the Shrivite took the Zirenian to Ariyeh. The E-T closed his eyes and his face turned beige for a long moment. "Yes, I taste-see you are the leader." He bowed. "Please take me to your other leader."

Ariyeh chuckled. "Will you know his face when you see him?"

The Zirenian changed to sky-blue, his version of laughter. "I knew his face before he was born."

Ariyeh clapped his hands. "Good, good. Come, you want to meet Yonan."

They went to the Ico centre, increasing numbers of people joining them on the way. There, Jonan was making such powerful strikes with a staff that the air was singing, but when he heard the excited crowd, he stopped and came out to meet them. Then, seeing how slowly the people were moving, he immediately knew why and pushed into the milling crowd. At its centre, Jonan stopped and put his green-fingered right hand to his heart.

The Zirenian didn't stop but came forward and wrapped his arms around Jonan's knee. "You called. I come. I have questions. You suggest answers."

Ariyeh thumped Jonan on the back with the exuberance of a Vulcan. "This was your experiment. Excellent, excellent."

Soon afterwards Evana and Vulcan directed two extreme tourists to Hebaron, and to his delight, Jonan was able to attune them to the Obelisk. Over the next five years, he continued to 'experiment'. Through the Obelisk he became a water diviner, an empath, and acquired the Tsadkah's uncanny ability to resonate to distant intelligences. More importantly, he increasingly 'saw' the individual as a node in a cosmic gestalt.

During this time, Ariyeh came to Jonan. "Hulva and I are ready for change," he said. "And you are ready to become the new Tsadkah."

"Me?" Jonan gasped. "But I'm not suitable. Just ask people."

"I have asked, and they have said yes."

"Oh!" But the new Jonan knew he was ready. Only the old one didn't.

With ease, Jonan/Yonan slid into the required role, that of teacher. He also continued to experiment until, one day he said, "The Obelisk's linking of minds is our subjective experience of quantum entanglement."

Yerudit sat silent for a long contemplative moment. "Since I understand neither," she said slowly, "yes."

Jonan seemed to flicker. "With practise the link becomes as natural as seeing or listening." His face glowed. "And we have only scratched the surface. We can resonate at deeper and deeper levels with the help of the Pillar of Frozen Light – a pillar that isn't light or frozen."

Yerudit nodded. "Ariyeh the Tsadkah would be truly impressed."

That year their first child was born. At the infant's first smile, Jonan sensed such a deep unity that he exclaimed, "Now, I see it! There *is* only one Obelisk!"

At the birth of their second child, he said, "Of course, we and the Obelisk are one."

Yerudit just smiled. And more so when Ariyeh and Hulva again broke their retreat in order to visit the children.

***

At the end of his twentieth year, Yonan the Tsadkah considered his adult children, and Yerudit the Tsadkot followed his gaze.

"They're too well adjusted," she observed. "Ariyeh, my father came from Terra. So did you. Is it time to send them?"

"Yes," Yonan replied, and they laughed with joy. "Terra will have at least one self-satisfied seal who still has the hunger."

END

# About the Author

Barry Rosenberg was born in London but moved to Canberra, Australia after completing a PhD on visual image processing. After becoming involved in meditation, he left research to pursue tai chi, yoga, and meditation. At this time, he began writing poetry, then plays, and then stories. After 12 years of being somewhat un-settled, Barry returned to Canberra to work in the Australian Public Service. Then, having taught himself picture framing so that he could frame his wife's fine art prints, he left the Australian Public Service in order to work a picture framing business from home.

Nowadays, Barry lives on the Sunshine Coast, Queensland, where he combines writing with woodwork. He mostly writes speculative fiction. Barry has had a number of stories published and has won a few awards.

CPSIA information can be obtained
at www.ICGtesting.com
Printed in the USA
BVHW051134060623
665472BV00014B/1296

9 781911 486374